Jersey Shore Cop

Captain William J. Halliday

NEWMAN SPRINGS PUBLISHING
320 Broad Street
Red Bank, NJ 07701

First originally published by Newman Springs Publishing 2020

ISBN 978-1-64801-125-2 (Paperback)
ISBN 978-1-64801-151-1 (Digital)

Printed in the United States of America

Contents

||||||||||||||||||||||||||||||||||||||||||||||||||||||||||||||||||||||||||||||||||||||||||||||||||||||||||||||||

Acknowledgments

My family and my desire to write helped me achieve a bucket-list goal with this book. My wife, Nancy, and daughters, Jeanne and Cissy, gave me the support and encouragement to attempt something I never thought I could accomplish.

My writing skills were limited to reports that were used as records of events and subsequent investigations. With the help of my daughters, Jeanne and Cissy, and my granddaughter, Lauren, I was able to write about the inside feelings and emotions of some of the witnesses and victims in my investigations.

Several friends have made helpful comments and suggestions. I am grateful for their support. I could not have written these adventures without the input from my law-enforcement colleagues—police officers, detectives, prosecutors, and judges. I cannot leave out defense lawyers; they all helped me become a professional police officer and later a police detective.

I also want to thank my snitches. They helped me solve many investigations. Thanks, Fast Eddie, Foxy, Ipana, and Big Louie.

Lastly, I received advice from my mentor, Ralph Simon, who was a Newark Police officer. He said, "Keep copious notes in a bound book with the truth as your guide. This book will never fail you." I have a record of my whole career in these notebooks, and they were my source for this book.

Prologue

The Jersey Shore is a beautiful place to live, work or play. It possesses an environment that makes life worth living. You can walk along the sandy beaches of the Atlantic Ocean or the bays of Sandy Hook. A person can take a stroll on the boardwalks with the amusement rides, games of chance or enjoy cotton candy while riding on a carousel.

Thousands of residents live here year-round. One reason is the excellent transportation choices, the wide variety of housing options, excellent schools and of institutions of higher learning.

Besides the allure of the ocean there are many other recreational activities and cultural events. Music, dance, nightclubs with Bruce Springsteen, Jon Bon Jovi, and the lovely voice of Taylor Tote. The Jersey shore offers racetracks, sporting events, and golf courses and fishing with party boats in most mornings. The shore is also a shopper's paradise with high-end malls, and antique auctions and bustling downtown stores

There are rolling hills with estates of the homes of the rich and famous. Horse farms for Monmouth Park racetrack. Farms that grow corn, soybean and a variety of produce. The governor of the state lives here.

Whatever your pleasure there is something at the Jersey shore for everyone. Within this idyllic setting there is crime. As long as there is opportunity for criminals to ply their trade there is a need for police. Bill Holiday and Vince Flynn have chosen to serve and protect the people of the New Jersey. Both started as patrolman and so distinguished themselves as crime fighters that they were promoted to detective. The brass with their expertise and insight put these two intrepid crime fighters together as partners.

Starting a New Job After Marriage

My life was going great. I had been married for three months to a wonderful girl, my high-school sweetheart, Nancy. We purchased a house just before we were married. It was an old house but was ours to own. We intended fix it into our dream house. Nancy was working as a secretary for a trucking company and I was working as a carpenter with a new home building company.

Life started to get a little unsettling. Nancy told me she was pregnant. We didn't plan on this so early. Nancy was able to work for the next six months. After that, we would have to rely on my salary. I really enjoyed the physical aspect of carpentry work, being outdoors and the comradeship of all the other construction workers. It was fun. The only problem was when it rained, or the jobs slowed down. When there was no work, there was no pay. When our construction crew got off work early, we would go to a local bar, usually a local go-go joint for a few beers. However, it was reflected at the end of a week with a reduced paycheck.

Nancy urged me to get another job that offered a steady salary and provided the health benefits a new father would need. Even though I didn't like the thought of leaving construction, I agreed to look for a new, steadier form of employment. I took employee-entrance tests for the phone company, the power company, the water company, the post office, and on a whim, the police department.

A month after taking the postal test, I received an offer of employment from the postmaster of the Belford post office. I started in September of 1961. I really didn't like the job because it didn't offer much in the way of challenges. After being there for three months, the assistant postmaster, an obnoxious, overbearing jerk, had to evaluate the time it took me to deliver the mail on my route. "Buttsy"

9

was his nickname. He walked with me as I delivered the mail. He said I walked too fast. What a creep! Delivering the mail was programmed to take five and a half hours. I did the route in the allotted time for the next few weeks. I like challenges, so I decided to do just the opposite and quicken my delivery pace. I delivered the mail in only two hours as a challenge to myself. It was fun, but I had to hide for a few hours before returning to the post office. One day, I was the recipient of a complaint because I walked on Mrs. Bossbeck's lawn while making her mail delivery. She called Buttsy. He was happy to reprimand me for my blunder. The next time I worked that route, I ripped up and threw away Mrs. Bossbeck's tax and phone bills. I didn't like the old bitch.

By spring, I was completely bored with the job. While walking the route one day, I came across a group of guys playing basketball in a school playground. The next day, I finished my route even faster and played ball with them. I hid my mailbag and changed into shorts and sneakers. When I returned to the post office, I was sweaty and a little disheveled. The postmaster commented on what a hardworking postman I was. Buttsy, however, looked suspicious. Thereafter, I played basketball almost daily until I got the call from Mr. Siefert, the town business administrator. It was a welcomed call and opportunity to change jobs.

A New Job

In mid-April on a Friday afternoon, I got home after delivering the mail. The phone rang and Nancy said, "It's a Mr. Siefert for you." Mr. Siefert was the business manager for the township. He said, "Hey, Billy Holiday, do you want to be a cop?" The department was hiring the top three on the civil-service list. I answered him that I definitely would try and then thanked him.

I hurried right to the post office and gave Mr. Johnson my two weeks' notice. He wished me well because he knew I wasn't destined for a career as a letter carrier. Buttsy frowned because he would have to find someone else to harass.

I was to report to my new job on Thursday, May 1. I was excited. Thursday morning, dressed in my only sport coat, I reported to police headquarters. The chief gave me my first assignment. "Go out for coffee and doughnuts for the brass." I got five cups and a box of doughnuts. I then passed out the coffee and doughnuts to the chief and the captains in the offices. No one offered to pay me. It cost me nine dollars. I wondered if this was the rookie initiation.

After waiting for an hour, the chief took me out for a tour of the township and the fourteen towns it encompassed. We stopped in four coffee shops. After lunch, the chief sent me to a uniform shop in the Newark for my uniform order. I got a police hat, two police shirts, two pairs of pants and socks. When I returned to headquarters, Lieutenant McKenna lent me a nickel-plated .38-caliber revolver and a gun belt that didn't fit too well. While practicing my marksmanship in the woods, I found the gun shot four inches to the left every ten feet. I didn't care—I wasn't planning on shooting anyone. I went home to put on my uniform. I looked like a cop (at least I thought I did).

I was scheduled to report on Friday to the patrol sergeant at four o'clock for the second shift. I was to be riding with a seasoned regular officer on patrol. I was to just sit in the car, keep my mouth shut, and assist the regular officer with his calls. These were my orders from Sergeant Murphy. I was going to work in the patrol division all summer. The next police academy class was scheduled for September.

Good luck to me.

My First Police Call

The next day, I was assigned the second shift by Sergeant Murphy to ride with veteran patrolman Al Cook (of course, nicknamed "Cookie"). Al was a ten-year officer and had always worked in the patrol division. We were assigned to District I. The township was divided into three districts with a patrol car assigned to each district and a roving car, usually the job of the senior officer or sergeant. District I was from East Keansburg to Sandy Hook and all the area in between. It comprised five separate towns and eighteen miles of major highway. Sergeant Murphy gave out the times for the dinner break. Cookie got 6:00 p.m.

At six, Cookie stopped at his home and told me to practice driving the police vehicle around the neighborhood. Cookie did not sign out. The dispatcher thought he was in the car when he sent the car on a call.

"Car 33, go to the Snug Harbor Tavern in Belford—there's a disturbance." I affirmed the call and went to the tavern, also known as the Bucket of Blood. When I arrived I called the desk, 10-4. At that time the sergeant and dispatcher thought that Cookie was with me. I entered not knowing what to expect or do.

The bar had about fifty drinking customers, mostly local commercial fisherman. These men started working at 4:00 a.m., usually finishing at noon. The rest of their day was spent in the Bucket of Blood drinking beer. Nobody seemed to pay attention to me at first. I asked the bartender, "What's the problem?" He pointed to a stocky man in the crowd he called George and said, "He was annoying other drinkers by stealing their drinks." I really didn't know what I was supposed to do, probably throw him out.

13

I approached George and asked him to leave. He paid no attention to me and walked toward the bar, where he took another patron's drink. The other drinker hollered for the bartender to stop him. I approached George. I grabbed his arm to escort him to the door. He shoved me away and then went to a table and stole another drink. He was drunk and wobbly, but he was big and looked strong as a bear. I attempted to grab him again, and he shoved me away again. I was pissed. I punched him in the chest, *thump* a hard right. That punch had little effect. *Uh-oh*, I thought. When I hit him again, he grabbed me and threw me on the floor. The fight was on.

In the next five minutes, my hat was gone and my pants were ripped. He threw me down to the floor. I got up and followed him through the crowd. The other patrons were evenly divided as to whom they were rooting for, but the fight amused them. When I caught him, I must have punched him ten times before he grabbed me and threw me into the jukebox. The force knocked the wind out of me. I got up and wrestled with him until I got him in a headlock. At this point, he tore my gun from its holster. The gun fell to the floor. I don't think he intended to take my gun; it was just where he happened to grab me. The gun belt was sliding down to my knees. I was out of breath, and he dragged me to the door and threw me out of the tavern.

Here I was, outside the bar—no hat, no gun, torn pants at the knees, bleeding elbow, and out of breath. While we were wrestling, he had ripped my holster, and now it was flapping. What to do? I could go to the patrol car and call for help. But how would that look? If I couldn't handle a simple call, they might think I was a wussy. Or I could go back in and try again. I was beginning to ache already.

Stupidly, I went back in. The patrons didn't seem to even notice. George was back at the bar, arguing with another drunk over a glass of beer he had stolen. I walked up behind him and sucker-punched him on the side of his head. Now I was in real trouble. The punch only got him mad. I started punching him again. He was bleeding, his face a mess. He didn't seem to want to hurt me; he just wanted me to stop bothering him. He finally grabbed me and wrestled me to the floor. He was sitting on me when the cavalry arrived. I heard the sirens during the fight. The bartender had called headquarters and told the desk sergeant that I was getting my ass kicked.

Patrolman Dom Furieto rushed in, saw me on the floor, and hit George with a baton on the side of his head, so he rolled off me. I heard the *boink* as the baton hit George. Furieto and Cookie hand-cuffed him and dragged him toward the door. Dom said to me, "Get your hat and let's go." The bartender gave me my gun that a patron had picked up. I tucked the gun in my belt and left to some cheers.

At headquarters, big George was booked and placed in a cell. He went sound asleep. I had to type a report.

At 8:00 p.m., I finished typing my report. Cookie picked me up and took me home to clean up and have dinner. I walked into the house and was met by my eight-month-pregnant wife. I told her, "I think I will like the job, but I won't last long if I have to fight like this every night." Supper was spaghetti, but looking at the red sauce, I couldn't eat.

I went back on duty at nine. The rest of my first night on patrol was quiet—but what an initiation to police work.

At Court with George

It was a Monday morning at nine. I wore my only other police shirt and trousers and waited in courtroom for my case. I spoke to the prosecutor. He told me my case was the second on the list. He said, "Relax, Bill, I'll handle everything."

Judge Kline arrived late. He looked grouchy and mean. He had the reputation of being tough on offenders.

The first case involved a shoplifter who had stolen women's stockings from Sears. He pleaded guilty. Judge Kline fined him five hundred dollars and threatened him with six months in jail if he would ever be in his courtroom again. The shoplifter paid the fine and hurried out the door.

My case was next. Patrolman Bob Olsen was acting as the bailiff. He went out to the cellblock to bring in George. When Patrolman Olsen brought in big George, the judge leaned over the bench.

Judge Kline acclaimed, "Hey, George! What are you doing here? Wait! Let me look at the police report." He talked to George like they were old friends. It so happened they *were* old friends.

Judge Kline fined George twenty-five dollars and ordered him to pay for a new shirt and pants for the kid (referring to me). I saw George gave money to Chief Hoyer. Earl Hoyer was our chief of police. He was sitting in the courtroom. I believe he was the custodian of the money received at court. Judge Kline then went on to the next case.

I didn't know what to expect from the court proceedings, but I knew assault on a police officer was a felony. The court dropped the case down to simple assault. I had no problem with the disposition. George was "bombed." He didn't want to hurt me. He just wanted another beer. I thought the disposition of the case was unjust, but I believed it left me in good stead with the judge.

In the next few years, I had several occasions to take disturbance calls at the Snug Harbor Tavern. However, I never had any trouble. The drunks knew they were going to behave or go directly to jail. I liked my reputation.

I never got my money for my ripped pants and shirt from the chief. Perhaps that's the life of a rookie cop.

Police Corruption?

I rode with veteran officers for the rest of the week. Harry Sage was the best of them all. He seemed to know everybody and did not issue many traffic tickets. He gave a lot of warnings. The following week, I was assigned to the midnight shift. Sergeant Battle was the commander. One of my jobs was to check the business places in District II. I started at the end of the highway near Holmdel and began rattling doors.

While I was checking the Harmony Bowling Alley, I found a side door unlocked. I called it in to the desk. SergeantBattle advised me to park my patrol car where I could watch the doors and wait for a backup.

Soon the roving car arrived. We entered the building and checked the interior. It appeared the proprietor forgot to lock the door. While I was checking the bar and office, I heard a strange noise. In the kitchen, that senior officer was using the slicing machine to cut roast beef.

The senior officer was making sandwiches for his kid's school lunches. "Would you like to have one?"

I replied, "No thank you."

The senior officer then called SergeantBattle on a landline. "Sergeant, mustard on your sandwiches?" I overheard SergeantBattle reply, "Yes, mustard on sandwiches. Don't forget to lock door before you leave. The owner's not coming to the bowling alley."

I wondered if this was a common occurrence. The next time I found an unlocked door, I checked the building myself and locked the door. I would leave a note for the owner. I was not going to steal food.

I was sent by SergeantBattle to a neighboring department to pick up a prisoner the following night. The usual practice was to send two men. This prisoner had been arrested on a violation of contempt of court for not paying a traffic ticket, so I was the only one sent. A nonviolent offense, I didn't need to cuff him, just transport him back to our headquarters. He was to be released after booking.

When I arrived, the desk officer asked me to wait a few minutes. They were having a problem making an arrest. Two officers dragged in a struggling and obnoxious drunk man. He was fighting and resisting. The officers put him on the floor and searched him. They took his wallet, his watch, his belt, and his shoes. They then put him in the holding cell before bringing out my prisoner. While I was waiting, I heard the three officers talking about dividing up the drunk's eighteen dollars and his watch. The two officers divided the eighteen dollars, and the desk officer took the watch.

I was dumbfounded. They stole his money. They saw me looking astounded. One of the officers said, "He won't remember what he had when he was arrested." His rationale for stealing the man's property was he deserved to lose his money for causing the trouble.

I hoped this corruption was not in my department. I believed my brother officers were basically honest. I would keep my mouth shut, as I was new to police business. Later on in my career, I would not allow any thievery. Soon, officers in other departments knew not to commit an offense in my presence.

Three Patrol Car Accidents in Three Weeks

||||||||||||||||||||||||||||||||||||||||||||||||||||||||||||||||||||||||||||||||||||||||||||||||||||||||||||||||||||||||||||||||

I was working the day shift at District III. There were five inches of snow on the ground with no sign of it stopping soon. Sergeant Mayo was in command.

There was a traffic problem on Holland Road. A car was stuck in the snow, causing a traffic hazard. The road was clear but narrow. While I was going to the call, traveling east around a bend, a vehicle traveling west struck the side of my patrol car. I was able to stop before the collision, but the other motorist could not. It was only a fender-bender, but I couldn't attend to the original call. SergeantMayo, the shift commander, had to come and investigate my accident. He wasn't happy.

I was on the midnight shift the following week. Roads were clear again, but the weather was below freezing. SergeantBattle was in command.

He usually went on the road at 3:00 a.m., drove to the diner for a coffee, and then parked behind his house and cooped. He didn't want to be disturbed.

At 3:30 a.m., the desk reported that a frantic woman was calling to report there was a burglary in progress. The dispatcher announced, "Car 31, burglary in progress. Briarwood Avenue, Leonardo. Step on it!"

Three cars were sent. I was close. I was in the next town north, Belford, but I had a clear shot on Leonardville Road to the location. While I was en route, the dispatcher had the microphone open, and I heard the woman screaming, "Someone's attempting to climb through the kitchen window! Please hurry!"

I was traveling at a hundred miles an hour when I observed a car coming from the opposite direction a couple miles ahead. I had the lights blazing and siren on full blast. The other car put on a left directional. I was sure that the driver would not turn in front of me. I continued on. The car was sitting there. *Blink, blink, blink,* the directional flashed. When I was about a hundred feet from the vehicle and doing hundred miles an hour, the driver suddenly turned. I slammed on the brakes but couldn't avoid hitting him. I swerved to the left but hit the other car on the side rear. I knocked off the rearside trunk and one back fender of the on the car. I actually ripped off the back of the car.

My patrol car continued after the impact; it rolled over and slid into a tree. I received only bruises and a mild concussion. The other driver, an eighty-seven-year old gentleman, suffered only few bruises. Both cars were totaled. He swore that he would never drive again. SergeantBattle was called to the scene. He was nasty and unhappy, as I had woken him up.

The following week, I was on the second shift. The roads were clear, but the outside temperature was still below freezing. Sergeant Mayo was in command.

I left headquarters to patrol District III. On a secondary road, I observed three teenagers pushing an older car out of a driveway. I stopped and pulled off to the side of the road. I was at the bottom of a slight hill. I hollered up and told the kids to push the car back into the driveway while I was walking toward them. They got behind the car and started pushing. The wheel turned unexpectedly. The car became out of control, heading down the grade with the three kids hanging on the back of the car and trying to stop it. One of the boys was very chubby. It was funny to see him dragging behind the car. There was nothing that I could do. I was a hundred feet down the grade. The car passed me and headed for the other side of the road, where it hit the curb it turned and then slid toward the patrol car. It struck my patrol car broadside.

I was not happy to call Sergeant Mayo and have him come out of a warm place to investigate. The car was unregistered, and the teens admitted trying to sneak out for a joyride. They were in trouble with their parents. I would be in trouble with Sergeant Mayo.

I was involved in three accidents in three short weeks. I thought I would be fired or be sent patrolling on Route 33 in the boondocks for the rest of my life. I didn't receive an official reprimand, just a warning. For months, I drove with extra caution.

I never had another police-vehicle accident in my career!

Handling Arrests of Female Offenders

I was on the day shift. Sergeant Battle was in command. I was on patrol and assigned to district three. A call came in from the dispatcher regarding a male driving erratically in a blue Chevrolet station wagon. A female passenger was assaulting the driver.

Lucky me! They were right in front of me. I followed the vehicle for a mile and observed the driver swerving while the woman was swatting him with a newspaper. Patrolman Bob Schnoor was called in as a backup. I turned on the overhead lights and stopped the car.

I asked the driver to step out of the car. He was about five foot eight and weighed two hundred pounds, balding, and wearing a Hawaiian shirt and shorts. The woman got out on the passenger side and came around to the back of the station wagon. Before I could say anything, she took the ice cream cone she was licking and smashed it on the driver's head upside down, with the ice cream dripping down the sides of his bald pate. I had a difficult time stifling a laugh. Suddenly she smacked him in the face as he was trying to back away. Patrolman Schnoor arrived at the scene. We arrested the irate woman. She tried to hit Bob, but he ducked the slap, and we were able to handcuff her. The man she assaulted was her husband. He said, "She is nuts!" We arrested her for simple assault on him.

At headquarters I was booking her at the front desk. While I was asking her for booking information, she kicked me in the shin. It hurt! Cookie was walking past, and he laughed. She then turned around and kicked him in the shin. He punched her in the face. The punch knocked her down. I attempted to help her up, but she tried to kick me again.

Cookie said, "Let me take care of her." She was very docile with him but stared daggers at me. There was a lesson to be learned here. Maybe it's that some women would only yield to aggressive men.

That same afternoon, I was dispatched to a disturbance on Chestnut Street, Hillside. Patrolman Schnoor was my backup again.

There was a crowd on the street of about forty people. They were in a circle. A man and woman were fighting at the center of the circle. The woman was about six foot tall and weighed two hundred pounds, wearing a brown wool dress; it went from her neck to the hem near the ground. She was dancing around in a boxer's pose. She was clearly the aggressor. The man looked just like the actor Sherman Hemsley (George Jefferson). He was backing away as she attempted to punch him. The crowd was hooting and cheering. Bob and I pushed our way through the crowd and told the onlookers to disperse.

The man ran behind us for shelter. She was chasing him around us and attempting, and sometimes succeeding, to hit him. We arrested her. Her name was Ruby Begonia. While transporting her back to headquarters, I received a call from Charlie 4. Charlie 4 was the call letters of the detective bureau. They told me to bring Ruby into the detective's bureau after booking. There was an active arrest warrant from the county.

I walked Ruby into the bureau. Lieutenant McKenna sat her down at a table with the secretary. I noticed Sergeant Gleason leaving the room. I left and went to the patrol officer's room to complete my report.

Soon after, I heard screaming and crashing coming from the bureau. I rushed in to help. The secretary, Margery, was on the floor. The table was knocked over. A file cabinet was knocked over. There were papers strewn all over the floor. The contents of the desktops were on the floor, along with the coat rack. Lieutenant McKenna, Sergeant Lutz, and Detective Olsen were on the floor trying to subdue Ruby. They finally got her under control and handcuffed her to the radiator pipe. They were all huffing and puffing.

Sergeant Gleason came back into the bureau laughing. Lieutenant McKenna was hollering at Gleason. Here's what triggered Ruby's wild tirade. It seemed that Gleason had gone outside the building by the window at the detective's office. He had partially opened the window and yelled in a strange, gravelly voice, "Ruby, they're gunner takes your chillin'!" That's when Ruby Begonia went wild. McKenna and Lutz were really mad. Olsen was still recovering from the tussle.

The social service division of Monmouth County had previously requested assistance with a planned interview they had scheduled with Ruby. They had information that she was not properly taking care of her five children. They had access to her now. The social service was notified, and they were sending a caseworker to headquarters with two sheriff officers.

I didn't like dealing with violent women. I was glad to return to patrol.

Burglary

Saturday, day shift, District II, Sergeant Scott was in command. The radio dispatcher announced that there was a 10-30 burglary in progress at 50 New Monmouth Road.

Patrolman Lanno was in car 31 and caught the call. I was the backup. I arrived as Lanno was heading to the front door of a ranch-style home. I parked in the driveway and ran around the back of the house. I saw a man run out the rear sliding door, headed toward the woods. I chased him and tackled him in the backyard near the rear chain-link fence. He surrendered with no real struggle. I cuffed him and took him back to the house. Patrolman Lanno had another person in custody. More cars, including the detectives, arrived. While checking the house, we found the rear door had been forced open and the inside of the home had been ransacked. The detectives took the prisoners.

Back at headquarters, while I was typing the offense report, I heard raised voices in the detective bureau. One voice said, "We have had several residential burglaries on the last four Saturdays. We know you did them."

I saw Sergeant Lutz and Sergeant Gleason leaving with the prisoners. Lieutenant McKenna told me that the prisoners were soldiers stationed at Fort Monmouth. The detectives were heading to the barracks at the fort to recover the stolen property.

I was scheduled to go off duty at 4:00 p.m. I stayed because the detectives brought back the soldiers with two bags of loot. It was my collar, so I wanted to find out what was recovered. I was in the property room when I heard Lieutenant McKenna hollering at one of the soldiers.

Lieutenant McKenna asked, "Where are the kerns?"

I heard the soldier was sobbing and crying. "We didn't steal any kerns."

Lieutenant McKenna was a friend of a victim who had their coin collection stolen in a recent burglary. The solders confessed to the burglary but denied stealing kerns. Lieutenant McKenna was angry. I went into the bureau. McKenna knocked the soldier off a chair to the floor. He picked him up and put him back in the chair. He asked the solder if he wanted to talk to a priest or minister. "Where are the kerns?" McKenna screamed. When the prisoner denied taking any kerns, he was knocked down again. This scenario was repeated several more times with his denial of stealing the kerns.

After Lieutenant McKenna stormed out of the office, I spoke to the scared soldier. I told him, "You admitted breaking into the house. You admitted and returned their jewelry. Why don't you give back the coins?"

His face lit up. The soldier said, "I have the coins hidden under my bunk in the barracks. But I don't know anything about kerns."

Lieutenant McKenna had a Bay Shore accent. He pronounced "coins" as "kerns." Somebody else should have done the interrogations. Sergeant Lutz and I took the soldier back to his barracks in Fort Monmouth and recovered the stolen coin collection. Lieutenant McKenna didn't seem embarrassed. In fact, he even praised my interrogation. Due to the lack of communication, the poor soldier took a beating for nothing.

I decided to go back to school (college) and take communication classes before taking criminal-law classes. I enrolled in the Ocean County College for the fall semester.

Drunk Drivers

My first opportunity to make a drunk-driver arrest occurred on a midnight shift in September. Sergeant Mahoney was in command. I was assigned to District I. I was patrolling Highway 36 near Sandy Hook of the Gateway National Park. I observed a vehicle come from the beach road and head north on the bridge. The car was weaving and driving on and off the sidewalk. The operator swerved and side-swiped a light pole at the bottom of the bridge. I called in the stop and pulled the vehicle over in the Highlands. Patrolman Bill Brunt was dispatched as a backup.

After pulling the driver over, I asked for his driver's license and registration. I could smell the odor of alcohol and observed a beer can on the car seat and empty cans on the floor on the passenger side of the car. He was alone in the car.

When Patrolman Brunt arrived, I requested the driver get out of the car. When he opened the door, he almost fell out. He was a short man with a craggy-looking face and very large ears. His clothes were dirty, and he didn't have shoes on his feet. I could not administer tests because he was staggering around on the highway. It was too dangerous. I arrested him on the spot.

Patrolman Brunt and I took him to the office of Dr. Marc Krohn. It was the procedure for testing drunks. The driver told us his name was Horace Jones from Newark. He said he was driving from a beach in Atlantic City after drinking a few beers. Dr. Krohn found him intoxicated. While Jones was leaving the doctor's porch, he fell. When we got him up on his feet, he fell again over a bush in the front yard. He wasn't hurt. He just had some dirt marks and scratches.

I booked him and put him in a cell. He fell asleep. I typed my report and went back on patrol. It was quiet for the next two hours.

At 4:30 a.m., I got a call to return to headquarters. Sergeant Mahoney was out on the road. Patrolmen Brunt and another patrolman, Bob Foster, were bringing my prisoner to the courtroom. I did not understand what was going on. Patrolman Lenny Moon was sitting on the judge's chair behind the bench. He had the judge's robe on. I knew this was going to be a little crazy.

Moon, acting in the role as judge, questioned Horace Jones. "Why were you in Atlantic City?"

Jones seemed confused and didn't answer. I was also confused. Moon found him guilty and announced, "I sentence you to one hundred years of hard labor."

Horace Jones was crying. Foster and Brunt dragged him back to his cell.

I found out that this was not the first time these police pranksters pulled the gag. When the case was heard in the real court, Horace Jones did not remember his early-morning court case. He never mentioned it. I was thankful for that. I did not want to lose my first DUI case. His defense was that he had only one eye. His left eye was made of glass. That's why he fell. The defense didn't work.

It didn't take long for my second drunk-driving case. I was working an extra shift for overtime on Sunday. I watched my softball team for a while in the morning and had lunch at 1:00 p.m. I expected a quiet day.

I received a call after lunch concerning a vehicle driving through backyards, crashing through fences and scattering families having a barbeque. The driver stopped when the front of the car crashed into a pool. When I arrived in the neighborhood, there was a crowd of angry people. The car's driver turned out to be a beautiful woman wearing dress clothes, silk blouse, short mini-skirt, and high heels. Her name was Susan Taylor. She was sitting in a lawn chair and crying. I asked her if she had had anything to drink. She said, "I had only one glass of wine and got lost and confused." She staggered when I asked her to walk and failed the other sobriety tests. I arrested her.

Back at headquarters, she refused to talk or take the breathalyzer. We had video cameras, and I taped her answers and actions.

I booked her and let her sit in the interview room. Someone was coming to bail her out.

I returned to the scene and gathered the names of witnesses. Most were eager to go to court. I had a good case for conviction.

The next week, I received two phone calls from prominent citizens asking me to give her a break. They said she was a legal secretary, a friend of many high-ranking police officers, and a personal friend of the Long Branch mayor. The arrest was legit. It's illegal to alter the circumstances of the case. All I could do was downscale my testimony. I would not perjure myself nor reduce or drop the charges.

It took ten months for the case to be scheduled. Judge Kline was presiding. The prosecutor called me as the first witnesses. I noticed everybody was being cordial. It was not what I experienced in previous cases. The prosecutor asked me to tell the court what had happened. I testified. The prosecutor didn't ask for other details. Now here came to my big surprise. Defense attorney Francis X. Moore, known for his ferocious cross-examinations, said he didn't have any questions. He just smiled at me and thanked me for my testimony. The prosecutor didn't subpoena any other witnesses. I wondered why.

Mr. Moore started the defense. He called the defendant, Susan Taylor, as his first witness. She looked glamorous. She was wearing a very short, tight black dress, and some makeup. She looked like Miss America. The judge was leaning over the bench, smiling at her.

Ms. Taylor testified that she had just been through a difficult divorce. She said, "I was supposed to meet a friend at Buck Smith's bar at noon. I had a glass of white wine while I was waiting. My friend called at 1:00 p.m. and had to cancel. I started to leave when a man who had been sitting at the bar approached me. He offered to buy me a drink. I thanked him but refused. I was getting up to leave when he voiced an indecent proposal. Because of my present situation, I became upset. I ran out of the bar crying. I got confused and lost while I was driving my car. Then that wonderful officer, Bill Holiday, rescued me. He comforted and helped me."

Ms. Taylor looked toward me. "Thank you," she said. Judge Kline smiled.

Moore inquired, "Have you heard Officer Holiday's testimony concerning your staggering?"

"It was because of my high heels. Could I demonstrate my walk while wearing those shoes?"

Judge Kline said, "Certainly!"

When she walked down the aisle, all the men in the courtroom stared, including me. She was a great actress and had a sexy walk.

Moore said, "No further questions."

The prosecutor also conceded. "No further questions."

At the back of the courtroom sat the witness, a typical barroom lizard—slick hair, baggy and shiny suit, mustache, and a sickening grin. He was Mr. Moore's next and only witness.

Moore called the witness. "Please describe what happened on that day when you met defendant in the bar."

The witness said, "I was at the bar on that day. I saw the defendant and offered to buy her a drink. She refused the drink, so I asked her if she would like to go back to my hotel room and have a drink with me there. She ran out of the bar."

Judge Kline glared at him. The witness looked scared.

The prosecutor had no questions.

The defense rested.

The judge smiled at Ms. Taylor, declaring, "Not guilty!"

Win some, lose some. I was in the good graces of the judge.

Urban Renewal

||||||||||||||||||||||||||||||||||||||||||||||||||||||||||||||||||||||||||||||||||||||||||||||||||||||||||||||||||

I was off duty on a Sunday morning and reading the newspaper. I read that a major fire had occurred in Lincroft at the Brookdale Horse Farm. A large barn used to store hay and horse feed was destroyed by fire. The barn was over a hundred years old. The paper reported the fire lit the sky for miles. Fire trucks responded from Lincroft, River Plaza, Fairview, and Red Bank. The fire was contained to only one barn, reported Sergeant Battle. He was shift commander that night. He had lived on the farm a few months ago.

Three weeks later, Sergeant Battle was again my shift commander. At 2:30 a.m., I was in the parking lot of the Action Auction business on Route 36 conversing with Patrolman "Posse" Richardson. Posse and I had been hired at the same time. My car was facing the highway, while Posse was facing the Action Auction building. A bread truck entered the parking lot, coming fast. The driver yelled to us that there was a fire at the canvas shop three miles south of us.

We raced out of the lot. I arrived first with Posse Richardson right behind me. I called the desk and said, "I'm going in the building." I knew the owner sometimes slept in the back room. The whole place was engulfed in flames. ButSergeant Battle, on the desk at headquarters, stopped me. He told me that the place was empty, and he already dispatched the fire company. "You and Posse direct traffic for the fire trucks." I wondered, since he wasn't on the site, how did Sergeant Battle know the place was empty? No problem, the building burned to the ground. The building had been old and ugly-looking but was still operating as a business.

Another three weeks went past. I was back on the midnight shift again with Sergeant Battle in command. At 1:30 a.m., I saw Sergeant Battle and his drinking buddy, Frank Johnson, driving on

Bray Avenue on East Keansburg. I didn't think they saw me. I continued patrolling Highway 36 and then went into Leonardo to patrol that area.

At 2:00 a.m., I heard a fire whistle far off. I called in, and the desk told me the fire was in an old, abandoned house on Bray Avenue. Coincidentally, the township was trying to get the owners to tear it down. Sergeant Battle's drinking companion, Johnson, who was also the township's building inspector, had given the owners a summons for failure to maintain the building. Johnson and Sergeant Battle were watching the fire when I arrived. While at the scene, a neighbor reported to me that he observed two men leaving the house just before the fire started. His description matched Johnson and Sergeant Battle.

At 3:00 a.m., I found the sergeant and Johnson at the VFW Building. They were inside and seated at the bar. I told the sergeant what was reported to me by a witness. He strongly requested I forget about the citizen's information. The citizen could not see that well in the dark.

I didn't make the report. Afterward, my work life seemed to be getting much easier whenever Sergeant Battle was the shift commander. I got the better patrol cars and the district I wanted.

The "urban renewal" continued until things got too hot. Insurance investigators were seen in the detective bureau. After that, no more fires for a while.

I believed my shift commander was a pyromaniac. He and his friend and partner were cleaning up old buildings by setting them on fire. I am sure they believed they were doing a public service. I kept my mouth shut.

First "Atta Boy" Letter from the Captain

||||||||||||||||||||||||||||||||||||||||||||||||||||||||||||||||||||||||||||||||||||||||||||||||||||||||||||||

I was on the four-to-twelve shift one summer evening in District I. Sergeant Mayo was in command.

Not many calls were coming in. It was untypically quiet for a summer evening. While on my patrol, I often stopped and conversed with citizens in the district. I came across a group of hikers near the river in Navesink. I spoke to a group of kids playing basketball behind Bayview School in Belford. I stopped in front of a candy store in East Keansburg at about 10:00 p.m. and talked to a group of teenagers hanging out on the sidewalk. I got out of the patrol car and stood close to the group. This group of kids appeared nervous and I smelled beer, although I didn't see any. I told them to be off the street by midnight.

I was ready to go off duty at eleven thirty when I was sent to East Keansburg on an alarm call. The alarm was going off at a liquor store on Ocean Avenue. When I arrived, the alarm was blasting, and there was no one in the vicinity of the store. I checked the front. The door was locked and the glass in front intact. I went around the back of the building. There was a six-foot fence. I could see over it standing on a garbage can. I spotted a window that had been pried open.

The owner arrived. He opened the front door and shut off the alarm. We searched the premises. It appeared nothing was taken. At the back of the store was a small toilet. Below the open window, the toilet paper holder was broken. A shoe was on the floor next to the toilet. The shoe had a distinctive large silver buckle. It looked familiar.

Earlier in the evening, I saw a similar shoe on one of the teenagers in front of the candy store. After securing the store with the owner, I had to return to headquarters to type my report. I was scheduled to

34

go off duty, but I requested Sergeant Battle to let me go back to the area to find the teenagers. He approved it without granting overtime.

After looking around for an hour, I found the group in a nearby car-repair garage. My suspect was bending over a car, looking at the motor. He was wearing a different pair of shoes. I requested backup. A patrol car with three police reserve officers responded. Without waiting, I entered and confronted the suspect. I had the buckled shoe with me. He resisted physically at first, but I wrestled him to the ground. He was a big kid, about 230 pounds. When the cavalry arrived, I made him take off one of his shoes and try on the buckled shoe. It fit. I arrested him.

At headquarters, Sergeant Mahoney called in Detective Bob Swensen. Bob was a twenty-year veteran and had recently been made a detective and department juvenile officer. Bob took the juvenile into the interrogation room with the shoe. To my surprise, he was "hammering" the kid's head with the shoe. This was an interrogation technique I had not seen before. After a dozen whacks with the shoe, the kid confessed. He also ratted out five other kids who were with him. He didn't plan the burglary, but he was the one who was caught. Bob asked me to come in back at nine in the morning to wrap up the case.

At 9:00 a.m., I met with Detective Swenson, and we went to the high school to arrest the other culprits. This was my first ride in a detective car and my first arrests at a high school. We made the arrests. Bob processed the juveniles, then telephoned the parents and made arrangements to meet with them to release the juveniles. I typed my supplementary report that went to my boss, Patrol Captain William Wilson, and to Detective Captain Red Woodruff. I left because I had to go on patrol at 4:00 p.m. No overtime was granted.

Two weeks later, I was given an "attaboy" letter from the chief, congratulating me on my fine police work.

Death by Auto: Drunk Driving

It was a Sunday morning in late fall. Nancy and I returned home from church. She was going to prepare a Sunday dinner for the four of us (we had added another baby girl to the family). I changed clothing and went to play touch football.

The game started last year with a few of us throwing the ball around in my backyard. Now we usually had ten to sixteen "over the hill" players. We would choose up sides and play at the high school field. I was always one of the last ones picked, but they needed me. I owned the ball. This Sunday was rough; it was nearing the end of the season. Big "Lumpy" Lesko knocked me silly with a pulling block, and now I was really sore.

I had dinner at 2:00 p.m. and reported for duty at 4:00 p.m. Sergeant Battle was in command, and I was assigned to District II. At 4:20 p.m., I received a 10-50 call. The location was on Highway 36 in the Highlands Hills. The desk dispatched an ambulance and fire trucks, then backup cars. I knew it wasn't going to be a routine accident.

When I arrived, there were two cars involved. It appeared one of the cars went out of control over the grass median and struck the other car head on. The paramedics removed two women from the car, and they looked dead. The driver of the car that crossed the median, a man named Robert Bosley, was crying for help. He was wedged in his car and jammed under the dash. He was bleeding from a head injury and had two broken legs. I could smell the odor of alcohol on him. I looked in his car and observed opened cans of Budweiser. He was taken away in the second ambulance.

While I was assisting the ambulance crew, others officers arrived. Patrolmen Lanno and Reilly were directing traffic. Lieutenant

Luker and Sergeant Battle were walking around looking officious. Highlands's police officers were also directing traffic. I started the investigation with Lanno. It took an hour to finish and clear the scene. We received information from the hospital that the women in vehicle 1 were DOA.

I asked Lieutenant Luker what was needed for the reports and investigation. He sent me to Riverview Hospital. I wasn't sure I knew what to do. The lieutenant went home, and Sergeant Battle returned to the desk at headquarters.

At the hospital I went into the emergency room. The victims were covered with a sheet in the emergency room. I peeked at one of them and almost got sick. I heard a commotion in the next room. Robert Bosley, now a manslaughter suspect, was screaming. He wanted sedation. Before any sedation, the nurse was required to take blood samples. I saw her take three vials. I requested to speak to him. The nurses didn't say anything, so I went to the gurney and asked how he was doing. He told me to fuck off. I asked him what happened and received the same answer. I asked him to allow the nurse to take another blood sample. He refused and told me to get out.

As I was leaving the room, I took one of the blood vials. The nurse and I argued about this. I told her it was evidence, but she said, "I cannot allow you to take the sample." Someone called the security guard. The guard, a former policeman who was at least seventy years old, declined to interfere. After some discussion with the head nurse, the emergency room doctor, and the security guard, I agreed to wait for the hospital administrator. I still held the vial of blood.

Mr. Blaze, the hospital administrator, arrived. We went to his office. I called Sergeant Battle. He was of no help. I called Lieutenant Luker. He wasn't sure what to do but said to keep trying. He wasn't coming to the hospital. Mr. Blaze called the hospital attorney. We decided to lock up the blood in a refrigerator with only Mr. Blaze having access. I was going to get a court order.

It was now 9:00 p.m. Lieutenant Luker authorized a secretary to assist me with the affidavit. I had never done one before and stumbled through. When the secretary, Mrs. Landry, was finished typing,

I called the local judge. He was not available. The protocol in this situation was to call a superior court judge. Judge McGann was on call.

At 11:00 p.m., I was at the judge's home. He reviewed my affidavit, told me how to type up the court order, and agreed to sign it when prepared. I went back to headquarters and typed the order.

Back at the judge's home, he wished me luck with the case and signed the order for me to seize the blood sample.

By 1:30 a.m., I was back at the hospital. Mr. Blaze, true to his word, returned and gave me the sample. He also gave me a container to transport the blood. I was really pleased that my efforts produced the desired results.

About 2:30 a.m., back at headquarters, I called the emergency number of the state police laboratory. They told me they would have someone at the lab to accept the blood. First, I had to type a request form for the examination. When this was completed, I drove directly to the state police laboratory in Trenton. The desk sergeant gave me an old patrol car for transportation.

At 4:00 a.m., I arrived at the lab and left the blood evidence. Because it involved two deaths, they would process it that day. At 5:00 a.m., I left Trenton.

At six, I was back at headquarters typing my report. It was a little sloppy because I was tired. I went off duty at 7:00 a.m. I was due back on patrol at 4:00 p.m. I went home and to bed, not sure I did things correctly.

At noon, Lieutenant Luker called. He said the blood report came back. The suspect was over the limit for blood alcohol. I needed to come to headquarters and sign complaints for manslaughter. The court clerk would type the complaints. I also had to issue a summons for reckless driving. I should also confiscate the beer in the suspect's car. My thought was, "What the hell was Lieutenant Luker doing?" It would be nice to get help and overtime money. I returned to headquarters in civvies and completed the investigation. The lieutenant used his influence to get me off my next shift. It was the least he could do. I was too tired to work anymore.

When Robert Bosley was released from the hospital, the detectives arrested him and brought him to the county jail. He did not make the million-dollar bail. I was subpoenaed to the grand jury. He was indicted, and a trial date was set. A week before trial, there was a hearing on the admissibility of the blood evidence. I was called to testify. It seemed this had never been done before and a precedent would set. The judged ruled in favor of the state. Once the blood was admissible, the defendant pleaded guilty. He was sentenced to ten years in state prison.

I got my second "atta boy" letter from the county prosecutor. I also got a letter of thanks from the family of the victims. I knew then I was a good cop.

The conviction was appealed on the admission of the blood evidence. New Jersey Appellate Court upheld the conviction. The New Jersey Supreme Court did not take the case.

My New Job as "Detective" Bill Holiday

In 1965, the town council approved a building program. They embarked on a program to build a new town hall, courtroom, and police facilities. The building was completed and furnished the following spring. The department was moving into a modern facility. The new headquarters had room for a chief's office, secretaries, and a modern dispatch system. On the lower level, there was a patrol squad room, patrol captain's office, locker room, and shower facility. The detectives had a squad room, captain's office, two interrogation rooms, an identification laboratory with a dark room, also an office for two secretaries. The traffic division had two offices. At the back, there was a large room for records, and evidence storage room with a large safe.

There was a reception area for citizen inquiries and directions to the office that would assist them. It was an ultramodern police facility, the best in the county.

On the day of the move, I was scheduled for a day shift on patrol. I was called in and sent to the detective's office at nine thirty. What did I do now? Lieutenant McKenna pointed to a desk and told me it was mine. He asked me if I wanted to be a detective. I was so surprised I almost fell over. I never expected the promotion. There had been rumors about promotions, but I didn't apply because I was too inexperienced and didn't have much seniority.

At least ten other patrolmen had requested transfers to the detective's division and sent their application letters to Chief Red Woodruff. I thought I could have a chance for the traffic division after I set a legal precedent the past summer, but I never sent in a request for a change of assignment. I loved being on patrol.

Also promoted was Patrolman Vince Flynn, a fifteen-year veteran. Vince was to be my partner. In the division were Sergeants Frank Lutz and Frank Gleason. Detective Bob Swensen was the juvenile officer. Allen Dodge was the photographer, crime scene, technician and department bookie. We had two secretaries, Gloria, who was a woman in her fifties with little experience, and Maryann, who was a stenographer. Lieutenant McKenna was the commander of the division.

I reported for work on Tuesday morning. I felt like a fish out of water. I enjoyed the patrol challenges and was good at my job. I didn't know much about criminal investigations.

A month later, Vince and I were sent to the New York City Police Academy for a four-week course in investigations. Being with thirty other officers from New York Police was a mind-enriching experience. They work in a different world. I envied their tasks.

We took the Bay Shore bus from Leonardo every morning. Then we had to take the crosstown subway to Second Avenue. Next step was the uptown subway express to 110th Street. This was an experience in itself. I felt safe carrying a gun during these rides.

After graduation from the academy, I had much more confidence in my abilities to work as a detective.

Nancy, my wife, was happy—no more midnights. My schedule consisted of two-week day shifts and one week of 5:00 p.m. to 1:00 a.m. shift. I was off duty most weekends and had more time with my family. I now had two baby girls to help raise.

My First Murder Investigation

It was quiet summer learning how to be a detective. Vince and I were working well as partners. I did most of the report writing. After our shift, I remained behind to finish reports. Vince headed across the street to Muldoon's bar. It was all right, except when we worked 4:00 p.m. to 12:00 a.m. He often borrowed my car for his nightly escapades. I would have to get a ride home with patrol. In the morning, the car was back at my house, returned during the night. I didn't ask him where he went or what he did. That was just Vince Flynn doing his thing.

The brass had been in turmoil. Chief Red Woodruff had announced his retirement. The captain candidates for the job had been jockeying and politicking for the position. The town council, with its infinite wisdom, had decided to give each candidate a one-month trial as "chief of the month." The acting chiefs had been suspending each other (with pay) when they were in power. Each suspension had hit the newspapers. What a joke, the department was the laughingstock of the state. The chief's job would be determined by an interview with the council. I believed the town council knew that the captains couldn't pass a written test by civil service. Most didn't finish high school. May the best man win.

These issues were not my concern; I wanted to solve crimes and be a detective.

My first murder investigation took place in November when Patrolman Eugene Armstrong checked a dirt lane on Van Schoick Road at 3:30 a.m. He shined his spotlight down the rutted dirt lane and observed something on the ground. In the darkness, he couldn't determine what it was. Taking his flashlight, he got out of the patrol car and walked in for a closer inspection. The dirt lane was a notorious as a trysting place for young lovers. He stopped dead in his tracks when he saw the body. It was a woman, half-naked. He approached and checked for a pulse but found none. The body was cold and unresponsive. Noting tire impressions and footprints around the body, he carefully walked out of the roadway and returned to his patrol car. He alerted Sergeant Battle, who was on the desk. Armstrong blocked off the dirt lane and waited for assistance from detectives.

I was called out at 4:00 a.m. I picked up Vince at his home. We arrived at 4:25 am. Lieutenant Lutz arrived to take charge. Shortly thereafter, Detectives McConnel and Schnoor were called to duty by Lieutenant Lutz. They arrived at 5:30 a.m. ID officer Dodge arrived with the ID van. The county prosecutor's office was notified, and Detective Sergeant Mannigrasso came to the scene. The medical examiner was called and arrived at 6:30 a.m. Van Schoick Road was blocked off, and all motorists driving past were stopped and questioned. We had a murder to investigate.

Vince, Dodge, and I entered the dirt road with the medical examiner. Both sides of the road were overgrown with brush, and the light was poor. Making sure nothing was disturbed, we escorted Dr. Gilmore to the body. He pronounced the woman dead and authorized the removal of the body. Now the grisly work began. I took notes while Dodge took the photographs. Vince rolled the body over. She had been lying on her side. Her hair was disheveled. She appeared to be in her fifties and weighed about 170 pounds. She had a coil of cloth around her neck. Her eyes bulged, and her face was a reddish color. Her striped blouse was torn and pulled up. Her bra was still hooked but pulled over her breasts. Her black slacks were torn, and the zipper was broken. They were pulled down to her thighs. Her granny panties were pulled down and ripped. Lividity was not present, but we noted bruises on her face and upper body. All indications were that a beating did not cause the death; we suspected she died of strangulation. We would learn more after the autopsy. We also wanted to know if she had been sexually assaulted.

On the basis of body temperature and outside temperature, the medical examiner estimated the time of death around 2:00 a.m.

There were no signs of a struggle on the ground; we believed the body was dumped at this location from a parked car.

ID officer Dodge photographed the shoe prints and tire impressions. With the assistance of the county detectives, plaster casts were made of the tire and shoe impressions. An ambulance arrived, and the body was removed. Under the body was a brown paper bag. It was a typical lunch bag. A flower was drawn on the outside of the bag, something a child might draw. Inside the bag was a paper coffee cup, three Sunny Dollar coupons from a Sunoco Gas Station, and four candy wrappers. We preserved the bag for fingerprints. A thorough search of the area did not produce any other physical evidence.

After the crime-scene search, we concluded she was probably killed in a car and dumped at the scene. The killer drove to the lane, stopped near the end, about a hundred feet from the roadway, then got out of the driver's side and pulled the victim out on the passenger side, thus the position of the body. When she was pulled out, the paper bag came out with her. We hoped the bag was part of the crime scene and not discarded by a previous person. The victim didn't leave any footprints. We did not know who she was or where she was from. There were no identification marks on her clothing or any pocketbook or purse at the scene.

Back at headquarters, Dodge developed a photograph of a facial shot he had taken. He made fifty copies. Our first task was to identify the victim. Lieutenant Lutz had me prepare a press release, hoping to get the papers to print the photo. The other photos were sent to local police departments.

I was off duty at 7:30 p.m. after a long day.

The Murder Investigation

I returned to headquarters duty on Sunday at 7:00 a.m. At home, I could not sleep. I know a case is best solved in the first forty-eight hours. I wrote reports and reviewed the evidence, then I went home at noon. I was back at the headquarters at 7:00 a.m. on Monday morning. Lieutenant Lutz called for a meeting at the squad room at nine.

Lutz assigned me to do the briefing. Present were Lieutenant Lutz, Detectives Flynn, Schnoor, McConnell, Swenson, Dodge, and Patrolmen Armstrong andStover on temporary assignment, and Detective Mannigrasso and Manning from the prosecutor's office.

I filled everyone in on what we had accomplished. A fifty- to sixty-year-old female was strangled and dumped on the dirt lane off Van Schoick Road. There was no identification as of yet. Photos would be given to each detective. Facial photo already sent to area newspapers. The press should have the picture in the paper today. Our first priority was the identification of the victim. All detectives were assigned to this task.

I also told all the detectives we also had tire impressions from the scene, footprints near the body, foot size about 9, and a brown paper bag next to the body. No fingerprints were found on the bag or contents.

Patrol Captain Wilson assigned two men to assist Detective Dodge in another search of the crime-scene area. He also had the area staked out when the searchers had left. It is a truism that the killer may return to the scene of the crime. We would have the name and address of anyone who would show interest in the lane off Van Schoick Road.

At noon, Detective McConnell calls in with a tentative identification from Sergeant George Preston of Keansburg Police. He recognized the photo. He believed the victim was Mary Russo, with no known address; she had been homeless for the past year. He described her as an alcoholic and a barfly. Her nickname was "Pissy Mary" because she would urinate while sitting on a barstool. She would hang out at local bars and go home with anyone who would give her shelter.

Together with Detective Sergeant Preston and Detective Beatty, I canvassed the local taverns. Some patrons at the Stagecoach Tavern remembered her being in the bar Saturday night. They gave us a list of the other patrons in the bar that night. This was a local watering hole, and everybody usually knew each other. Some recall a young man they didn't know sitting at the bar that night. His description was of a white male, early twenties, slight build, black hair, wearing a blue jacket and blue slacks. Witnesses saw the bartender check his identification. Whitey Baccara was tending bar that night. Sergeant Preston said he would locate him right away.

The bar witnesses recall wasn't good due to the consumption of beer that night, but the consensus was that Pissy Mary walked out alone around midnight. The stranger left about 12:30 a.m. A composite photo of the stranger was made by Detective Dodge from the witness descriptions.

Back at headquarters, I shifted assignments. Schnoor and Manning took the plaster casts to local automobile-tire dealers for identification. McConnell and Manigrasso took the shoe plaster casts to shoe stores for information. Vince and I worked on the bag contents. Detective Stover and Swenson were on other investigations, as the murder didn't stop other crimes. Schnoor also had the task of looking at the records of known sex offenders in the county.

Tuesday morning, Sergeant Preston still could not the locate bartender, Whitey Baccara. Preston thought he was avoiding talking to us. There was nothing on the candy wrappers in the bag. The Sunoco Sunny Dollar coupons came from the Sunoco Gas Station on Highway 35 Holmdel. The owner could determine when he had issued them. He also had no idea who got them. The coupons were given to all who purchase gas. He had given out thousands. The paper coffee cup had a serial number on the bottom. We tried to find the out who made it. One of Mary Russo's male friends was picked up by Sergeant Preston. Stanley Hawkins of Keansburg allowed her to sleep on his porch when she didn't have a place to go. He did not have a car, and his foot size was big, a least a size 11 shoe. He was not a suspect at this time.

On Wednesday, fourth day of the investigation, Sergeant Preston finally located Whitey. He would meet us at the Stagecoach bar tonight. He wouldn't tell Sergeant Preston where he was living. We went to work on the paper cup. It was manufactured in Syracuse, New York. Syracuse Police notified for assistance. Detectives from Syracuse Police contacted the manufacturer. They cooperated and sorted through records as to where the cup was shipped. McKenna, acting chief at that time, called me in from Keansburg headquarters. He had information that could solve the case. *What's with that?* I wondered.

At 1:20 p.m., Vince and I went to the chief's office. He introduced us to Mrs. Elsie Ruheimer. The chief had us bring her the crime scene photos and the reports. He also wanted us to take her and her husband to the crime scene. Mrs. Ruheimer was a least eighty years old and her husband older. She told the chief she had psychic powers and would tell us who committed the crime after she visited the scene. I told the chief we had a meeting with Sergeant Preston and suggested he take them. I don't know how we got out of that assignment; I think the chief knew we thought Mrs. Ruheimer was a nut and waste of time.

At 10:00 p.m., we met with Whitey at the bar. He was afraid of us because he was booking sports bets at the tavern. After we threatened him, he agreed to cooperate. He checked the license of the young man to determine his age. He said he didn't remember anything else. He did give us a description that matched the description given by other patrons. He observed Pissy Mary ask the stranger to buy her a beer but the stranger refused. Whitey did not see them talking again. Whitey also liked the composite made by Detective Dodge.

Thursday at the headquarters, Detective McConnell, known to us as "the Badge," received a call from Syracuse detectives. That paper coffee cup was shipped to one of three businesses in Monmouth County, New Jersey: a rug-manufacturing plant in Freehold, a coffee plant in Freehold, and a perfume-manufacturing plant in Holmdel. Badge would follow up this lead. Detectives Schnoor and Manigrasso found the four tire imprints to be of different makes and models—two Goodyear, one Michelin, and one of unknown make, possible a foreign tire. All the tires were low on tread. An indication that that suspect vehicle that dumped the victim was possibly and old junker.

Vince and I went to interview Whitey again. We were hoping maybe his memory had improved. Vince talked him into being hypnotized with the proviso that we would not ask anything about bookmaking. Whitey was afraid of Vince for some reason. At 3:00 p.m., we were at Dr. Motell's office. The good doctor assisted the police on investigations. The hypnosis was somewhat successful. Whitey recalled the year of birth on the suspects driver's license. It was 1945, indicating our suspect was twenty-three years old.

It was Friday. We got nothing from the newspaper copy on the posting of the photograph of the paper bag. I was hoping some parent would recognize their child's drawing. At 9:00 a.m., the chief sent for Vince and I. We were dreading this meeting for we knew Mrs. Ruheimer would be there. She was smiling and confident. She told us the killer was a big, husky man in his fifties who was a heavy drinker and a women abuser. "There you are," said the chief. "Go get him." We thanked the chief and Mrs. Ruheimer and got the hell out of his office. That was the chief's contribution to the investigation.

Badge reported to us that the perfume factory did not allow their cups to leave the cafeteria. One ounce of the perfume base was worth thousands. The cafeteria was guarded by their security staff. Interesting information, I thought.

By Saturday, six days into the investigation, we had a list of persons of interest—persons in the tavern when she left Saturday night, persons that allowed her to stay in their homes, persons she slept with for shelter or money. No one stood out as a suspect except the young stranger in the bar.

We took Sunday off. Vince and I have been working sixteen hours a day since the murder. We noticed the identikit composite was in the Sunday papers, along with the victim's photo and the paper bag.

Monday morning, we had a meeting at the squad room. Lieutenant Lutz let me take the lead again. We decided to concentrate on finding the stranger. We had his composite, we knew his size and clothing, and he drank beer. That's it. Vince and I decided to check the perfume factory. If the only person able to take out a coffee cup was a security guard, did they have a guard that matched the composite photo?

The security manager was a retired police officer from Asbury Park, a retired detective named Johnny Parsons. He looked at the composite and said it resembled a guard on the night shift. I asked for information on this guard. At that time, he knew the employee was twenty-four years old and lived in Asbury Park. He drove an old Chrysler. He had been employed for six months, and his last employment was with the US Army. He looked like a real good suspect. He was due to work at 4:00 p.m. on Wednesday. His name was Henry Johnson. Parsons would arrange for Vince and me to interview him at the plant. Tomorrow we would look for his car. The prosecutor's office would check his military records. This guy was looking better and better.

The Arrest

Tuesday morning, Vince and were I excited at the prospect of solving the case. Johnny Parsons called. It's great to have a former police detective assisting. He found, through other employees, that the suspect's car had been impounded in Ocean Township. It had broken down on Park Avenue with a flat tire. With the car being on the street overnight on a busy roadway, the police impounded it and had it towed. I called Detective Rogers of the Ocean Police. He said, "They had the car and would hold it for us."

Vince and I went to Ocean Township Police headquarters. Assisted by Detective Charlie Rogers, we viewed the car in the impound yard. The tires seemed to match the photos we had of the crime-scene tire impressions. Vince noticed a place on the dashboard that had a piece of tape stuck to the chrome, possible where the paper bag was hung. Detective Rogers would guard the car while we returned to our headquarters to obtain search and seizure warrants.

I prepared the documents, while Vince contacted the judge. After the orders were signed, Vince and Detective Dodge went with a tow truck and seized the car. We took the tires off and sent them to the state police lab in Trenton.

Wednesday morning, we prepared for our meeting with the suspect. We suspected he was the person at the Stagecoach bar who had talked to the victim. We would confirm this with a lineup tonight. His car tires matched, but this was not confirmed yet. His physical size matched the person at the bar. In his capacity as a security guard, he would have been able to take the coffee cup from the plant. We would seize his shoes when we meet him. We were ready for the interrogation.

At 3:30 p.m., Vince and I were at the perfume plant. Parsons had us wait in his office. At 4:10 p.m., he introduced us to Henry Johnson. He was a small man with dark hair and a ruddy face. I thought the composite fit perfectly. He seemed nervous but under control. As per union rules, we had to wait for the shop steward to be present. I advised the shop steward he could be called as a witness to this questioning. He didn't object; he didn't know the situation.

The first question I asked was, "Henry, do you know why we are here?" He said no. I asked him if he was at the Stagecoach bar Saturday night, November 5. He said he had never been in there. I asked him if he would voluntarily stand in a lineup, and he agreed. The shop steward asked why we wanted to do this. When I told him it was a murder investigation, he look shocked. Henry turned gray and came close to passing out. The shop steward said he would contact a lawyer for Henry. I told him to have the lawyer contact me before the lineup was conducted and I would wait for him.

At 7:00 p.m., back in the squad room at headquarters, lawyer Martin McCall arrived. I didn't know him, and I was sure he wasn't a criminal attorney. He voiced a mild objection to the procedure, but I explained to him what was going to happen. The detectives found seven other persons of the same race, size, and age of the suspect. I stood them in a line at the back of the squad room. Each held a card with a number. I asked McCall where he would like his client to stand. He objected again, and I told he didn't have to be present and not to say anything to the witnesses. He seemed a little overwhelmed but followed my rules. He chose position 7 for Henry. We photographed the lineup for court.

The lineup consisted of three police officers who were in civilian clothing and not known to the witnesses, a Coca Cola-machine repairman who was making a repair to the machine in the foyer, and three men who were patrons of Muldoon's tavern. The three volunteered at Vince's request. Vince brought in Whitey. We had him view the lineup, and I gave him a form to fill out. Swenson had picked up two witnesses who were at Stagecoach that night. They viewed the lineup and were given the form. The forms asked two questions: (1) "Do you recognize anyone in the line?" and (2) "How do you know this person?" I retrieved the forms. The witnesses were thanked for their service and transported back to home or the bar. The officers changed to uniforms and went back to patrol.

Henry and his lawyer were placed in an interrogation room. We took the suspect's shoes. Again, McCall mildly objected.

The three witnesses were sure Henry was the stranger in the bar. The shoes were the same size as the shoe impressions at the crime. We had enough evidence. Vince was happy to make the arrest. He booked Henry and set up a court appearance for the morning. McCall said he was not going to litigate the matter and Henry would have to arrange for a criminal attorney.

Off duty at 11:30 p.m., I went to Muldoon's tavern to celebrate with the detectives. They had a raucous time recapping all that they did. I quietly left and went home.

On Friday morning at the headquarters, Lieutenant Lutz and acting Chief McKenna found out we had made an arrest, and they were elated. The chief wanted the information for a press release and a perp walk. The detectives were sitting around, drinking coffee, patting themselves on the back. I don't begrudge them, they worked hard, but I was the one doing the necessary paperwork. At 10:00 a.m., Vince and I decided to interview Henry before his initial court appearance. Badge took him from his cell and placed him in the interrogation room. Vince was the first interrogator. He was hollering and screaming at Henry, calling him a murderer of women. This went on for twenty minutes. I was next, the good guy. The old routine of "good guy, bad guy" works.

Henry was crying when I went in. I offered him a cup of coffee, which he declined. He was sitting across from me, a table between us. He was wringing his hands and softly moaning. I spoke to him, telling him I understood his situation. I was soothing and understanding. I reached across the table and held his hand. "What happened, Henry?" I asked. He confessed.

I called in Vince and the stenographer Evelyn. Henry was going to give us a statement. After the routine questions at the beginning, I asked him to tell us what happened.

He began by saying that after work, he went to the Stagecoach bar in Keansburg. He had heard of the bar from fellow workers. The bar had country music, which he liked.

I asked him, "What happened at the bar?"

"I was having a beer when this older lady came over and sat next to me. She smelled awful. She wanted me to buy her a beer. I refused and moved away from her. A little later, I saw her leave. She staggered and was unsteady when she left the bar. I had another beer then left."

Vince asked, "What time did you leave?"

"I left about 12:30 a.m., and when I got outside, it was drizzling. When I got to my car, I opened the door and she was sitting in the passenger seat. She asked me to take her to my home. I refused and told her to get out of my car. She pleaded with me and asked me to drop her off at the Holly Hill Motel on the highway. I felt sorry for her and drove to the motel. When we got there, she wanted me to get a room. She had no money and would sleep with me if I paid for a room. No way was I going in a room with her. Henry didn't need any prompting. He continued.

"She asked me to take her to a friend's house up the road. She directed me to this dirt lane. There weren't any houses nearby. She wanted me to have sex with her. I told her to get out of the car, but she refused. I got out and went around to the passenger side, opened the door, and dragged her out. She fell on the ground, I got back in the car, and I left. That's all."

I told him I had just a few follow-up questions. Vince left to get the paper bag. I asked him if he ripped her clothing. He denied this but said she pulled up her striped shirt when she asked him for sex. Vince came back with the bag. When Henry saw the bag, he said the bag was his and it must have fallen out of his car when he pulled the woman out.

I had no further questions. Vince wanted to question him more, but I thought if we pushed him, he might not sign the statement or recant some of it. I didn't believe his sad story, but we had plenty for a trial. Henry seemed very relieved. I requested the judge to wait for an hour before the arraignment. I told the judge the defendant's lawyer was en route. He was from the public defender's office.

At 12:30 p.m., Henry was charged with murder. The judge set bail at a million dollars. The public defender objected to no avail, and Henry was remanded to the county jail.

At 2:00 p.m., the paperwork was completed, and Henry was leaving for the county jail. The chief walked him from the cellblock out the front door to a waiting patrol car. Someone had notified the press, I wonder whom. The press took photos of the chief and Henry, and they were on the front page. The *Asbury Park Press*, the *Red Bank Register*, the *Courier*, even the *Newark Star Ledger*, printed the photos and the story of the arrest. Vince and I were mentioned somewhere in the article.

Case closed pending court.

Case of Arson!

Fire broke out in a church on a Sunday night in the fall. An unidentified man stood in the woods across the street, gazing at the burning church. He watched as the fire trucks arrived and the firemen spring into action. The nearest hydrant was 330 yards away, and a lot of hose had to be laid. By the time the water was turned on, it was too late. Nothing could be saved except the foundation.

Fire trucks, police cars, and an ambulance blocked the roadway. Cars were stopped, and a crowd started to gather. The unidentified man (later identified as Fred Craft) masturbated and then joined the crowd. His eyes were still gleaming when he attempted to assist the fireman put the hoses back on the trucks. They chased him away.

When the fire was reduced to white smoke and flying ash, Fred walked away. His gait was fast on short, stiff legs. He walked north for three miles until he reached the highway. He turned east and walked to a nearby strip mall. On the corner of the mall was a pool hall. Detective Swenson worked part time in the pool hall for extra money. He had six kids.

Fred ran into the pool hall hollering about a fire in the dumpster behind the mall. Fred said, "I am a state trooper. Call the fire company." Swenson called for fire trucks and went out back to check the fire. The dumpster was engulfed in flames. It was a Sunday, and it hadn't been emptied for three days.

The fire trucks arrived with very tired firemen. They had just returned from the church fire. They quickly put out this fire. Patrolman Bob Foster was at the scene. He and Swenson looked for the state trooper who reported the fire. They wanted to know how he was able to observe a fire behind the mall. Swenson was suspicious of him; he was young and didn't have the look of a law-enforcement officer.

Fred had hitched a ride. He went to his home in Toms River, where he lived with his parents.

Monday morning, Chief McKenna was wild. The mayor was coming in for information. The town council was worried. The church was in a neighborhood of upper middle-class homes. The church had been in this location for over a hundred years. The parish supported a small group of black people that lived on Church Lane. The roadway next to the church had small homes occupied by the same family line since the Civil War. Developers tried to buy their property many times. The houses were old wood-frame types, but the property was very valuable. The politicians didn't want any hints of racial strife. The chief told us to solve this arson as quickly as possible.

Vince and I went to the church first thing in the morning. Meeting us was Fred Dispensier, the county arson investigator. In the ruins, we a found kerosene can in the area where the fire started. The kerosene smell was strong. No doubt an arsonist started this fire. We took some samples of the wood for evidence.

The next three months, Vince and I checked on every known firebug in the county. We went to almost every fire. We expanded to fires in other parts of the state. We found nothing. Reading the *Teletype* one morning, we saw where the state police had arrested a person for setting grass fires in Burlington county. They set a date for other agencies to interview him. Vince and I called and responded. We met with Fred Craft that day. He was a five-foot-six white male with a fifth-grade education. He admitted starting the grass fires. But the state police suspected more.

I introduced myself and Vince. I asked him if he was in Monmouth County three months ago. He said, "I hitchhike all over. I might have been there. Do you have many fires there?" I asked him if he set a church on fire one night about three months ago. He answered, "Oh no, I won't do that to a church. I am a Catholic and Father Corrigan would be mad." He was taking a polygraph on other fires, and I requested the trooper examiner to ask him about our church fire.

The polygraph expert, Trooper Jimmy Murphy, gave us his opinion. There was no deception in the church fire. Freddie tried to hide his involvement in other fires, but Murphy easily deduced this. Later in the day, Freddie confessed to setting other fires. His bail was increased, and he was placed back in the Burlington County Jail awaiting trials. We left, but he was still on our suspect list.

Another three months went past. The church parishioners were having services in a nearby Methodist church. The pastor, Reverent Eziekel Perkins, was as gracious and understanding as anyone I ever met. He said, "I forgive the arsonist for he did not know what he was doing." There was no pressure from the pastor or his congregation, but the politicians were still demanding the chief solve the case. The chief was asking me daily what I was doing. He was angry when I had nothing to report. He threatened to replace all the detectives.

A few weeks later, Vince and I were shuffling through reports and my notebook. We didn't have any other cases that needed imme-diate attention, so we decided we needed a ride. We went to the Burlington County Jail to talk to Freddie again. We asked Freddie to take a ride with us. He readily agreed. He wanted to get out of jail for a while.

On the ride back to the township, Freddie admitted to setting other fires. He used to hang out near the firehouse in Silverton, where he lived. He would set fire to crow weeds and run back to the firehouse. When the whistles went off and the fire trucks raced to the fire scene, Freddie ran after them. He often got to the fire before the fire trucks arrived by taking shortcuts. He could do this because he set the fire. Because he was a likeable kid and only sixteen years old, the fire company made him a junior fireman. They didn't suspect him at this time of being a pyromaniac. This gave him access to the firehouse. Two weeks later, the firehouse caught fire, and there was major damage. Freddie saved the fire truck. Freddie was the suspect, but they couldn't prove it. Freddie was dismissed from the company. Freddie told us he set that fire and laughed about it.

Back in the township, I purposely drove past the burnt-out church. Freddie got excited and said, "I set that place on fire." I asked him how he did it. He said, "I was walking down the road from the Garden State Parkway. I saw a white building, no one was around. The back door was unlocked, and there was kerosene stove in the room and kerosene can near the stove. I spilled the fluid on the floor and set it on fire." He was getting excited as he told the story. He was dribbling and shaking. I requested he give us a written statement, and he agreed.

At headquarters, Detective Swenson identified Freddie as the person who reported the fire behind the pool hall. Freddie admitted that too. Vince and I took a statement on both fires. I gave Freddie a soda and some bubble gum I had in my desk. He was delighted. I called Billy Eastmond, a reporter for the local newspaper, and had him meet Vince and me at the church. He took a photograph of Freddie, Vince, and me as Freddie pointed to the church a where he started the fire. Handcuffs were on his wrists. The picture was very graphic. We scooped the chief and Captain Lutz. The chief would have wanted to be in that photograph.

En route to the Burlington County Jail, Freddie was in the back seat blowing gum bubbles. Near Fort Dix on a lone stretch of road, Freddie said he could conjure up a fire. I told him to go ahead. A few miles later, I heard sirens ahead. At the next intersection, two fire trucks roared through. Freddie said he started the fire. What a scary dude!

We were hailed as competent detectives by the media. Little did they know we could have solved this much earlier. Freddie didn't know the white building was a church. He never looked up to see a steeple and cross. We wasted time looking in other directions when we had Freddie right in front of us. I felt good about the arrest but stupid for the mistake. Thank goodness, no one knew about this except Vince and me. I am not as smart as I pretend.

When we went to trial on this case, the defense was trying to prove Freddie was incompetent and should not have been allowed to confess. He was too stupid to know what he was doing. This defense was sound but didn't work for Freddie. When he was in jail, he sent me four letters. He was receiving information and help from inmates who were jailhouse lawyers. Freddie wrote Latin terms and lengthy legal sentences and used police terminology. I was sure he didn't understand what he was writing. I saved the letters and produced them at the trial. Freddie admitted sending the letters and told the judge he understood everything he wrote. I didn't understand all he wrote. The defense attorney asked him why he wrote letters to Detective Holiday. He said, "He was a nice man and gave me bubble gum."

The judge ruled him competent. This decision surprised me. The judge found him guilty but mentally ill. Freddie was sent to the Vroom hospital for the criminally insane. The term was undetermined and dependent on his mental condition.

Every Christmas season since his incarceration, I would receive a Christmas card from Freddie. On the front is a candle burning. Inside, it says, "Merry Christmas. Freddie."

Case closed.

Witchcraft Investigation

Do you believe in witchcraft? Diane O'Neil did. Diane had been afflicted with diabetes since childhood. She had been injecting herself with insulin for fifteen years every day. She had been depressed for years. Diane was in her senior year at Villanova University. She was majoring in literature and journalism. She had tried everything medicine offered.

When a distant aunt suggested she contact someone from the Wicca religion, she agreed. Her aunt gave her the phone number of a priestess called Ms. Kitty in New Jersey. Diane called Kitty for an appointment. Kitty invited her to her home for a discussion and the possibility of a cure.

In March, the university was on winter break. Diane and her fiancé, John Barr, drove to Monmouth County and registered at the Howard Johnson Motel in Middletown Township. Tuesday morning, John drove Diane to Kitty's home. It was a run-down bungalow on the beach. Kitty told her she would ask the good witches to cure Diane. She said, "I have to go to New York City and purchase curing potions." These potions would cost ten thousand dollars. John thought that Kitty looked like the bad witch of the north from the Wizard of Oz. He believed she was a fraud, but he could not convince Diane.

After the meeting with Kitty and the witch, Diane and John went back to the motel. Diane called her aunt to borrow the money. The aunt agreed to loan her the money and send it by wire. Diane called Kitty. John tried to object, but Diane was adamant. She was going to try the witchcraft cure.

Kitty told Diane to come to her home that night with the money and be prepared to stay the night. John was to remain at the motel.

Thursday morning Diane called John. She told him they had a ceremony in a black room. She was certain to be cured. She had not taken insulin since Tuesday. Kitty told her, "I need more money because the bad witches found out about the ceremony and will cast a spell." She needed an additional five thousand dollars for more of the potion. Diane asked John to call her aunt for the money. She was staying with Kitty overnight again. She would call tomorrow for the money.

Friday morning, John heard from Diane. She sounded weak, and her speech was slurred. Diane wanted John to bring the money as soon as possible. John asked her about her insulin. She said, "I don't need it anymore."

At noon, John Barr made an important decision. He went to police headquarters for help. The desk sergeant sent him to the detective bureau. All the detectives were at lunch, so I interviewed him. He informed me what was happening. When Vince returned from lunch, I had him check on the background of Kitty. I took a statement from John Barr.

Kitty's real name was Mrs. Catharine Gorinske. She had a lengthy arrest record. She had been arrested for shoplifting many times, but lately she had been involved with fraud. She had two pending cases on fraud using the pigeon drop game. Her husband, Igor Gorinske, was her accomplice. With this information, I drew up an application for a search warrant. I was looking for evidence of witchcraft being used to defraud. The judge found the request for the search unusual but gave us the warrant.

At 6:00 p.m., we planned the raid. John told us he heard dogs barking when he was at the house. I requested the dog-control officer to accompany us. A reporter from the local paper was in the bureau at that time. She heard us discussing the raid and requested to go. I allowed her to go with one stipulation. She was to keep silent and just observe. It was Friday the thirteenth. I decided to go at midnight, which, under the circumstances, seemed appropriate.

At midnight my group drove near the bungalow. We parked three houses north on the same side of the street. Detective McConnell was assigned to break down the door if necessary. We didn't have a no-knock warrant, so I lightly tapped on the door. There was no answer, but the dogs in the backyard started barking loudly. It sounded like many dogs. Badge kicked the door in. It broke easily. Vince and I entered with Detective Schnoor, reporter Nancy Smith and John Barr right behind us. They were all in the living room. We really surprised them. Diane was on the couch and appeared asleep. We ordered Kitty and Igor against the wall for a weapons pat-down. Special Officer Veronica McNair searched Kitty. John and I tried unsuccessfully to wake Diane. I called for an ambulance and urged them to hurry.

John and Diane left in the ambulance for the hospital. We arrested the Gorinskes and started the search. There was a small dog in the house without eyes. The dog control officer found eleven other dogs in a filthy kennel in the rear yard. All the dogs were malnourished and without eyes. The animal-control officer had to call for more trucks to transport the dogs. In a separate room off living room, we discovered a room with an altar with a goat's head on top of it. There was an open book in front of the goat's head. The book was about witch ceremonies. Two lit candles were on each side of the book. The walls and ceiling and door were painted black.

I placed Kitty and Igor under arrest. Kitty asked if she could change her clothing before she went to jail. She was wearing a black belted gown. I had Badge search her bedroom first. Disguised reporter Nancy Smith stood by the bedroom door as Kitty went in to change. We confiscated her black robe. We also confiscated the black robe that Igor wore, a devil's mask, and some jars with powder inside. We found eight thousand dollars in an envelope on her dresser. As we left, Kitty announced, "I'm putting a spell on you!" She got angry when we all laughed.

Back at the headquarters, I called the chief and Lieutenant Lutz. I gave them the information for a press release. The *Courier* newspaper would have the scoop, but the other papers would want this story.

Saturday morning, I called the hospital. Diane was taken off the critical list. John Barr was at her bedside. He saved her life by coming to us. I needed him for another statement. A meeting was set up for Monday morning.

On Friday morning, the chief called Vince and me to his office. The Gorinskes made bail. They then went to the prosecutor's office to file complaints against Vince and me and all the others who were on the raid. She charged us with sexual harassment. She said that we forced her to disrobe in front of everyone and made lewd and lascivious remarks about her body. When I informed Chief McKenna that we had a female reporter with us, he was elated. He had been feuding with the prosecutor for months. He called the newspaper and requested Nancy Smith to come into headquarters.

Ms. Smith stated, "The police actions were proper and professional." The chief had me take her statement. He called the prosecutor's office and told them, "Go to hell with your complaints."

Without the chief's knowledge, I called the assistant prosecutor handling the case. I wanted to avoid unnecessary work from both camps. I told Assistant Prosecutor Folet of my newspaper witness. He became interested. He asked for her statement. He said the complaints would be voided when he received Ms. Smith's information.

The next day, Assistant Prosecutor Folet called the chief. He said the Gorinskes complaints were dropped. The chief wanted the Gorinskes charged with making false charges. That was not to happen. The chief was not happy.

Case closed pending court.

The Murder of Fourteen-Year-Old Jane Durra

Keansburg High School was in the third week of classes. Jane Durra, a student, attended all her classes. After school, she went to the first football game of the season. It was a home game in the athletic field behind the school. Jane was living with an aunt and uncle in New York City until she was accosted in the hallway outside of their apartment. She escaped the mugger unharmed but frightened. The family moved her to her older sister's home on Forrest Avenue, Keansburg.

After the game, she walked home to Forrest Avenue, two blocks from the high school. She ate a sandwich, changed her clothing, and left her sister Janet a note saying, "I am walking to Della's home on Essex Street, East Keansburg." Della was her aunt. Jane would go there often. She never arrived at Della's house on Essex Street.

Janet telephoned Della at 8:30 p.m. She wanted to know when Jane was coming home. When Della told her Jane had not been there, Janet became alarmed. Her husband, Gus, took a flashlight and walked the route Jane would have taken. Their house was next to the railroad tracks; the shortest distance to Della's house was along these tracks. The night was dark, and there was little light along the tracks. The batteries in the flashlight were also weak. Gus saw nothing.

Janet called Keansburg Police to report her missing. Sergeant Loader responded and took the report. Because her destination was Essex Street in East Keansburg, Middletown Township, police were notified. Patrolman Vince Zemo, Sergeant Loader, Gus, and Janet walked the railroad tracks (the route Jane would have taken) from Forrest Avenue. Della and her husband, Jack, joined the search walking from east Keansburg west. They met in the middle; there was no sign of Jane.

Police patrolled the area looking for her all night. With the exception of service calls, they continued searching. No one had seen a fourteen-year-old girl walking the streets on or near the railroad tracks.

By 6:30 a.m., Janet was frantic. With a better flashlight, they walked the tracks again. Halfway between the homes, Gus spotted a small plastic container in the weeds ten feet off the tracks. The brush and been knocked down, and Gus and Janet followed the trail. Twenty feet away, they found Jane's body.

Gus stayed at the scene; Janet ran back to call headquarters. Patrolman Beaver and Patrolman Killian responded. An ambulance was also dispatched. Patrolman Irv Beaver knew he had a murder scene and immediately taped off the area. Detectives and superior officers were notified.

I was called from the police desk at seven twenty. I picked up Vince and arrived at seven forty-five. Detective Dodge was called for photographs and crime-scene identification procedures. Lieutenant Lutz arrived at 8:10 a.m. Even Chief McKenna stopped outside the tape. No one had been inside the scene except Gus and Janet, Vince and me.

When Vince and I examined the body, we took Detective Dodge with us. The victim was on her back. Her shirt and jacket were next to her. Her skirt was pulled up to her waist. Her panties were torn and pulled down to her ankles. Her socks were on; one shoe was off near the body. She had a large bruise on her face and discoloration around her neck.

The medical examiner, Dr Gilmore, arrived and examined the body. He pronounced her dead and authorized the removal of the body to the morgue. We could now do a thorough search of the area. We used string cord to separate the area into ten-foot squares and searched. The Keansburg police and county detectives assisted us.

In any homicide, the first suspect is the person who finds the body. Lieutenant Lutz and Vince took Gus to the county offices for a polygraph test. I worked the crime scene. At 3:30 p.m., Lieutenant Lutz and Vince returned. There was no deception on Gus's test.

We had little physical evidence—the victim, her clothing, and her plastic sewing kit container. We did not find any weapon that could have caused the bruising on her face. We suspected a fist caused the damage.

At 6:00 p.m., Lieutenant Lutz called for a meeting in the conference room. At least thirty police officers were present. We planned our strategy and listed our tasks. Chief McKenna would give a press release in the morning. When the meeting was over, I went to my desk to prepare my reports. I finished all the paperwork by 10:30 p.m.

Friday, I called Vince, and he met me at the dinner. We ate and went back to the crime scene. It was another black night. I could understand why Gus would miss the location of Jane's body. We searched until 2:00 a.m. We went home, but I couldn't sleep.

Saturday morning, I was really tired. We organized another search of the crime scene. We had many volunteers looking for anything that might be evidence. We searched for a possible weapon. We did not find anything that would help us.

We started with possible sex offenders. We picked up anyone known to us as a recent offender. We requested the assistance of the state police for criminal files. Thirteen suspects were interviewed and released. They had alibis for the period in question.

Keansburg High School principal Gene Bulmer was contacted. He opened the school and helped us round up Jane's classmates. We interviewed them in the school. We worked all weekend without receiving any information that would help.

On Monday afternoon, we received the autopsy report. The victim was raped and beaten. The cause of death was strangulation. It was undetermined if an instrument was used to cause the facial damage. The medical examiner believed it was probably a fist. Blood was found on her clothing. The time of death was before midnight.

The rest of the week's work was interviewing the high school students. Many had seen her at the football game. She was alone when she left the game and walked east toward Forrest Avenue. We interviewed all of Jane's family members and took their statements. At the end of the week, we had conducted over two hundred interviews.

We were getting calls about suspects. My list was growing. Detective Sergeant Preston of Keansburg Police Department called with information about a mentally disturbed person. Vince went on the interview. The person, Charlie Fenton, confessed. This turned out to be a waste of time. He confessed to most murders that were in the newspapers. During the course of the investigation, we took two false confessions.

Vince and I went to New Your City. We went into the criminal files and found the complaint and details of Jane's encounter with the mugger. We interviewed her uncle and aunt. We interviewed Jane's brother who lived with them, but he did not have any information.

Local suspects were running out. We checked them all. Lieutenant Lutz and Vince even went to Florida to interview a suspect. Detective Schnoor and I went to Zanesville, Ohio, on information that two convicted sex offenders from New Jersey were in the area at the time of the crime. This lead did not pan out. Later, I went with county detective Charlie O'Conner to investigate a suspect in Denver, Colorado.

Keansburg police Detective Sergeant Preston, Vince, and I worked diligently for six months without getting anywhere. We decided to start all over again from the beginning. It was tedious and difficult to continue. The only person of interest was a stocky man wearing a light-colored raincoat, spotted north of the school on the tracks at 6:00 p.m. The witness said this unknown person walked fast and was last seen on Main Street in Keansburg. We couldn't find him. The investigation drew to a crawl. As information came into the bureau, we investigated. We uncovered nothing for months.

I told the family I would never forget and never stop looking for her murderer. I was determined to get this killer!

Scrambled Eggs on a Chief's Hat

Deputy Chief Bill Smith passed away. I don't know how old he was, but he had previously told me, "I became a patrolman around the time your grandfather was arrested for bootlegging." He was a hard-drinking man, somewhat like my grandfather. The deputy chief told me he was a drinking buddy of my grandfather, and they often hung out at my uncle's tavern. He was tough and nasty to rookie patrolmen but never hassled me. I guess it was because of family connections. I never saw him do anything but write the shift names in the docket and read the newspaper. He was loyal to the department and popular with the rank and file. We would all miss him.

Services were to be held at the Pryer's Funeral Home. A problem occurred when Smith's widow wanted to set up a memorial table in the funeral home. She wanted to place the deputy's photograph in uniform, a chief's hat, his VFW hat, and his badge on the table. The deputy didn't have a chief's hat and the widow asked to borrow Chief McKenna's hat for this table. McKenna hesitated because his hat had the original hat badge that dated back to the 1920s. He relented to the widow's wishes and lent her the hat and hat badge, assigning Lieutenant Freibott to deliver and retrieve the hat.

Vince and I attended the services in the morning. I noticed the memorial table; it was a fitting tribute to the deputy. We were subpoenaed to the grand jury and had to leave early. We arrived at nine, participated in the service until nine forty-five, and left for court. When we left, the hat was still on the table.

We arrived back at headquarters at 3:30 p.m. The place was swarmed with newspaper reporters. They were buzzing around like bees near a fallen hive. Cops were in small groups, whispering. Curiously, I gathered information from different sources. The chief's

68

hat had turned out to be missing. He asked Lieutenant Freibott for his hat; he didn't have it. Freibott ordered Patrolman Parsons to get the hat, but when he looked for the hat at the funeral parlor, it was not on the table. The chief called all participants to headquarters. All the pallbearers denied seeing the hat. The hat disappeared after the services. The chief suspected someone put the hat in the coffin before the funeral director closed the lid.

It was rumored that the chief called the funeral director and requested that the hat be retrieved. The chief sent a "flunky" special officer to the cemetery to meet with the director. The state of internment was unknown.

Special Officer Steve Lemko returned with the hat. How he got it was unknown. Only Lemko, the funeral director, and the chief know how it was retrieved. Someone had tipped off the press, and they were waiting for Lemko at headquarters. I arrived shortly after the chief got his hat back. The chief would not talk to the press. Under the chief's orders, Lemko was hiding.

The next day, the hat story was on the front pages of all the newspapers in New Jersey. The press had an inside informant. The story was on the Associated Press; thus, it was printed in the New York papers and other papers throughout the country. The *New York Times* and *Los Angeles Times* had the story. I was also told the incident was reported in the London and Tokyo papers. The chief and department were ridiculed by radio personality Don Imus on his morning show. Our agency was global news. Anywhere I went for the next month, people wanted to know what happened and who threw the hat in the coffin.

To this day, I am still asked about the hat. The widow threatened to sue. The chief said he had investigated but never solved the mystery.

I am so thankful I was at court that day.

The Police Chief's Army

These were my working conditions. I was a ranking soldier in the chief's army. It's my job to make things legal, so said the chief. I was the only person in the agency who had a criminal-justice degree. The chief frowned and discouraged his cadre of men from attending college; not many wanted a college education, anyway. For some reason, he did not attempt to stop me in my pursuit of knowledge. I believe it was because I write many of the reports of our activities that end up in court.

The army consists of sworn sixty-five regular officers. The majority of his army were "special" officers—that is, veteran groups, senior citizens, and some service-club members. His nonregular police-officer army was extremely loyal and ready to move into action at his biding. He had over a hundred loyalists.

A group of antiwar protestors requested a permit to demonstrate in front of the naval base at Earle. Before the application was considered, the group set a date to demonstrate. The naval base was a depot used to ship arms, ammunition, and supplies overseas. The war protestors wanted to disrupt this activity.

The chief was determined to disallow this. He surreptitiously called the VFW, American Legion, and the Marine Corps League and asked them for a counter-demonstration. We, the regular police officers, were in the middle although it was easy to discern where our loyalties were. The demonstrators were on the side of the highway in front of the depot. The counter-demonstrators were driving up and down the highway in pick-up trucks, waving American flags and hurling insults and curses at the war protestors. It was starting to get ugly. There were about one hundred protestors and three hundred promilitary people hurling insults at them.

The chief showed up with two buses. He arrested all the antiwar demonstrators picketing on the highway. The navy would not let them on the base. The navy had a contingent of marines at the front gate. The chief ordered all the demonstrators on the bus. The chief told them he was taking them back to their cars, which were parked nearby. But instead, the buses went directly to police headquarters. All the demonstrators were arrested, placed in the courtroom, and held for processing and bail.

The press had been tipped off and showed up at police headquarters with cameras and notebooks. The chief ordered me to prepare the charges and make them legal. He did not want me to confer with the county prosecutor, as he was feuding with him. I did consult with the town attorney. I charged the demonstrators with disrupting traffic on a highway and failure to disperse. However, I didn't recall anyone asking them to disperse.

All the demonstrators were photographed, booked, and individually brought before the municipal judge. He released them in their own recognizance and set a date for the court trail. I knew we would have to contend with powerful lawyers. If we escaped without a major lawsuit, we were lucky.

A week later, two patrolmen arrested a group of hippies for speeding on the highway. When the Volkswagen van was stopped, the officers searched the van. Marijuana seeds were found on the floor, and all eight occupants were charged. They were released on summons. The chief was delighted with the arrest and told me to assist the patrolman with the reports (and to "make it legal"). The chief didn't believe in the recent Supreme Court decisions. He allowed me to use "creative writing" in the reports. I absolutely refused to allow perjury, but I helped the patrolman to craft their words for a legal stop, search-and-seizure arrest. We had been making these arrests for the past year and had gained a reputation. The "drug culture" adherents had been warned to be wary of our department.

This last group of pot-smokers complained to the press. They also made it known that a group of them and their friends were going to town hall for the next public meeting. They were going to complain to the mayor and council about police harassment and misconduct.

When the chief learned the plans of the hippies, he went into action. He called upon his army of senior citizens. The chief visited the senior citizens often and was a frequent guest speaker. He had me speak on occasions. The seniors met often and discussed many topics. Politics and crime interested them. They loved the chief. When he told them a group of pot-smoking hippies were going to protest police arrests and searches, they were outraged. They soon organized.

The night of the meeting was a warm and comfortable evening. If was almost impossible to get near the town hall. The meeting room was full at six thirty even though business was scheduled to start at eight. Outside, the crowds of senior citizens were becoming noisy and rowdy. There were a least thirty posters being held on sticks supporting the chief and department. There must have been five hundred people outside the meeting room that only holds one hundred fifty people. There was standing room only.

At 8:10 p.m., a psychedelic painted van and an old car pulled into the parking lot. A group of ten persons headed for the hall. They looked like they were in their twenties. They had long hairs and were dressed in hippie garb. We needed uniformed police officers to escort them. The calls from the crowd were shocking. You wouldn't think that senior citizens would use foul, vulgar, and threatening language. Once inside, we arranged for them to have seats in the front row. When the mayor called for the public portion of the meeting, the crowd screamed for the hippies to leave.

The meeting could not be held due to the behavior of the seniors who had filled the seats. After some futile attempts of the mayor to listen to the hippies, he cancelled the meeting. The crowd cheered and chased the hippies back to their vehicles. A marked police car had to give them a safe escort out of town.

On the steps of town hall, the chief, in full uniform, thanked the people for supporting the police department. The press was present but didn't print his remarks. The press reported us as being overly aggressive in car stops and searches.

There were a number of senior citizen high-rise buildings in the township. The senior apartment buildings are located near major shopping centers. Many apartments have windows that overlook the parking lot and stores in the shopping center. The chief organized some of the residents to watch over the center. He made them special officers. He gave them binoculars, clipboards, and police stationary radar to record incidents in the centers. They were to call the police desk when they observed any suspicious activity. These resident calls drove the patrols nuts. They called for everything. Cars double-parked, cars in the fire zone, cars parked in handicapped spaces, and any suspicious persons. There was an eye on the shopping center from early morning until the seniors went to bed. The calls were numerous. They kept the patrolmen very busy. If the patrol didn't respond quickly, they called the chief. He raised hell with the shift supervisor. This was not a popular program with the patrolmen. It did reduce crime in the shopping centers and increased the chief's army.

The state of New Jersey has statutes concerning police departments and police officers. These statutes specifically state the requirements necessary to be a law-enforcement officer, a person qualified to enforce the law, keep the peace, and carry a gun while performing these duties. The training is also specific and must be done at a state-approved academy. I am a certified instructor for the state.

There is also a provision for special officers. The duties are specific as well as the training. Special officers are sworn in by the chief of police, and they are required to have the same training as a regular police officer but can receive this training over a longer period. Many academies in the state have a night program for these part-time police officers.

The chief ordered me to train special officers in the township. He arranged for this training to take place in one of the local high schools. He had 175 people he wanted trained. This was to take place in the evening, one night a week for four weeks. I advised the chief that the state required the applicants to be trained for four nights a week and every other Saturday for nine months. He scoffed at this training and told me to do it in "his" allotted time. I had a copy of the police-academy curriculum and asked him what he wanted me to teach. He refused to look at the state's mandates and ordered me to "just teach them." I followed the orders.

The persons applying were already doing different police duties, mostly in trouble areas where these citizen cops reside. If a citizen complained about a neighborhood situation, the chief would make him a special officer. When this complainant left the chief's office, he would have a badge and the paperwork needed to purchase a gun. This is the start of the chief's army. I couldn't mention the liabilities of these tactics because the chief didn't want to hear them.

I started the classes. The students, mostly seniors, sat at tables in the cafeteria and ate snacks and drank coffee. They were polite and listened to my lectures. They signed in at the start of class but left when they wanted to. The chief said no tests. After four weeks of listening to me, the chief came to the last meeting. When I finished the lecture, which he cut short, he had them all stand. He swore them all in as special police officers! I cringed at some of the new special officers; they were a danger to themselves, to the regular police, and to the public. Only a few were to be paid for specific duties. Most of the specials volunteered their services. They were the last part of his private army.

Is it a defense to say I was following orders? I was in his army. Do you think the chief was brilliant? The crime rate was the lowest in the county. The police budget got passed each year. Our police salaries were the highest in the county. My chief, with only an eighth-grade education, was one of the most powerful men in the county. He could make or break a politician; they knew it and he knew it. His influence could garner any number votes for a political candidate.

These were the conditions of my work.

God bless America.

Hypnotism

Annabelle Rearden went to work on Saturday night. She was a waitress at a steak house in Rumson. Annabelle was a blue-eyed blonde with a smile that could light up a stage. Only eighteen years old, she was a gorgeous beauty who wasn't aware of just how beautiful she was. A vivacious teenager, she was popular with everyone who knew her. She lived with her sister, Sarah, and their parents.

On Sunday morning, Sarah returned to their home after a two-day ski trip. Sarah had to teach her kindergarten class early Monday morning. When she entered the house at noon, she found Annabelle under the dining room table. Annabelle was curled in a fetal position with a severe bruise on her face. She was still wearing her waitress uniform. She was conscious but incoherent. Sarah called 911 for an ambulance and police. Police officers arrived with first responders.

Patrolman Dan Manley interviewed Sarah and investigated the circumstances. He did not find a forced entry. There was nothing missing from the home. Sarah did not know of any reason for the assault. Manley went to the hospital but was not allowed by the doctors to interview Annabelle. Sarah called her parents, who were also away from home for the weekend. They returned immediately. Patrolman Manley notified Lieutenant Lutz. He decided to wait until Monday for a complete investigation.

Monday morning, I was assigned the case. After reading the report, I went to the hospital with Badge (Detective Pat Connell). He was given that nickname because of his demeanor. Badge hated anybody who was not a white Anglo-Saxon American male. He was god-fearing police officer. That sometimes scared me. Although he was gruff in appearance, he always had sympathy for victims of crime and was basically a good cop.

At the hospital, Annabelle was in room 223. At her bedside were her parents, Steve and Maureen Reardon. She was sedated, and I couldn't interview her. Steve and Maureen couldn't believe she was assaulted. Everyone loved Annabelle. The treating physician told me she had a broken cheekbone and severe bruising on the left side of her face. He suggested a closed fist as the instrument that did the damage. I requested Steve to accompany me to his home. Detective Dodge would meet us at the house.

Detective Dodge dusted and found six fingerprints in the common places. He lifted the prints and assisted us in a search. Nothing was found outside the house. No signs of forced entry as in Patrolman Manley's report. Steve reported nothing was missing or disturbed. I had a major mystery.

Later in the afternoon, I interviewed Sarah while Badge checked the neighborhood. Sarah had nothing to add, and the neighbors did not see anything suspicious on Saturday night.

On Tuesday, I was able to talk to Annabelle at the hospital. Maureen was present.

I questioned Annabelle. "Do you remember what had happened to you last Saturday night to Sunday morning?"

She answered, "I remember I was going to work, and that's all."

Her mother had nothing to help me. Back at headquarters, I recalled an incident where a bartender could not remember the information on a driver's license he inspected. His memory was important to my murder investigation. A psychiatrist named Dr. Motell, a trained hypnotist, assisted me in that case.

I contacted Dr. Motell and explained the situation with Annabelle. He said he would assist me. Dr. Motell worked for the prosecutor's office as a consultant. The prosecutor approved. Now I had to obtain permission from her parents and doctors.

With permission granted by both Annabelle parents and her doctors, I picked up Dr. Motell at his office on Wednesday morning. Badge met me at the hospital. Dr. Motell explained the procedure he was going to us before we went into Annabelle's room. Dr. Motell would hypnotize Annabelle, and I would assist him with the questions. Her parents would be in the room, sitting quietly off to the side.

We started to hypnotize Sarah at 11:30 a.m. We dimmed the lights, and the doctor put Annabelle in a state of hypnosis. When she was relaxed, the doctor asked Annabelle the questions that I prepared.

"Annabelle, did you work Saturday night?"

"Yes."

"Did anything happened at the restaurant?"

"No".

"Did anybody annoy you or bother you?"

"No."

"What did you do after work?"

"I drove home."

"Did anybody follow you?"

"I don't think so."

"When did you get home?"

"About eleven thirty."

"Was there anyone at your house or any cars in the driveway?"

"No."

"What did you do next?"

"I tried to go into the house but the fu…key wouldn't work. I told Dad to fix the lock. The f—in' key was stuck. F—k, f—k. Okay, it turned. I am in."

"Is anybody in the house?"

"No. I am tired I am going to make myself something to eat. No, first I think I will take a shower."

"What did you do?"

"I am going upstairs to…"

Annabelle started screaming and crying. Her parents rushed to her side, and Dr. Motell brought her out of the hypnosis. It took twenty minutes to calm her down. Steve Reardon was very upset.

I conferred with Dr. Motell, and we believed that the incident occurred when she went up the stairs. We both thought we should try again. It was difficult, but Dr. Motell and I convinced the parents we should hypnotize her again. Annabelle wanted to try again. We let her rest for a couple hours.

At 3:00 p.m., we tried again. The same procedure was used. The same questions were asked and answered. I could see her parents were embarrassed when she used obscenities at the front door. She was frustrated when she had such a difficult time opening the door. We decided to change interview strategies. We changed questions.

"Annabelle, was anyone in the house?"

"No."

"Did you go to the kitchen?"

"No. I want to shower first."

"Go to the stairs."

"Okay."

"Do you see or hear anyone?"

"No."

"Go up one step. Anything happening?"

"No."

"Go up another step. Anything happening?"

"No."

"Go up the third step. Anything happening?"

"No. I am tired. The restaurant was busy tonight."

"Go up another step. Anything happening?"

"No."

"Go up another step. Anything happening?"

"Bruce is here."

"How do you know that?"

"I smell his awful cologne."

With that answer, I signaled the doctor to stop. Annabelle was brought out of the hypnotic state.

Outside in the hallway, I asked the parents, "Do you know who Bruce is?"

Annabelle's parents answered, "He was her sister Sarah's former boyfriend. They broke up a month ago and have been arguing ever since. Bruce is a senior student at Monmouth University. He lives in a dorm on campus and has been to our house many times."

I told them I would question him right away. I left the hospital to take Dr. Motell back to his office. I called headquarters and requested Badge to pick up Bruce. While I was returning from the doctor's office, I received a radio call from Badge. "I got the maggot, Lieutenant. He confessed. I am bringing him in."

At 5: 30 p.m. at headquarters, Badge and I took a statement from Bruce Kentington. He admitted to the assault.

Bruce said, "I went to the house because I knew nobody would be home. They left a key hidden under the front door mat, and I went inside the house. I have given Sarah a gold bracelet, and I want it back. She doesn't deserve it. She broke off with me. She wouldn't give the bracelet back. I went there to get it. Annabelle came home early. I got scared. I didn't want to get arrested for burglary. When Annabelle came up the stairs, I was hiding behind the door in Sarah's room. When Annabelle passed the room, I hit her and ran. I had my car parked around the corner. I went home. I knew you would catch me. I was going to turn myself in, but I just couldn't. I am afraid I would go to jail."

Bruce Kentington was arrested and booked. His parents bailed him out that night. He had a clean record and was known to be a responsible person. He would plead guilty and take his punishment. His parents were supportive of him and cooperative with us.

Annabelle's parents were angry but understanding. They wrote a great letter of thanks to the chief and the prosecutor.

Case closed.

A Nightclub Singer Is Murdered

The old Stagecoach bar and grill was sold. The Stagecoach had two pool tables, shuffleboard, two dartboards, and the best wings in the area. On Saturday nights, they would have a country Western band that drew a big crowd of good ole boys. Sunday was sports events on the four televisions. The new owner changed the name to "the Midnight Club." The motif was changed to disco and dancing. A new and different clientele was expected. We fingerprinted and did a background check on Dominic Denuccie aka "Nick the Nose." Nose was the new owner. He also hired a new group of bartenders and waitresses. All had clean records and were issued permits to work in a liquor establishment. The state police organized-crime task force said the Nose had associates in organized crime, but he did not have any convictions." We could not deny him a liquor license.

The opening night was observed by Detective Steve "Greek" Crapapolis. Greek said it was a typical nightclub setting with low attendance for the first night. Nose told Greek his weekend entertainment came from New York. No problems were foreseen in this area. The Nose expected the crowd to pick up when the place became known.

On the fourth Saturday night, an incident occurred. Lead singer Lauren Gold just finished her second set and went outside for a smoke. Her boyfriend, Robbie, the manager of the band, followed her outside. They argued about her smoking and song selections. He was also jealous of her flirting with customers. They had been fighting for a month. Lauren had threatened to move out of his apartment and leave the band. They had been living together for six months.

At midnight, she didn't come inside for her final set. The group played without her. Robbie went looking for her at 1:30 a.m. He couldn't find her. She was not in the van, and she didn't know anyone else in New Jersey. He thought she might have taken a taxi home.

On Sunday late in the afternoon, Scott Ward was scrounging firewood in a wooded area off Portland Road. He saw what looked like a foot in a mound covered in brush. When he looked closer, it was a human foot. He drove quickly home, a mile away, and called the police.

Patrolman Sage got the call. He met Ward in a cleared opening on Portland Road. Ward showed him the body. Patrolman Sage backed out of the woods and called for the detectives. He preserved the crime scene.

I arrived with Detective Vince Flynn. Patrolman Sage had cordoned off the clearing. We examined the crime scene. The body was a young white female. She was naked and covered with brush and leaves. We called for the medical examiner and more officers for a search. I notified the chief and Captain Lutz. They did not come to the scene. I notified the prosecutor's office; they would send detectives to assist in the morning.

Portland Road was not a busy street. There were no sightseers, and the press didn't show up. We didn't find anything of value with the first search, so I suspended activity for the night. It was a dark night. We would only destroy the scene if we continued. I stationed Detective Schnoor in the clearing for the night. Sometimes a perpetrator returns to the scene of the crime. The clearing was made because a home was going to be constructed on the lot. There were woods on both sides of the clearing. Our preliminary suspicion was that the victim was dumped from a car that parked in this clearing. She was in the woods fifty foot from this cleared area. Detective Dodge took photographs of the victim and tire imprints. There were so many tire tracks I didn't think we could identify the perpetrators tire imprints, but we had to try.

On Monday morning, Detective Dodge and a team of searches returned to the scene. I was scheduled to witness the autopsy at noon. A call came into headquarters about a missing person. Robbie Finklestien said his girlfriend didn't return from the engagement at the Midnight nightclub. He last saw her at 11:30 p.m. behind the club in the parking lot. I telephoned him, and I requested him to come to police headquarters for a report. I didn't tell him about the body found off Portland Road.

Vince and I went to the autopsy. Detective Mannigrasso from the prosecutor's office took photographs and secured any evidence on the body. Dr. Gilmore, the medical examiner, said she died from strangulation. From the neck coloration, he believed the perpetrator strangled her from behind with an arm-bar hold, a martial-arts type of death grip. I noticed a black grease stain on her heels as if she was dragged through a grease pit.

Robbie met us at the headquarters. His description and photograph of Lauren Gold matched our victim in the morgue. Vince and I took him to the morgue for the identification. When we lifted the sheet on the body, Robbie passed out. Jones, the morgue attendant, was prepared. We carried Robbie to a couch outside the autopsy room, and with smelling salts, Robbie woke up. He cried and was hysterical. It was his girlfriend, Lauren Gold, on the slab.

The detectives assigned had a lot of work. All the people who attended the nightclub had to be interviewed, if they could be found. Vince and I concentrated on the Nose. He had an unsavory reputation and demeanor. He saw her leaving that night walking south out of the parking lot onto the highway. He was mad because she didn't sing for the last band set. He paid the band to have a female singer. She left at somewhere around midnight to his recollection. He agreed to take a polygraph test. We set the test up for Friday morning.

All week, interviews were taking place. Robbie returned from New York and gave us a statement. He took the polygraph test on Friday afternoon. Both he and the Nose passed without any deception. On Monday night, Vince and I met at the parking lot of the Midnight Club at 11:30 p.m. After searching the lot, Vince walked north on the highway. The only place open was the Oak Diner. The people working at the dinner were different from Saturday night. We would have to return. I walked south and found all the businesses were closed. The Exxon Gas Station, a mile from the club, was closing at midnight. I didn't get an opportunity to speak to the attendant. We would have to stop back there when it opened.

A break came in the case came when Captain Sam Bottone of Atlantic Highlands Police Department called to tell us that women's clothing had been found in a dumpster behind the First Aid Building. The clothing was noticed because the sequined black dress found was of good quality and not something usually thrown away. There were also high-heel shoes and panties. Lauren Gold had left that night wearing a black sequined dress.

Detective Dodge and I headed out of headquarters to retrieve the clothing and investigate. It was seen first by a first-aid member who went to the dumpster to deposit trash. He notified Atlantic Highlands Police.

En route, there was a call on the police radio of a domestic disturbance in River Plaza. Patrolman Paul Graves was dispatched. When he arrived, he peeked through a window to determine what was happening, a smart maneuver by an experienced officer. A few minutes later, he called for backup. He had observed a man with a gun in a rear bedroom. The man was pointing the gun at a woman and a young girl. The man was searching the bedroom while guarding the victims. Patrolman Graves was observing them while waiting for backup.

Detective Dodge and I turned from our route to Alantic Highlands and went to River Plaza. When we arrived as backups, the house was surrounded. The house was a ranch-style building with a front door and a side door on the right from a kitchen. The call had come from a person driving past the house, who had observed a man struggling with a screaming woman on the front porch. The witness reported the man forced the woman back inside the house as she was trying to leave. He called it in as a domestic disturbance.

The perpetrator came out the front door holding the woman hostage. When he saw us, he dragged the woman back to the front door. He had pointed the gun toward the woman's head.

A patrol car was in the one-car driveway. It was blocking a Volkswagen parked in front of a garage. More officers arrived. I was the ranking officer and in charge. Badge arrived and was standing next to me on the front lawn behind a tree. The perpetrator came out dragging the hysterical woman. He threatened to shoot her if we didn't move the police car out of the driveway. I ordered Detective Deickmann to move the car.

The perpetrator pulled the woman off the porch and dragged her toward the Volkswagen. He was waving the gun at us and back at the woman's head. Officers had their guns drawn. Badge and I were seventy feet away. Graves was closer but on the side of the house and blocked by the Volkswagen. I carry a snub-nosed Colt .38. I couldn't shoot for fear of hitting the victim. Badge had his (baby) .357-Magnum 6-inch Colt revolver. He was taking careful aim and, in the proper shooting position, still and poised. I was wavering and just pointing my weapon. I knew I could not shoot.

The perpetrator dragged the woman next to the car. He opened the door. The door covered most of them. As he attempted to force the woman into the car, his gun went off. I thought he shot her as she fell to the ground. I ordered Badge to shoot. He shot the perpetrator right through the neck. When Patrolman Graves heard the shot, he fired three times and hit the Volkswagen three times. We rushed toward the perpetrator; he was down and bleeding profusely. The victim was not injured. The perpetrator had accidently fired the gun when he tried to push her into the car.

The scene was secured. The perpetrator was a burglar. We had a rash of burglars in the past month. The burglar was dropped off at a cased home, then picked up after the theft by an accomplice. In this instance, the burglary was interrupted when the home owner returned. The department placed a police guard on the burglar at the hospital. We identified him as John Case, a criminal with a long record. Badge went back to headquarters to prepare the reports and make notifications. I would review and assist in the report-writing when I returned from Atlantic Highlands First Aid Building.

We recovered the clothing and shoes. Robbie would have to identify them for us. It was interesting where they were found. The dumpster is only a mile from the crime scene.

Reviewing the reports on Monday morning at a strategy meeting, Detective Schnoor brought up the list of persons he encountered at the crime scene after dark. He checked on six cars that drove into the clearing Sunday night and two cars that drove into the clearing on

Monday night. On one of the stops on Monday night, he questioned an eighteen-year-old from Atlantic Highlands. He told Detective Schnoor he stopped to urinate. His address was near the First Aid Building. I assigned a detective to investigate the other persons. Schnoor and I checked on Stuart Woods from Atlantic Highlands. He had a clean record and was not known to the local police. Captain Bottone, Detective Schnoor, and I interviewed Woods. He lived with his mother and recently graduated from high school. He didn't have any close friends or a girlfriend. He worked at an Exxon Gas Station on Highway 35. The gas station was a mile south of the Midnight nightclub.

At the gas station, Mr. Werner, the manager, told us that Stuart Woods was working alone in the gas station the night Lauren Gold was murdered. Woods was supposed to close the station at midnight. That's when I saw the oil-changing bay. The floor was covered with oil and grease. I could picture the victim being dragged through the bay and getting the grease on her heels. I had the feeling the case was about to be solved.

Badge and the Greek were sent to pick up Stuart Woods. He came in with his mother. After advising him of his rights, we presented him with the evidence. We told him we had a witness who saw him dump clothing. The police can lie to a suspect when attempting to get a confession. He said, "The witness lied when he saw me dump the clothes." But that shook him.

After an interrogation with his mother present, he made a confession. He said, "She walked in just as I was closing." She "came on" to him at the station after he had turned off the lights. "She wanted rough sex, and the lovemaking got out of hand and she strangled herself with her own clothing." It was a preposterous statement, but he did implicate himself in her death. (This murder occurred at the same time as the infamous New York City Central Park murder). I didn't believe him, but I took his statement and charged him with murder. He had a baby face and could put on an innocent look. He said, "It wasn't my entire fault, and I'm going to ask the judge for mercy after I plead guilty."

He was convicted as the killer. Because of his age and clean record, however, he was sentenced to only twenty years. I was disappointed. The Lauren Gold murder case was closed. Lauren's boyfriend, Robbie, was outraged at the sentencing.

John Case, the burglar in the other case, was charged with burglary, kidnapping, and attempted murder. He didn't go to trial because he was paralyzed from the neck down from the gunshot. His family threatened Badge with phone calls. We notified the prosecutor's office. His family was mostly criminals and cowards. We weren't worried. Badge boasted, "Bring them on, and I'll shoot more of them." Two exciting crimes committed and solved within the month.

Cases closed.

The Riots

Chief McKenna came bursting into the detective bureau. "Get ready! We are going to Newark!" He then dashed out.

We knew Newark was in a full-scale crisis with street assaults, looting, and burning. The police were unable to handle the situation. Their cars were overturned and set on fire when they entered riot areas. It was national-television news. Reporters were interviewing residents who stated their fears. A few looters were caught on camera carrying loot out of stores. They were laughing and running through the streets carrying televisions and appliances. The city was in turmoil.

We had riot gear. Sergeant Skip Murphy was in the patrol division but with other assignments. Skip was the arms and range instructor. He was also the director of civil defense. In his position as civil-defense director, he had the capacity to tap into the state and federal budget for equipment. Skip was good at this; he supplied us with riot helmets, shields, batons, and uniforms. He also purchased two military 2.5-ton trucks, a jeep, and an armored personnel carrier. We never used the APC. He bought shotguns and nonlethal weapons, such as bean-bags guns. He had one hundred body bags.

Skip had it all; he was prepared for war in the streets, and he stored his arsenal and equipment in a warehouse at the range. We policed a suburban area of middle-class homes, a resort beach area, and rural area that had farms. How Skip obtained all this gear was unbelievable, but we had the equipment we needed.

The National Guard was called into Newark, Jersey City, and Camden. We were not needed there. The chief was disappointed because he wanted to go. I don't know how our little police force could make a difference, but the chief wanted to do anything that could help in a riot. We could only send about twenty-five men if we were called upon. The chief would use special officers to patrol the streets while we were gone.

A week later, Asbury Park had a riot. Their chief of police requested assistance from neighboring police departments. Chief McKenna took two patrol shifts, twelve men, seven detectives, and two men from traffic, Lieutenant Lutz and Lieutenant Collins. He was in command. We piled into Skip's trucks and headed for Asbury Park. Skip had one of the trucks loaded with riot gear and ammunition.

We arrived at noon on a sunny day. We could see smoke and smell the burning when we pulled up at the railroad-station staging area. A few Asbury Park Police officers were there. They appeared exhausted. They had been on duty for twenty-four hours. We formed a group of about forty police officers, our men and officers from Brielle, Point Pleasant, and Neptune. We loosely marched into the riot area on Springwood Avenue. We followed one of our trucks with the chief riding shotgun and Skip driving.

There were a few people on the sidewalks. Faces appeared in the open windows along Springwood. They were cursing us and telling us to go home. I noticed many stores had been looted. Some stores had a whitewashed sign on the window that said "Black Owned." These stores were not looted. Plenty of garbage were strewn on the street. Three blocks into Springwood Avenue, we saw an Asbury Police car turned over and burning. A fire truck came from the opposite direction. Bricks and stones were hurled at the fire truck. A hoodlum ran behind the truck and grabbed the hose. Three others joined him. They pulled the hose off the truck and ran with the hose attached to the truck. The fire truck sped forward, dragging the hose with men hanging on. It passed in between our group. When the rioters saw us, they ran the opposite way. It was not funny, but we had to laugh seeing the truck racing down the street dragging the one hundred foot of fire hose.

A brick was thrown and hit the front of our truck. The chief jumped out and hollered, "Get the bastards!" Some of us started shooting at the people peeking over the façade on the rooftops. Some cops shot at windows. At least fifty shots were fired, including shotguns. When the shooting stopped, it got quiet. A state police car and an Asbury Park patrol car arrived. They were not needed. Our detail of officers had this area under control. This shooting made us realize we were in a combat zone.

We were divided into units and assigned to different areas. I was given command of twenty officers and sent to the intersection of Prospect and Springwood Avenues. On Prospect, there was a shoe store and liquor store. Across the street was a small grocery store. We were assigned to protect these businesses. I formed a line across the street using fifteen men with shields and batons. Behind them was Schnoor, with a bean-bag gun and another gun that shot wood blocks. Behind the line, PatrolmanSage had a shotgun and tear-gas gun, along with a Brielle officer who had tear-gas canisters. My orders were that the street was closed to vehicles and pedestrians.

There were no further problems until about 4:00 p.m. A large group of people had gathered on Prospect Avenue in front of a housing complex. They walked toward our line. There were a few rocks thrown at us. The group was mostly teenagers; some appeared intoxicated. With a bullhorn, I warned them to stop. There were about two hundred people. I called for reinforcements.

Within a few minutes, Chief McKenna, Lieutenant Collins and Captain Johnson of Asbury Park Police arrived. They brought ten more officers. A large black man wearing a colorful dashiki shirt emerged from the crowd. He was with another man in shabby clothes wearing a clergy collar. A third man, wearing gangster tattoos and dreadlocks, stood with them. They said, "We are representing the neighborhood."

The six of them had a conversation, which I overheard. The crowd edged closer. The men wanted the police to vacate Prospect Avenue or there would be violence. The leader said, "We will not be able to control the crowd if you don't back up." The mob wanted to loot the stores that "Whitey" owned. The chief and captain refused. While they were talking, Lieutenant Collins backed up and accidently tripped over the curb. The chief saw him fall and thought he had been hit or struck by someone in the mob. The chief hollered,

"They got Frank!" He then hit the leader on the head with a baton. He fell to the ground bleeding, and the mob charged us. I had our men organized, but they just went wild. They beat the charging mob with batons.

Schnoor fired tear gas into the mob. They quickly retreated with our men chasing and assaulting them. We chased them for about hundred yards until they dispersed. We arrested the ones that were on the ground and called for an ambulance. A few of the mob were on the ground and bleeding. The ambulance refused to come into the riot area for the injured. A few officers were bruised from thrown objects and close fighting but nothing that required first aid. Some of those from the mob filtered back and helped their injured friends. It was all over in thirty minutes. The stores were defended. We took six men, one woman, and five teenagers into custody.

Our area was relatively quiet for a while. A Salvation Army truck drove into the intersection, and we had drinks and sandwiches. Two blocks farther west on Springwood Avenue, Skip had a situation in which looters were running into stores and stealing. I heard a noise that could only be a Thompson machine gun. Chief McKenna had told Skip not to bring that weapon. I learned later that a looter had been shot and had two .45-caliber bullets in his legs. Skip denied shooting him. The issue was not pursued, but the chief took the Thompson machine gun and put it back in our equipment truck.

It got dark around 8:00 p.m. We had a few skirmishes with looters. Back on Springwood Avenue, half our group was sent to protect the stores that were not looted. Sage went into a looted candy store and put a quarter in the jukebox. Lieutenant Collins ordered him to stop the music playing. Sage fired at the jukebox with his shotgun and blew it apart. There were no repercussions for our actions. The constitution was suspended in a riot situation (we believed.)

Patrolman Bill Thorne and I were patrolling on Springwood Avenue on the sidewalk near the buildings. Someone dumped hot, soapy urine water on us from a window. One of the cops on the street fired a tear-gas grenade into the window where the dumped the fluid came from. We ran around to the back of the building and saw the occupants running out coughing with tears flowing. We laughed and called out to them. We were having fun. I started enjoying the riot.

At midnight, we were relieved and returned back to our head-quarters. The chief asked for volunteers for a return the next day. Almost all wanted to go back.

On day 2 at noon in Asbury Park, we arrived back at the staging area. The chief, Sergeant Freibott, and me were the ranking officers. We brought nineteen men. We were sent back to Springwood and Prospect Avenues intersection. The stores that we protected yesterday had been broken into and looted that night. The shoe store had hun-dreds of old shoes and sneakers on the floor but not one new shoe or sneaker. Boxes were strewn on the floor and chairs turned over. The counter was turned over and the cash register missing. The liquor store was emptied of every bottle and can. The grocery store was torn apart with bags and boxes open. The cash register was also missing.

After we left on the previous night, the Asbury Park mayor and council with the Asbury chief and the county prosecutor's office decided it was too dangerous to have a police presence in the riot area. They pulled the police back to the east side of Ocean Avenue to defend the big stores in the center of the city. Macy's, Steinbeck's, Sears, and other retailers had to be protected. It was ironic that the looters destroyed that portion of the city where they lived and shopped.

While meeting at the railroad station, Asbury Chief Jones and Chief McKenna arranged for us to walk to a nearby diner for a break and food. Outside the dinner, Chief Jones said we could order ham-burgers and coffee. At the entrance, our chief whispered, "Order any-thing you want to eat." Most of us ordered the steaks and the best desserts. Asbury Park was paying the bill. The dinner looked like a movie set with all the weapons, helmets, and gear on the hooks and tables. I saw a similar scene in a World War II movie.

At nine o'clock, we were asked to leave. We had filled the jail, and the emergency room at the hospital was packed with the injured looters and exhausted personnel. We emptied the diner of food. We were not requested to return. Detective Dodge, who came on day 2, took a lot of photographs. We especially enjoyed the picture of

Sergeant Freibott riding a broken old bicycle on Prospect Avenue. It was hilarious.

We quelled the riot. Looking back, it was both a dangerous and adventurous time.

Riot over.

Armed Robbery and Murder

After a busy summer, I was hoping for a quiet fall. The cool weather and rain stopped the riots. Schools were back in session, and football was the talk of the students and parents. Stores were busy again with fall shopping. Crimes were lower, and there was less work in the detective bureau.

On a cool November afternoon before Thanksgiving, the Two Guys department store was crowded with customers. It was raining lightly when Johnny Booker dropped Roy Fox off in front of the Food Circus store. It was a store on the highway opposite the Two Guys store. Johnny Booker and Terry Keenan then drove to Twin Brook Avenue and parked the car on the street facing the highway. They crossed the street into the parking lot of the Howard Johnson Motel. They passed behind the motel and climbed over a four-foot chain-link fence leading to the parking lot of the Two Guys department store.

Johnny went inside the store on the pretext of seeing his girlfriend. She was employed as a salesperson. He walked past the office and then went to his girlfriend's counter. From this counter, he could observe the front doors and the office.

Outside the store, Terry Keenan was loitering in a phone booth near the entrance next to the front doors. He was talking to Roy, who was across the highway in a phone booth in front of the grocery store. Roy could observe the highway from this location. They were positioning for a robbery.

At 4:00 p.m., the armored truck from Wells Fargo arrived and parked near the front entrance. Two uniformed security guards armed with sidearms exited the truck and went inside the store. The guards went into the office. Johnny was watching them. The guards left the office carrying bags that appeared to be stuffed with money. Johnny followed. The guards went out the front door.

Roy, who was on the phone, told Terry all was clear on the highway. Terry stepped out of the phone booth and confronted the guards with a .40-caliber handgun. Johnny was behind them. The guards dropped the bags. One guard started to jump into the truck. Terry shot him and then shot the other guard who was standing with his hands in the air. Johnny picked up the bags, while Terry shot the guard in the truck again.

When the shots were heard, customers started rushing in and out of the store, running and screaming. It started to rain heavily. Johnny and Terry ran down the sidewalk toward the fence. They dropped a couple of bags. They climbed the fence and ran to their car. The car was started, and they raced toward the highway. The light was turning red for them, but they went through the light and turned north on the highway. Roy ran from the phone booth in front of the grocery store when he saw the robbery. Johnny and Terry picked him up on the highway, and they sped away.

Police cars were dispatched to the scene. The first officer that arrived was besieged by the chaos. Patrolman JJ Smith attempted to stop the bleeding of the security guard lying on the ground on the side of the truck. An EMT was inside the store at the time of the shooting and came out to help.

The officer was surrounded by people yelling and offering information and advice. A second officer arrived the same time as the ambulance. It was difficult to corral the witnesses and protect the scene. The rain got worse. People were handing the moneybags and bullet casings to police officers. The crime scene was out of control.

When I arrived at four twenty-five, the store was closed off. The witnesses were inside store. The front entrance was taped off. I assigned the detectives to do the interviews as soon as they arrived. Those witnesses who actually saw the victims or perpetrators were taken back to headquarters for questioning and statements. The other store patrons were let out the side door and escorted to their cars.

Outside, Detective Dodge arrived for the ID work. At 4:40 p.m., he took photographs of the scene. He collected the evidence. We picked up six shell casings on the ground and two in the armored car. We had two moneybags that were dropped by the perpetrators while they were running away. One of the perpetrators lost his watch cap while running. Most of the evidence was tainted because we were not sure who originally picked the evidence off the ground and handed it to the officers. We did have a small piece of cloth torn off from one of the perpetrator's coat as he jumped the fence into the motel parking lot.

Before being taken from the scene, the badly wounded guard told one of the officers that the shooter came out of the phone booth in front of the store. I directed Detective Dodge to secure the booth for prints. Because it was raining so hard, I called headquarters and requested Sergeant Scott on the desk to call the phone company. I wanted the booth taken to the police garage for evidence. When Sergeant Scott called back he said the phone company would remove the booth in three days. I then requested a township truck to the scene. I went inside the store with Detective Oswald and got bolt cutters and wire cutters form the hardware section. Outside, Oswald and I cut the booth loose, and when the truck arrived, Oswald escorted the truck and telephone booth back to headquarters.

I arrived back at the bureau at 7:00 p.m. We had statements to take from at least ten witnesses. Detective Crapapolis, known as "the Greek," came into the office. He had been off duty. He had been on the highway with his wife in his own van at 4:05 p.m. He observed a car speed out of Twinbrook Avenue and to the highway-heading north. The car went through a red light. Detective The Greek got the plate number and noted that a local hoodlum was driving. He suspected it was Johnny Booker. The Greek was going to issue a traffic summons when he returned to headquarters. He later heard of the robbery and murder while at the shopping mall. It was a lucky break in the case.

Booker was known to most of the detectives. I assigned four of them to hit the road and find Booker. The store security manager knew Booker as the boyfriend of one of her clerks. I assigned two detectives to pick her up. The county prosecutors sent three detectives to assist. We were moving fast on the case.

Lauren Ward, Booker's girlfriend, was picked up at home. During her interrogation, she stated Johnny was in the store at 4:00 p.m. and left her counter just before the robbery. She added that he appeared nervous and didn't say much to her. She denied knowing anything about the robbery. She was very scared when I suggested that she was an accomplice to the murder. She gave us a statement, and I let her go home.

Detectives Mulvey and Manning called in to the bureau. Manning said that Booker was not at home. They developed information that he was traveling with Roy Fox and Terry Keenan. I knew Fox usually hung out at O'Reilly's bar in Keansburg. I had all detectives assigned and the clerical staff working; office chaos ceased. At midnight, I called Detective Sergeant Preston and asked him to meet me at O'Reilly's bar. Detective Oswald was with me. I needed to get out of the office and on the road, looking for the suspects.

We arrived at the bar at 12:30 a.m. Sergeant Preston wasn't there yet. Oswald and I went into the bar. The street was well lit, but the bar was dark. Our eyes had to adjust to the dim light. There were two men at the front of the bar and three on the backside. I couldn't identify them because of the dim lighting. We were only three steps into the bar when O'Reilly rushed over to us and asked us to come into the backroom and his office. He appeared extremely nervous.

I thought he had information on the crime and our suspects. When he closed the door, I asked him what was happening. He stammered and looked around the small and cluttered office. I thought he was going to have a heart attack the way he was breathing and wheezing. He reached into a corner next to a file cabinet and picked up a rusted, old .22-caliber rifle. He said, "I found this on the beach and wanted to turn it in to the police."

I told him, "Cut the crap, O'Reilly. What do you know about the robbery?"

He said, "It's all over the local radio. That's all I know."

He calmed down and seemed relieved of something. When we left, the three men that were on the far side of the bar were gone.

Sergeant Preston arrived, and I filled him in on our conversation. He suspected that O'Reilly knew more than he told us.

Friday noon, the Badge and Oswald picked up Fox at his parents' home. After advising him of his rights, it did not take long for him to break. He confessed to being the lookout. He said, "I didn't know that Terry Keenan had a gun. Johnny Booker went into the store to follow the guards out once they had the money bags." He added, "I didn't know Terry was going to shoot anybody." He admitted he was at O'Reilly's bar last night with Terry and Johnny. Terry was seated next to him, telling him he was going to shoot me first, then Detective Oswald. "O'Reilly saved you both from being shot when he took you to his office. You should thank Genie O'Reilly. You and Oswald would not have had a chance."

Fox was charged with being an accomplice and put in a holding cell. I prepared warrants for Booker and Keenan.

On Friday, at 4:00 p.m., we surrounded the Booker residence in Leonardo. Johnny lived with his parents. We were armed with arrest and search warrants. The parents cooperated, and we found Johnny hiding in his bedroom closet. He was arrested and advised of his Miranda rights. The search produced the clothing he wore at the crime scene. We didn't find the gun. He refused to make a statement.

It was Friday evening at 10:00p.m. Keenan lived in an apartment over a garage in Keansburg, near O'Reilly's bar. Along with Sergeant Preston and a contingent of officers, we attempted to enter his apartment. Assistant Prosecutor Carton was with us, armed and assisting on the entry. Lights were on, and we could see through the window there was movement in the apartment. Sergeant Preston learned that Keenan lived with his wife and baby son. There was only one entrance to the apartment. It was up a flight of stairs. The situation was dangerous. We should have called on his phone and demanded he surrender, but we didn't. I didn't want to be a hero, but I led the group up the stairs. I was first, followed by Preston, Oswald, and the prosecutor. The prosecutor had his gun in his hand. I was as scared of the prosecutor as I was of Keenan. I never saw the prosecutor being trained with a weapon.

I pounded on the door. I melted against the wall as close as I could. I was expecting a hail of bullets to come through the door. After a few minutes, Alice Keenan answered my pounding. I called out, "Police! Open up!" She opened the door a crack and peered out. I didn't see Terry. She said, "He isn't home." I told her I had a search warrant, and she let us enter. We found his coat, the one he used during the robbery. We had fiber evidence from the chain-link fence he jumped over that caught part of his coat. We found .45-caliber ammunition, but we didn't find the gun. Alice was cooperative and said: "I don't know where he might be hiding." She knew he was wanted. He told her the police would be coming, but he didn't tell her why.

We had two of the three in custody. Facing two counts of felony murder, and after consulting with his lawyer, Booker confessed. He said, "Terry did the planning and the shooting." He also said, "I saved your life."

I was dumfounded. "How would that have happened?" I asked.

He said repeated his earlier story that on Thursday night, the three of them were in O'Reilly's bar when Oswald and I came in. He said, "Keenan saw you and took his gun out and held it under the bar. Keenan was going to shoot you. I stepped between Keenan and you guys until O'Reilly ushered you into the back room."

He wanted me to be grateful; I wanted to beat his ass. We took his confession, and he was transported to the county jail awaiting court.

Monday morning, Booker and Fox were arraigned at the municipal court, and bail was set at a million dollars, no 10 percent. The case was sent to a grand jury. Keenan was declared a fugitive and the F.B.I. was requested to assist in the hunt.

The Fugitive

It's January 1975. It has been six weeks since the Two Guys store was robbed and the security guard murdered. The three culprits had been indicted by a grand jury. Booker and Fox were in the county jail under a million-dollar bail. Terry Keenan was still on the run and had not been seen in New Jersey.

On Monday morning, I called Alice Keenan and requested an interview. Sergeant Preston and I went to her apartment at 11:00 a.m. We went up the same stairs that I was so apprehensive about when we attempted Keenan's arrest. This time, Alice answered on the first knock. Her girlfriend, also with a young baby, was with her. After a long conversation, we convinced Alice that it would be better for Terry to surrender. He might fight his arrest, and because of the charges against him, the police would not hesitate to shoot. Alice reluctantly agreed and said she would cooperate.

Alice told us that Terry calls her least once a week. His last call was on New Year's Eve. He told her he was well and would send for her when he was able. He told her he was in Texas. She said she would try to get him to surrender.

I requested a telephone trace on her incoming calls. She made me promise for the tenth time that the police would not hurt him, then gave us the go-ahead for the line trace. I returned to headquarters for the paperwork on the trace. After contacting the phone company, Mrs. Dundee, the New Jersey Bell Telephone representative, said, "The trace will be set up by this weekend." I submitted the paperwork. She had to call Alice for her consent.

The following Monday, Alice called and said, "Terry telephoned last night." Mrs. Dunn called and told us the trace on the phone went through and the call came from a public phone booth on Highway

75, north of Tulsa, Oklahoma. With this information and the prosecutor's order to apprehend Keenan, two detectives were authorized go to Tulsa by Chief McKenna. The specific permission was for Sergeant me to accompany county detective Andy McCormick on the investigation. I was elated and anxious to go. It's my case.

On Tuesday afternoon, we arrived at the Tulsa airport and rented a sedan. We went to the Tulsa Police Department and enlisted the assistance of Detective Bonny Pollard. We showed photos of Keenan around cheap hotels and rooming houses without any success. We had flyers prepared, and Bonny Pollard sent them to all precincts and police departments in the county. On Wednesday, we found the phone booth where he made the call to Alice. It was inside a truck stop on a major highway, Route 75, north of Tulsa. No one in the restaurant or gas station recognized the photo.

The next two days, we drew a blank in the Tulsa area, nothing on Keenan. We were about to give up when Lieutenant Lutz called—Keenan had called home again. The call originated from a public phone booth near Springfield, Missouri. Andy and I headed north.

On Route 65, outside of Springfield, we found the phone booth. It was another truck stop. What was he doing? How was he traveling? Where was he getting the money to eat and travel? As in Tulsa, no one recognized the photo. At the central police headquarters in Springfield, we received the assistance from their fugitive squad. We spent two days searching for Keenan in the Springfield area. The FBI was now helping; two agents were with us.

Lieutenant Lutz contacted us at Springfield Police headquarters. Keenan called home again. This time from one hundred miles north of Route 65, just over the border in Illinois. We drove north and continued the search process. We checked into the local Holiday Inn and waited for him to call again. We felt we were close to him and he was in the area.

That evening, we went out for dinner and a little relaxation. On the drive back to the hotel on the highway, Andy saw a sign outside of a nightclub that said "If nudity offends you, don't stop." Andy slammed on the breaks. We went in and got a table at the back of the room. We ordered beers, and the MC came on the small stage. He introduced the first dancer. She was a little heavy and not a very good dancer, but it didn't take too long before she was naked. After about five minutes of her lumbered dancing, a skinny guy who quickly became naked joined her. The female dancer left the stage, and a guy even skinner joined the first guy. Now there were two naked men on stage. They danced and fondled each other to the raucous applause of the crowd. Shit! We were in a gay bar. We put ten dollars on the table and got out. Bad experience. No more bars on this trip.

The next day, we searched the area for any sightings of Keenan. That evening, Lutz called. Keenan had called from Ottumwa, Iowa. He was heading north again. I couldn't figure any pattern to his travels only that he was headed north every three days. What was he doing?

Further bad news from Lieutenant Lutz, Alice had withdrawn her permission for the phone trace. He told us to come home. We drove north toward Davenport, stopping off in small towns to leave photos and flyers. After eight days of wasted effort, we came home.

The next morning, during a meeting with the chief, the prosecutor, and Lieutenant Lutz, they agreed that I should apply for a wiretap on Alice Keenan's phone. It's a lot of work preparing the affidavits for a phone tap. I did the work, and Judge Yaccarino signed the order. We were ready to go again.

We set up the equipment in Keansburg headquarters. The phone and tape recorders had to be manned twenty-four hours. Keansburg officers, county detectives, and our detectives were the listeners. It was a tedious assignment.

Three days later, he called. He told Alice he was renting a room on the south side of Chicago. He had the money for her bus fare, and he was going to send it through Western Union. The call came from a public booth in a pharmacy on St Marks Avenue. We immediately alerted the Chicago Police and the FBI.

During his conversation with Alice, he told her he quit his job with the circus and was going to get a local construction job. I felt like a fool. I was riding high with my hard work to solve the case. Dumb me—I saw the circus advertising posters in my travels through the Midwest but never figured he was traveling as a circus worker. I learned my lesson. Leave no stone unturned. I was humbled.

Chicago staked out the neighborhood. They got him on the street. There was no problem with the arrest. They had plenty of cops to make the grab. They applied for a warrant to search his room. They didn't find the gun. He waived extradition and was transferred back to the Monmouth jail awaiting trial.

The trial started in March. He appeared in court with a shaved head. Part of our evidence were the hairs found in the cap he lost at the crime scene. No problem, our evidence was strong. Fox testified for the state. Booker refused to testify, but we had his confession implicating Keenan. The public defender, Bill Wilson, made a valiant try but couldn't mount much of a defense. The jury was out for deliberation for three hours before bringing in a guilty verdict. Three weeks later, he was sentenced to life plus thirty years. Now I felt satisfied. Determination and hard work paid off. Booker received ten years and Fox five years.

Case closed.

Juvenile Court

Juvenile court is held in the county. This court and the grand jury are the only courts held in private and secret. The only persons allowed in the courtroom are the defendant, the parents, the defense attorney, the prosecutor, and the complainant. In many cases, the complaint comes from the police. The judge has the discretion with respect to who are allowed to be present during the hearing.

In our county, the judge was the Honorable Murray S. Klein. The judge was a small man in his sixties, bald with a gray pallor. He was known for his compassion and skill in handling juveniles. His problem was that there were not enough facilities for incarceration or other alternative remedies. The police believed him to be too soft, and the corrections and probation departments felt he was too emotionally involved.

The judge's clerk, Bertha Broomly, aka "Big Bertha, zealously guarded the courtroom. Broomly would sit at her desk in the anteroom of the court. She admitted the participants for each hearing. A court officer had a small desk in the room with her. Broomly was a large woman who was usually disagreeable with all who entered her domain. Close to three hundred pounds with short hair and horned-rim glasses, she was quite formidable and a little scary. Witnesses who were subpoenaed must sign in at her desk by 9:00 a.m. She would pay the witness two dollars and order them to wait outside in the hallway until the court officer would call their case.

For some reason, Broomly had a personal vendetta against police officers. She hated us. We usually had to sit outside at the courtroom all day. Many officers grumbled and griped, but secretly they were happy because they were getting overtime. I also pretended to be angry, but this time was great for me—I could work on my college assignments.

I was subpoenaed for a shoplifting arrest I had made. Four weeks ago, Sergeant Skip Murphy and his patrol shift broke up a beer party held in the woods. Sergeant Murphy signed complaints against eleven juveniles for consumption and possession of alcohol. This offense is usually heard locally in a meeting between the chief and the parents. In this case, however, there were so many involved that the juvenile court wanted the case held in county court. I believe Judge Klein wanted to inconvenience the parents.

Sergeant Murphy was subpoenaed to juvenile court with eleven separate subpoenas. He signed in at 9:00 a.m. and presented them to Big Bertha. She refused to pay Skip for eleven and said, "I'm only paying for one because they were all for the same incident." They had a terrible argument, hollering and screaming at each other. The argument was heard out in the hall and waiting room. As usual, Skip had to wait in the hallway until the case was called. It was last on the court calendar. I wondered why. After his appearance, Skip went to the assignment judge and county court administrator and filed a complaint.

I saw him when he returned to headquarters. I never saw him so mad. He notified Chief McKenna. The chief got angry and told Skip he would make some phone calls and write a letter of complaint. The county was "screwing around" with our department.

A week later, Skip stopped in my office. He was elated. The assignment judge ordered Big Bertha to pay for all subpoenas. He was going to the county just to collect his twenty-two dollars. I knew this would cause us a lot of trouble. Big Bertha would make it as difficult as she could, but then again, it couldn't get much worse.

Two weeks later, Vince and I were assigned to the 5:00 p.m. to 1:00 a.m. shift. At 10:00 p.m., Vince said he didn't feel well, so I dropped him off at headquarters. He clocked out, and I returned to road. At 11:30 p.m., a call came over the radio of a stolen car out of Union Beach. There was the car right in front of me on the highway. I called for a backup, following the car until a patrol car arrived. We stopped the car.

The operator was a young female. She told us the car was her sister's and she had permission to use it. She was sixteen years old without a license. We locked up the car, and I transported the juvenile to headquarters, with a patrol car following.

She called her sister at headquarters. Her sister, Penny Jones, reported her younger sister, Susan, stole the car. I offered to release her to Penny. When Penny arrived at headquarters, I was spellbound. She was gorgeous. Penny was doing an internship at Monmouth Medical Hospital, her last year before becoming a registered nurse. She would get home at 11:00 p.m. That's when Susan stole her car. I wanted the chance to see Penny again, so I signed a complaint that would go to juvenile court. I called Penny the next day before she went to the hospital. I told her to tell her parents they didn't need a lawyer. I would recommend the judge to reprimand her sister to scare her. Penny was relieved and agreed with my strategy.

I received a subpoena for juvenile court. Five other police officers with subpoenas rode together with me to court. Detective Bob Swansen had cases concerning two runaways. Two patrolmen had a drug case, and Sergeant Skip Murphy had a burglary case. I really didn't want to go to court the same day as Skip, but it happened. We signed in. Bertha glared at us, paid us, and growled for us wait out in the hallway. When Susan, Penny, and their mother arrived, I told them to report to Big Bertha. I sat with them in the hallway. Penny had to study for a test. So did I. I took her to a room set aside for waiting police officers. We chatted and studied together.

At about 9:45 a.m., the court officer found me in the waiting room. He had an order from the judge that I was not allowed to leave the building. He told me that all the police and officials that signed in that morning were to be in the judge's court after the day's cases were finished. He didn't tell me why. I was disappointed because I couldn't have lunch with Penny and her mother. I had to stay in the building.

It didn't take long before the incident causing our detainment was revealed. Big Bertha kept a ceramic frog on her desk. The frog was about ten inches high and had a large mouth. Big Bertha kept her candy in the frog's mouth. That's what it was designed for. Some unknown culprit placed a ten-inch dildo in the mouth of the frog. I didn't hear the screaming, but the other cops near the office said she went wild, demanding to know who did it. It spread through the whole courthouse. A lot of people—cops, court officers, and even a couple of judges—were laughing. Of course, Judge Klein didn't think it was funny. He ordered all of us to be in his courtroom at 4:00 p.m. He also wanted the prosecutor present, not just one of the assistant prosecutors.

At 4:00 p.m., there were about forty people gathered in the courtroom, mostly cops but some probation officers and a couple of other court officers. The judge entered and stood behind his desk. He picked up that ten-inch rubber dildo and waived it at us. He was red in the face, his hair was sticking up and his ears wiggled. "I know one of you did it!" he repeated three times. "I will find out, hold you in contempt of court, and put you in jail. You are all officers of the court and duty bound to tell me who did this."

I wondered if he really expected one of us to rat out the culprit. Whoever did it was our hero. The judge told us to get out, and he stormed out of the courtroom. Big Bertha sat there and glared. I never saw anyone so angry.

Everybody suspected Skip. He was a cop and smart enough to know never to say anything. The judge never found out who did it. It took a couple of months for the clamor to subside. Detective Swenson, our juvenile officer, said Big Bertha had mellowed somewhat, but we still were last on the calendar.

Susan Jones was given a lecture on the evils of car theft, and then my case was dismissed and closed. Later, Penny Jones became a valued informant.

The Floater

Our jurisdiction covered the Navesink River, parts of the Shrewsbury River, Raritan Bay, and the Atlantic Ocean. It also included the reservoir and some lakes and creeks and streams. We had to investigate "floaters"—dead bodies found in these waters. Bodies of bridge jumpers in New York City float through the Hudson and East River into New York Bay. Then the bodies float into the Raritan Bay then get hung up on the sands of Sandy Hook. This is a multijurisdictional location where the deceased were usually processed by our detective bureau. We had plenty of experience in this area.

I was on the road with Vince when we received a radio message from dispatch. Chief McKenna wanted us to go to Chris's Marina in River Plaza, where Chris De Fillipo owned a small boat marina and deli. He had a problem with a bad odor coming from the meadow next to his boat dock. The boaters complained to Chris, who called the chief.

When we arrived, Chris pointed in the direction of a marsh area on the north side of the dock. He was excited and agitated. He said, "The smell is coming from within the crow weeds near the bank of the river." It didn't take long to catch the odor. I knew right away it was a floater.

We would keep short boots in the trunk of the car for emergencies and this type of investigation. Donning the boots, Vince and I pushed our way through the crow weeds until we saw a body. It was in a deteriorated condition. It must have been in the water and on the riverbank for a few weeks. The body was putrefied and had been eaten by crabs and other critters that abound in the area.

When we came out of the crow weeds, Chris and some onlookers wanted to know what was happening. I told the people to stay on the dock and not to venture near the body. Chris wanted to know who was dead. I told him, "It was hard to tell but looked like an older male, wearing a dark shirt and tattered jeans." Chris was the unofficial mayor of River Plaza. He said, "I know everyone in the area. I want to take a look." I strongly advised against it.

Before I could stop him, he bounded into the crow weeds. After a couple of minutes, I heard Chris coughing and vomiting. Vince and I had to help him back to the dock. After he recovered, he said, "That's George Tash." George was a sixty-year-old alcoholic, usually homeless and drunk. George lived in Red Bank, in a shack just next to the river. He came across the river on occasion to purchase wine at Chris's deli. Chris chased him away most of the time. He didn't have much money and asked people to buy him wine and cigarettes.

I called for the medical office to respond. A body cannot be removed until the coroner arrives and pronounces him dead. I explained the circumstances to the secretary in the office. She relayed back to me that Dr. Beck would not have to examine the deceased; he would send his assistant.

The meat wagon from the medical examiner's office arrived, a black van with man named Smitty driving. Smitty was the ME assistant and was usually sent to pick up the floaters. He requested help picking up the body. He said, "Just put this Vicks VapoRub under your nose, and you won't smell anything." Yea, like I believed that. I thought, *Great, this is really making my day.*

Smitty, Vince, and I went into the crow weeds. It was difficult to walk in the marsh; you sunk into the goo six inches with every step. Smitty laid down the rubber bag next to the body. He grabbed the top, and Vince and I each took hold of a pant leg. When Smitty said, "Lift," we did. George fell apart. Vince and I had the bottom part of his body, and Smitty had the top. Vince barfed and ran out of the weeds. I stood and couldn't move. Smitty stuffed both parts into the body bag, and I helped him carry it out.

The dead body odor was still on us, so we stopped at our homes to pick up a change of clothing. At headquarters, we took a long shower and hung our smelly clothing outside near the police garage. Eventually I threw my clothes away.

Now the paperwork. Since Vince didn't like to make reports, the task fell on me.

The next morning, the medical examiner, Dr. Stanley Beck, called. He requested information on the deceased and a detective at the autopsy. I sent Detective Dodge. Al Dodge had an iron stomach; he could probably eat an egg-salad sandwich while taking photographs of the procedure. Since Mr. Tash was living in Red Bank, their agency had his vitals. I called the Red Bank detective bureau for assistance. They offered me their file on George Tash. Vince and I went right over to their office.

Captain Krackie met us. He was the senior officer in the bureau, ready to retire. He did not know what we needed or why we requested information. While we were talking to the captain, Detective Herbie Swan came over to us and said he would handle the matter. Herb got Vince coffee and left us in their bureau office while he retrieved the file from the records bureau. Herbie and Detective Bob Claymore had a suspicious smile on their face. They seemed to enjoy the fact that we had to prepare the reports and attend the autopsy. They gave us the information and wished us well with a smirk. George had a lengthy arrest record for drunkenness and public disorder. He also had to be taken to the hospital often for detoxification. At sixty years of age, the Red Bank Police knew he wasn't going to live much longer, and they didn't care. His death didn't surprise them. He didn't have any family or relatives. We didn't have anyone to notify of his departure.

On the way out of Red Bank headquarters, we met Patrolman Reggie Brown. He asked what we were doing. When I told him about George Tash, he laughed until he bent over holding his side. "What's so funny, Reggie?" I asked.

He said, "I heard George died two weeks ago at the back of his shack in the shallows of the river. I also heard that Herbie and another detective pushed George a few feet farther into the river so that the next tide would carry him away. They knew that the body would float across the river and become stuck in the marsh near Chris's Marina." They were happy to get rid of George and the paperwork involved.

Vince and I went back inside the bureau. I confronted Herbie. He denied moving George's body but was laughing hysterically. All the Red Bank detectives were laughing. They did it. I know it. They had won this time, but I would get back at them. I would have to do all the reports.

The medical examiner ruled Tash died of natural causes and alcoholism. There was no mention in his report concerning how Tash got into the river

A couple of years later, Herbie and I attended a three-day seminar together. On the third night, after quite a few scotch and sodas, he admitted to the deed. It was okay. Police do those things to each other. Herbie was a good cop. It was actually very funny.

The Toe-Sucker

It was a full moon that night, and I expected some interesting events to take place. After reading the morning reports, I found the case. A local resident reported a person entered his home after two in the morning. The culprit pried opens the sliding glass door to the recreation room. Then he came into the master bedroom where the victim and her husband were sleeping. The pervert was on his knees at the foot of the bed and pulled up the blanket and sheet. He was sucking the victim's big toe when she woke up and screamed. Her husband woke up and saw the pervert at the foot of the bed. The perpetrator ran. The children woke when they heard their mother screaming. She calmed them down and called 911.

Mr. Colmorgan, the husband, reported that he jumped out of bed after hearing his wife scream and gave chase. The perpetrator ran out of the front door. The husband was barefoot and could not catch the pervert. He went back into the house and put on a bathrobe and slippers. The victim had already called police headquarters. The husband went back outside to look for the perpetrator. The victim's home was in an upper-middle-class housing development off Highway 35. There was only one road into the development, and the victim's home was the first house on the entrance road. While outside, the victim's husband observed a new Lexus SUV speeding from inside the development toward the highway. The car driver was the culprit. He didn't get the complete license-plate serial, just "NJ" and three numbers, 154. The vehicle was unique in color and style. Lexus did not make many of them.

Mr. and Mrs. Colmorgan both said, "We could identify the culprit. We saw his face." Mrs. Colmorgan was taken to the hospital and treated for hysteria. Mr. Colmorgan was furious. The children were checked by the first aid and found to be all right.

Vince and I were just finished with a floater, and Captain Lutz wanted us to investigate this case. When Vince finished his morning coffee, we called the victim for an interview. The report made by the responding officers was our starting point. The victims gave us full cooperation and support. They wanted an arrest. The assault seemed incredible, although I read about similar cases in police journals. We had a description of the perpetrator and his vehicle.

Back at headquarters, we put out a Teletype to all the police departments in the county. We described the event, the perpetrator, and his vehicle. Later that afternoon, we received a call from Sergeant Gilbert of Little Silver Police Department. A matching vehicle was parked at the train station in Little Silver. Vince and I took Mr. Colmorgan to the train station. He identified the car, everything fit with its description. Motor Vehicle Bureau gave us the name and address of the owner. A David McClain, Waterview Avenue, Rumson.

Mr. McClain's home was a Tudor-style home in a very expensive neighborhood. We knocked on the door. A well-dressed woman answered it. She asked, "What do you want?" After identifying ourselves, she invited us into her home. She offered us tea and cookies and asked us how she could help us. I asked her if her husband was home. She answered, "He is at work." I asked her what car he was driving. She answered, "A Lexus and it should be at the railroad station. Was it stolen?" I told her it was still at the station. "Then what is it you want?" she asked. I asked her if her husband was home at around 2:00 a.m. That's when she broke down. She said, "I knew it! He has a girlfriend! What happened?"

I asked her about last night. She said, "He went out about 1:00 a.m. for a drink and cigarettes. We had an argument about his going out since there was liquor and smokes in the house. After he left, I went to bed crying. What did he do?" I couldn't tell her because she was such a nice person. I asked her to have her husband call us.

Back at headquarters, our secretary Veronica left us a message from a Mr. Gladstone, a lawyer, requesting an immediate call back.

He could wait. I was expecting a call from McClain. It was after five, and we were going off duty.

The next morning, Vince and I arrived for work at our usual 9:00 a.m. Before we got settled, a Mr. Vernon Gladstone was on the phone wanting to talk to me. He said, "I am with a New York law firm," then and rattled off some names of which I could care less. He said, "I represent a Mr. David McClain." He said Mr. McClain was going to sue me, the chief, and the police department for harassment. He advised me to stay away from Mrs. Mary McClain and Mr. McClain himself and that I would regret it if I contacted them again.

"I am going to call the New Jersey attorney general and report your impertinence and unprofessional conduct," I told Mr. Gladstone. "I will follow your advice." I thanked him for his call and sprinkled the conversation with a lot of "yes sirs" and "no sirs."

Vince was listening to the call and was laughing. This lawyer, Gladstone, must be some jerk. He was attempting to intimidate us. He was screwing with the wrong detectives. One thing about Chief McKenna, he backs up his men. Now we were really mad.

I called the prosecutor and told him the facts of the case and the investigation. He advised me to get an arrest warrant and lock McClain up. He would enjoy prosecuting McClain. I called Mrs. McClain and told her I was going to arrest her husband. I told her what he did, and she was actually relieved that he didn't have a girlfriend. She told us that he would return from the city on the 6:10 p.m. train and she would not warn him of the impending arrest. She really was a good woman. She said, "My husband needs help."

When the 6:10 p.m. train arrived at the Little Silver Station, Vince and I were there to meet McClain. As he was entering his car, we approached him and placed him under arrest. He looked shocked and angry. "I thought Gladstone took care of this matter," he said. What he got were his rights read to him and handcuffs on his wrists. We brought him back to headquarters, booked him, and placed him in a cell. He made a phone call. He said, "Gladstone wants to talk to you." I told him, "Have that asshole lawyer call me in the morning." The judge set his bail at fifty thousand. He would spend the night in jail. I called Mrs. McClain to let her know what was happening.

Next day, the first order of business was for Vince and me to interrogate McClain. When we put him in the interrogation room, he said he would tell us the truth even against the advice of his attorney. He seemed very sorry. He admitted to the offense and confessed to two other incidents. We took a written statement, and after he signed the statement, he called his wife. We bought coffee and rolls and had breakfast together. He said, "I'm feeling much better now that my problem can be fixed."

While we were in the interrogation room, Gladstone arrived. I made him wait in the hallway. He had his hat in his hand. He had a different attitude this morning when I threatened him with unethical conduct. He still was a jerk. He wanted to know if we could work out something to help his client. I told him we had to include the victims with regard to any decision made on this matter.

The Colmorgans were delighted with the quick arrest and would attend the meeting with the prosecutor. Gladstone wanted the meeting held at his office in New York City. I said, "No way." He would have to travel to the prosecutor's office in Freehold.t

We met the following week a Prosecutor Coleman's office. After a discussion, the prosecutor offered a plea bargain. It consisted of three-year probation and three year psychiatric counseling with monthly reports to the sex-offenders unit. I thought it was a generous offer. McClain accepted, and the Colmorgans agreed.

Case closed.

Big Louie

I received a message from secretary Ronnie. "The chief wants you in his office right now." *What's this about now?* We didn't have any major cases pending. Didn't the chief know there were eleven other detectives available? The chief called these assignments "vest pocket assignments." I catch them too often.

Well, I beat it up to Chief McKenna's office. Captains Lutz and Gleason were present. The chief told me, "Contact Mrs. Margaret Van Arsdale immediately! She has a problem that must be handled with the utmost discretion."

Mrs. Van Arsdale was a pillar of the community. She was the chairman of the local Republican Party and on many charity boards. She was rich and powerful and had been a big supporter of the chief and the police department. The chief and brass dropped this problem on my lap. *This can't be good.* I called her for a meeting. She requested I come to her home, a mansion on the river, as soon as I could. "Please come alone," she insisted. *Uh-oh, this is going to be worse than I thought.*

When I arrived, the maid greeted me at the door. She ushered me into a sitting room, which was large with books on two walls and had a wet bar and a large array of windows facing the Navesink River. Mrs. Van Arsdale arrived within a minute. She was a fine-looking woman for her age, early sixties. She was wearing an elegant silk suit with high heels and had long, straight blond hair and little makeup. We had met previously at charity or club functions. I was the guest speaker at her women's club last year. The topic was the death penalty. Why these women wanted information on the death penalty surprised me. When I finished speaking, I found them to be strongly in favor of the penalty. They wanted murderers hung. They were a formidable group.

"Please call me Margaret," she said. She offered me a drink, which I declined. I saw her fill up a glass with ice and a lot of Jim Beam. She began praising me, saying that she knew of my reputation as a detective. She said, "I made a dumb and stupid mistake. I need your help. I need your confidentiality and advice." I promised her discretion and said, "I don't judge people. I will try to help." I could tell she was tense and apprehensive.

After a long pause, she sat up straight and said, "This is embarrassing, but I will tell you all. I was attending a fund-raising for the visiting nursing association at the Molly Pitcher Hotel a month ago. While there, I met the bartender hired by the catering service. He was entertaining all the people at the bar. He was mixing drinks and flipping bottles around like Tom Cruise in the movie *Cocktails*. He was very handsome and about thirty years old and not wearing a wedding ring. I had a charity dinner coming up in my home the following week, and I asked him if he would bartend at my home for the event. He agreed and asked if he could stop at my house to look over the bar and give me the order for the beverages needed.

"He came the next afternoon. We discussed the party and guest list and the drinks that would be served. He was so charming. My husband, Richard, was not home. Richard, who is my third husband, is a pilot for a major airline. He has been a pilot for thirty years. He flies to Europe every week and is gone for three to four days. I get very lonely in this big house. The bartender's name was Ricky, and he said he was from Texas. We talked all afternoon about nothing that I can remember. We had some wine and ended up in my bedroom. I slept with him. How stupid of me!"

"The night of the dinner party, Ricky was at his best. He was the highlight of the event with his bartending antics. My guests loved him. Richard was in Paris. When the party ended, Ricky never left. We slept together again.

"The following week, Ricky called. He said, 'I am in trouble and need some money. He asked if could I loan him five hundred dollars. He said he would pay me back after the next party he worked.

116

I told him to come over and pick up the money. He asked for cash. He came to the house that evening. Richard was not home again. We slept together again. The next morning, Ricky was gone before I woke. I noticed the drawer on the bed stand partially open. Richard kept a gun in that drawer. The gun was missing. I knew Ricky stole the gun. Ricky called later that evening. He said, 'I am in trouble again and need more money.' He wanted ten thousand dollars. I said I wanted the gun returned. He admitted taking the gun. He also said, 'I have a tape recording of our sexual activities in bed.' He had surreptitiously hidden a tape recorder in his jacket pocket, and the jacket was next to the bed. I told him I would pay, but I was scared and I would need a couple of days to get the money. That's the story, Lieutenant Holiday."

I told Margaret I needed that drink she offered when I first arrived. We discussed the situation. She pleaded, "Please help me. My marriage and reputation are in jeopardy".

"I'll figure something out. Stall Ricky for a day. I need to get his background information." I finished my beer and left a very distraught Margaret Van Arsdale.

I returned back to police headquarters. I searched the criminal record file and other files I could access. There was nothing under the name of Rick Gregory. I was sure that the name was fictitious. I contacted his employer, the catering service. They gave me the information on his application and told me he had been employed with them for two months. He was thirty years old and lived in an apartment in Asbury Park. He listed bars and restaurants in Dallas, Texas, for previous employment. The catering service did not check his background. They did have his social security number, which they gave me. They considered him a good employee, personable and reliable.

On Wednesday morning, I called Margaret. She did not hear from Ricky yesterday. I told her, "If he calls, set up a meeting. You should tell him that you plan to grocery shop today and that you have the money. You will meet him in the parking lot at the grocery store at noon. The store is the Acme on Route 35. Call me back as soon as he calls, and I will set up for the meeting. Don't worry, we will handle him."

Ten minutes after I hung up, Margaret called back. She advised me that Ricky had called and agreed to the meeting but seemed suspicious. She said, "I will go, but I will be really scared."

We had a meeting at the detective bureau and ninety minutes to set up the snare. I put DetectiveSchnoor at the store, wearing a store apron, and his guise was as a store employee picking up the carts in the parking lot. He was also to notify the store manager of our activity. On the opposite side of the parking lot was a two-story bank building. I assigned Detective Badge at the bank. He was to observe the parking lot from an upstairs bank window. I assigned Detective Swenson, aka "Fish," and policewoman Evelyn Wilton to be at the parking lot with a basket of groceries. Vince and I would be on the south side of the parking lot, hiding behind a little patch of woods. The patrol division would assign two cars at the highway to block the exits when he arrived. I advised the team, "The suspect is armed and we do not know much about him. Be careful."

We were set up at eleven forty-five. We were all in radio contact. I could see everyone from my position. Badge had the best view of the parking lot. At noon, he radioed the team that Mrs. Van Arsdale had arrived and parked at the center of the lot. At 12:05 p.m., the suspect arrived in an old blue Chevrolet and parked next to Margaret. I radioed for the team to converge on the suspect. When I got to his car, I saw him lying on the ground with Fish standing over him with his foot placed on the suspect's neck. Fish had yanked him out of his car and slammed him to the ground. I told Margaret that she could leave. She mouthed a "Thank you" and was gone. We searched the suspect and his car. We found the gun but not the tapes. I noted that Badge was not in on the arrest. I wondered why. Where was he?

Back at police headquarters, Rick Gregory was booked and placed in a cell. I called Margaret and told her, "We have the gun, and Rick is in a cell. I will interrogate him after lunch." She said, "I want to buy the team their lunch and thanks again." We had a great lunch at Applebee's for a successful mission.

Fish brought Rick Gregory from the cellblock to the interrogation room. Rick denied everything. I told him he was to be charged with theft, seduction, and attempted kidnapping. We were going to recommend thirty years imprisonment. He cracked open like an egg. He was almost in tears. He was afraid of Fish, who was hollering and stomping around the interrogation room. He wanted to know what kind of deal we could make. This alerted me that the police had interrogated him on previous occasions. Knowing that Mrs. Van Arsdale wanted to keep this incident from her husband and friends and especially the newspapers, I knew I had to make some kind of deal.

I asked him where the tapes were. He told me they we in his apartment and offered to give them to me. I got his keys and sent Badge and Fish to search his apartment and retrieve the tapes and tape recorder. I then took a statement from Rick. He admitted to the seduction but said, "She gave me the gun and offered me the money as a loan." I knew he was lying but took his statement.

He wanted to know how he could help me. He said, "I know of an impending home invasion and robbery." He said he would give me all the information. The robbery was planned for next week in Long Branch. I notified Long Branch detectives. I got Ricky dinner, and we waited for Detectives Mike Irene and Pat Joyce from Long Branch. When Irene interrogated Ricky, he got all the information he needed. Ricky even offered to go with the crooks during the robbery. I called the prosecutor, and he agreed. We got the gun and the tapes on my case, and I released Ricky to Long Branch. There was nothing on record. I didn't sign complaints, although Rick didn't know that. He believed he was released under his own recognizance.

Thursday morning, Jimmy Lesconso, the manager of the bank where Badge was assigned, called and told me how all the secretaries and clerks in the bank had a good laugh on what happened to Badge. He was standing at the window, looking out over the lot, holding a radio and a shotgun. The bank workers were watching him from their desks. It was exciting to them. They heard Badge call us that the suspect had arrived. Badge then ran toward the exit door to assist on the arrest. He went into the wrong door. He entered the ladies' room by mistake, which was next to the exit door, totally embarrassed when he realized what he had done. He banged the door open and ran out. He dashed out to the exit and was gone. He was too late for the arrest. When he went out the exit door, the whole room broke out with laughter. They saw the look and scowl on his face as he raced out. Now I know why Badge was not there for the takedown. I couldn't tell him I knew.

Two weeks later, Irene called. The robbery was on, and Ricky was going with the bad guys. Ricky was given the code name Big Louie, his choice. I went along with Fish to observe and assist if necessary. The target was staked out. When the robbers arrived and kicked in the front door, they were met not by the homeowners but a detail of Long Branch detectives. It was a great arrest. Ricky was arrested along with the other three. He was placed in a cell with the others. A couple hours later, a police officer took him out of the cell and said loud enough so the others could hear that Rick's lawyer had arranged his bail. He was never suspected as the informant. He followed that by assisting other agencies as an informant. He was instrumental in breaking up a large drug ring, assisting the state police.

He wouldn't do the undercover work without consulting me. He was making me famous with other police agencies. He gave me information on criminal activities all over Central New Jersey. Most of the time, I told the agencies that the information came from Big Louie. Many of them wanted to use him, but he was my informant.

When not making money as an informant, he went back to bartending and making porno films. He didn't tell me about making films until I needed him to hang out in a bar for information. He said, "I can't because I have a job in New York making a porno film." His films were in theaters in the city. I saw the advertisement for the show, but I never saw the movie. Rick "Big Louie" Gregory was a police informant in Monmouth County, a great bartender and a porn-movie star.

College

Chief McKenna frowned on any police officers attending college. He said, "It only puts farts in your head." I was working part time at the Sears store as a security officer. While working, I saw a notice on a bulletin board concerning a college scholarship for employees. It mentioned a competitive test for the tuition payments. I passed the test and was offered the scholarship. I didn't tell the chief. It was not a requirement to notify the department. I started attending evening classes.

In a time of national turmoil, studies were conducted concerning riots, poverty, and drug abuse. Congress formed a committee to investigate the problem and offer solutions. This committee put forth five separate publications. The first was titled "The Challenge of Crime in a Free Society." In this document, they recommended the police officers to be professional and educated. As a result of this study, President Lyndon B. Johnson pressured Congress to pass a bill for funding police education. His funding bill passed in Congress. The federal government would pay the tuition for any police officer who enrolled in college.

I knew our department could benefit from this new legislation, but I was the only one to take advantage. The chief discouraged college, and my colleagues had a disdain for academics. They preferred recreational activities to advancing their education (e.g., bowling, shooting, pool, and drinking). Not one person in the police department had a college degree. By taking college courses, I learned the new laws, new court decisions that impacted my work and how to behave and act professionally as a law-enforcement officer.

During my early years at the detective bureau, I was the go-to guy for the chief when there were problems. Using my education,

I assisted other officers in report-writing and making their actions legal. I wouldn't condone perjury. I used what might be termed "creative writing." I was the only person capable of preparing search warrants even though the chief didn't think they were necessary. Because of my success helping the chief, I became a benefit to the department. He didn't try to discourage me from attending night classes in college.

After finishing community college, I registered at Stockton State College. I was attending evening classes with colleagues from the county—two chiefs of police and two police captains. The criminal justice department at Stockton College, chaired by Professor Wisnewski, was happy to have us.

We registered in the fall term together. We attended two classes on a Wednesday evening. One class was in criminal justice; the other class was a math class. We all passed easily. The spring classes came quickly. On registration night, we were at the auditorium looking over the offerings. A class on organized crime was offered at 6:00 p.m. We signed up for the class together.

While trying to decide on the second class, I saw a vision of beauty. A tall redhead wearing a white blouse, red mini skirt, and three-inch heels. She was in her midtwenties. I wondered what class she was going to register for. When I saw her go behind a table, I realized she was teaching a class. I went to her table. She was better looking than I first observed. She had sparkling blue eyes and a knockout smile. Whatever she was teaching, I was taking. It was French 101. The college required a language, and this was going to be my language. The other police lummoxes (my buddies) signed up for the same class.

The first night of French class, we all sat across the front row. Our teacher, Ms. Midgely, appeared somewhat nervous. She was drop-dead gorgeous; it was difficult to concentrate on the lesson. We were the only police officers in the class of thirty students. We dominated the discussions. We really enjoyed the class.

After three weeks of classes, Professor Wisnewski called me at work. He said Ms. Ridgeley was thinking of resigning. She was intimated by our presence in the classroom. I told the professor, "I will take care of the problem. Ms. Midgely is our reason for taking this class."

On the ride to the college, I told the other cops about the problem. We decided on a strategy to keep Ms. Midgely in the classroom. When we entered the classroom that night, we all sat in the last row. We didn't say a word all class. That night went smoothly for Ms. Midgely. The next week, we employed same strategy.

After two weeks, I called Professor Wisnewski. He said she was impressed and she would continue the class. I told him, "We will behave and continue to make her comfortable."

After the fourth class, Ms. Midgely spoke to me after class. She said, "This is my first time teaching at a college level." She was a high school language teacher and recently received her master's degree, which qualified her to teach on a college level. She said our group was her first class and she was intimidated. We had a long chat, and I assured her we would support her; she was doing a great job teaching. And she looked so sexy. I didn't tell her that last part.

After the sixth class, we all had a chat with Ms. Midgely. We invited her to Mulligan's Bar and Grill. We usually stopped by at the bar after class. The bar was located near the campus and on our route back to the Garden State Parkway. She declined.

After the tenth week of class, Ms. Midgely (now Susan to us) agreed to stop at Mulligan's after class. She said she felt very secure walking into place with us. We all had a great time. She was a delight. This occurred after every class thereafter. She was very good at shooting darts too. I know we all looked forward to Wednesday evenings with Susan.

Too bad, the semester ended. I received an A grade; so did my colleagues. We had a good friend on the faculty. I saw her on campus a few times after classes. She said, "I still go to Mulligan's bar on occasion, but it's not as much fun without you cops."

Spring Semester at Stockton State

January 1974 was the start of the spring semester at Stockton State. Our same group got together for registration, six police officers from Monmouth County. We wanted to take six credits, that is, two courses on the same evening. Last semester turned out great with adjunct professor Susan Midgely. We all signed for a criminology course at 6:00 p.m. At 8:40 p.m., there was a class in advanced math and a class titled Human Sexuality. Tom Wallace and I registered for the human sexuality class. Neither of us liked math classes. The time and date fit with my schedule—police softball league on Tuesday evening, college on Wednesday evening, and bowling on Friday evening.

The first night of class was interesting; I knew I could learn enough in criminology class to help me in the detective bureau. I was interested in predicting crime trends and motives for the commission of crimes. It was going to be a very educational class.

Then I went to the human-sexuality class. The class syllabus didn't offer much to me except for the sex-crime class. This class was going to be difficult for me because I lacked interest. The instructor was Professor Marcia Muller. She was a tall and heavy woman, with iron-gray hair pulled back from her face and coiled at the nape of her neck. Her features were severe—strong, jutting jaw, lips drawn into an uncompromising line, heavy eyebrows above thick glasses. She wore a long sleeve dress of a heavy fabric, even though the weather was still warm. She had a slight accent, probably German. "Take notes!" she bellowed. "They will be important." Our class had fifty students evenly divided between male and female. She dismissed us early the first night.

The third week, the criminology class was going well. The human-sexuality class assignment was to discuss porno films and actors. Ms. Muller only had information from the textbook. I added information concerning the industry. I received my knowledge from the arrest last fall of Rick Gregory. Rick, aka Big Louie, made two films that were being shown in New York City at the time. After class, Ms. Muller asked me where I received my information on the porn industry. I told her about Big Louie. She said she had never met a porn star. Her interest was piqued. That's when I offered her a deal for Tom Wallace and me. The course required a term paper of twenty pages. In lieu of the paper, I would arrange for Big Louie to be a guest speaker. She accepted. I would set the date.

At the fifth class in human sexuality, I introduced Big Louie as the guest speaker and his manager, Ron Goldman. Big Louie was Rick Gregory; "Ron Goldman" was Detective Ron Oswald. Rick and Ron got together for the ruse. They thought it would be fun. Rick was an actor. Ron was a con artist. Ms. Muller was delighted.

After the introduction, Big Louie started his talk. He had two films playing in New York City theaters and gave the address of the theaters. Before he got rolling, a student raised her hand. She was a beautiful nineteen-year-old coed on her second year at Stockton. She asked, "Why do they call you Big Louie? I was nervous; my college credit was in jeopardy. I kept my fingers crossed waiting for his answer. I saw Tom Wallace laughing. Rick said, "It's not because of the length of my tie." The class had a good laugh, even Ms. Muller.

Big Louie was in front of the class for an hour. He was funny, articulate, and entertaining. He sounded like a professional porn star. He gave his salary and working conditions. The students listened with rapt attention. I had never seen students so attentive. They listened to every word. He was a huge success. Then Ron took over. He put a phony Manhattan address on the board. He told the students, "If you are interested in a porn career, send me a resume." He added, "Include frontal and rear nude pictures." He was pushing it a bit, and I got nervous again. Tom Wallace was straining not to laugh out loud.

After class, Ms. Muller approached me to thank me for the guest speaker. She asked for his address and telephone number. She wanted to have him return for her other classes. I told her he was doing me a favor tonight. She said, "I can get him a stipend for future appearances." I told her I would ask Rick.

On the ride home, I asked Rick if he wanted to do it again, for pay. He said, "I would be happy to do it and take the money."

I got an A grade in both classes, and I did not have to do a term paper. I know Rick called Professor Muller to set up his guest appearances for next semester. Good luck to both of them. I was done with that ruse.

Bar A

It was four thirty on a Sunday morning. The phone rang. It was Chief Phillips of Holmdel Police Department. The chief, Bruce Phillips, and I were personal friends. He said, "One of my patrols found two bodies in a ditch." He requested my help with the investigation. He already called one of his detectives, Jimmy Smith, and the county prosecutor's office.

I arrived at the crime scene thirty minutes later. Two patrolmen and Jimmy Smith were protecting the scene. Detectives Andy McCormick and Detective Johnny Mannigrasso arrived the same time as me. Andy and I went into the ditch to examine the bodies.

Both victims were Caucasian males. They appeared to have been shot in the back of the head. They each wore dark suits and dress shoes. They both had their wallets in the back pocket of their trousers. Their identification was in the wallet, along with money. It was not a robbery. It looked like a mob hit. The county medical examiner arrived and authorized the removal of the bodies. The county identification van was at the scene and took photos and casts. There were tire prints and footprints. There was evidence left by the killers.

The victims, Vincent Montenegro and Paul Simonetti, had Newark addresses. Back at Holmdel headquarters, Andy notified the state organized-crime task force. I called my contact in the Newark Police Department. Detective Ralph Simon knew both victims. He said they were mob wannabes hanging out with known mobsters. He would call back with further information.

On Monday, I notified my boss, Chief McKenna, of the situation. He told me to continue assisting the county detectives and Holmdel police. It wasn't until Wednesday that information started to come in. The task force found through informants that the victims had recently taken a road trip to Florida. They suspected it was to purchase and transport drugs back to New Jersey. Detective Simon said Newark Police found out that the victims were seen at the Bada-Bing Bar on Friday evening. They were with another wannabe a hoodlum named Billy Delaney. They were talking about taking a trip to Atlantic City.

The task force confirmed Simon's information. The three, along with the Gaducci brothers, went to the Resorts Casino in Atlantic City to sell the drugs. There was a problem with the amount of cocaine the victims had in their suitcase. Some of the drugs were missing. The Gaducci brothers reported to the boss. They suspected that the murder victims took some of the drugs to sell on their own. Sunny Après, the mob boss, told the Gaducci brothers to take care of the problem permanently. The organized-crime task force had this phone call taped through a wiretap.

The next step was to find and question Billy Delaney. On Saturday, Simon found Delaney at a bar in Newark. He brought him in to headquarters for questioning. Lieutenant King of the state police task force questioned Delaney with Detective Simon. Both officers were skilled interrogators. Faced with a life term for conspiracy to murder, Delaney confessed. He was promised safety from the mob, maybe even placement in the witnesses protection program. Chief Phillips was notified.

On Monday, the chief asked me to accompany him and Detective Smith to pick up Delaney from the Newark jail. The charges against him were made by the Holmdel Police Department and Monmouth County Prosecutor's Office. He was charged with being a material witness to a double homicide. Delaney had to return to the Monmouth County, where the crime occurred.

En route back to Monmouth County, Delaney gave us the whole story. He said Sonny asked him to drive Tony "the Priest" Gaducci and his brother "Fat Frankie" with Vinnie and Pauly to Atlantic City. They used his Chevy suburban for the ride. They planned to stay overnight. He didn't know they were going to make a drug deal. He waited in their room when the four went out that night. When they returned, the four of them were screaming at each other. They were arguing about the deal and making phone calls. After doing some gambling and having dinner, they headed home. While on the Garden State Parkway, the arguing continued. Then he heard two shots. Tony told him to pull off at the next exit. They drove to a rural area a mile from the parkway. Tony told him to stop and park with the lights out. They made him help pull out the bodies and dump them in a ditch. He found his way back to the parkway and went north. He dropped the Gaducci brothers off at the Bada-Bing and then went home.

Delaney was afraid to go to the county jail. He knew that once the mob found out that warrants were issued for the Gaducci brothers, his life would be in danger. He agreed to stay in the Holmdel jail until the grand jury met. Then he would be needed and ready to testify at the trial. Detective Simon learned that the Gaducci brothers had fled to Florida. That was good information because as soon as they were indicted, we could get the FBI involved. They would be declared fugitives.

Chief Phillips was happy the case was just about solved; his problem was what now should he do with Delaney. It had been three weeks and Delaney was living in the cell at Holmdel Police headquarters. Bruce brought him a television for the cell, and he ordered his meals from the menu at the local diner. Bruce even had him at his home for dinner on occasion. It's not a good situation but would have to last until Delaney's grand jury testimony.

Tuesday night and we had a softball game against PBA Local 184, the Point Pleasant team. Bruce was our catcher. He was driving tonight and picking me up in his police car at my headquarters. It was 6:00 pm. Bruce pulled up in front of the headquarters. He had Jimmy Smith, our second basemen, in the car. Also in the back seat was Billy Delaney. This was not good.

The field was off Ocean Boulevard in Point Pleasant. We were now bringing criminals to the game. I played the outfield and got three hits. We won the game. After the game, it was customary to go to Bar A for pizza, wings, and beer. Other police teams in the league would be there for the party. It's usually a big crowd of cops, friends, and groupies. It's the highlight of the week for most of us.

That night, the beer flowed. We were in first place in the league, one game better than the state police south team. State police had three teams on the league—a north team, a central team, and a team from South Jersey. The night progressed as usual. At one point, I saw Delaney dancing with a pretty blonde named Marilyn. She and her three girlfriends were there almost every Tuesday night. They loved to dance. They were popular with all the cops.

At 2.00 a.m., the bar was starting to close. However, the owner never pushed out the cops. The other customers were told to leave. At 2:30 a.m. I found Bruce and dragged him out the door. Jimmy had left earlier with a pretty, buxom secretary from the prosecutor's office. When we got outside, Bruce's police car was not in the parking lot. He said Delaney had the car. Delaney had left at one thirty to take Marilyn for breakfast. I looked around; it was almost 3:00 a.m. We were alone sitting on the curb in front of Bar A. Our only choice was to sit and wait. We waited until Delaney drove into the parking lot at 3:30 a.m. What a relief for both of us. I got home at 4:00 a.m. Good thing Nancy was sound asleep. I would have some explaining to do. It didn't turn out to be just another night of playing softball.

Prisoner Escape

On Sunday, June 6, the department of corrections issued a BOLO ("be on the lookout"). There was an escape from Trenton State Prison. This is the most secure institution in the state. There had not been an escape in thirty-five years. This prison housed the most incorrigible New Jersey inmates for the past hundred years. The escaped prisoner was Terry Keenan, white male, thirty years old, six foot two tall, and two hundred pounds. He had been at Trenton State Prison for the past three years. He was serving a life sentence plus thirty years.

I was at a party for my older sister at her home in Belford. She was turning thirty-five years old. The desk sergeant tracked me down at her house. A lieutenant from the Department of Corrections wanted to meet me at our headquarters. I left the party and went to work. My wife, Nancy, was not happy; I had been called in to work the last two weekends.

At headquarters, I waited for Lieutenant Anderson. He arrived with three other correction officers. I was the complainant and lead investigator on the crimes that Keenan committed. Lieutenant Anderson believed I would have knowledge of his habits and hiding places. Detective Schnoor was on duty. I sent him along with two of the correction officers to the Booker family residence in Leonardo. Johnny Booker was in Rahway prison doing twenty years. Booker was involved with Keenan on a previous case I investigated.

The Fox family from Port Monmouth was instrumental in the crime that sent Keenan to prison. I went to the Fox family residence with Lieutenant Anderson. The Fox family were respected members of the community. Dan Fox was extremely cooperative. He blamed Keenan for leading his son astray. He said, "If I hear anything about Keenan's whereabouts, I will call you and help capture him." No one in his family even knew he escaped. Detective Schnoor called. The Booker family didn't know of Keenan's escape. They would not hide Keenan for fear of violating the law. They already had enough problems. I didn't think staking out their residence would be beneficial.

Our groups met in Keansburg headquarters. Sergeant Preston gave the correction officers the location of Keenan's hangouts and a list of his friends. Keansburg officers and correction officers searched the "Burg" for Kennan or information regarding who might be hiding him. We checked his last address, an apartment behind O'Reilly's bar. The apartment was vacant. We learned from O'Reilly that his wife, Jeanne, moved from Keansburg last year. O'Reilly told us; "She is living in Woodbridge with her mother. He hasn't seen her in a year."

The DOC made up "Wanted" posters. Keenan's photo and record were in every police department in Monmouth County. Lieutenant Anderson reported at our department and Keansburg headquarters for the next two weeks. No one reported sighting Keenan. All our informants were looking. I was pretty sure he did not return to his home area.

Before Lieutenant Anderson left Monmouth County, I asked him how Terry Keenan escaped. He said, "Keenan hid in the yard sometime during the day exercise period. They believe he hid in the cleaning room. His cellmate put pillows in his bunk and covered them, making it appear that Keenan was in his cell and in bed at the nighttime check. The midnight-shift officer, while checking all the locked cells, noticed something suspicious in the cell. He called for assistance and unlocked the cell. He found the ruse. Keenan's cellmate would not say anything. The prison was searched. On the roof they found a blanket covering the barbed wire on the top of the wall. They found scuffmarks on the inside wall between the wall and a brick smoke stack four feet from the inside wall. Keenan shimmied between the stack and the wall for over forty feet. It was a feat prison officials could hardly believe. But Keenan was strong and agile. After going over the wall, they believed he had an accomplice pick him up in a vehicle. An alarm was sent to the Trenton Police and Hamilton Township Police, to no avail.

Terry Keenan had made a daring escape.

The Badge

Pat McConnell was sworn in as a police officer two years after me. He is a big man, 6 foot tall and 220 pounds. Pat was recently discharged from the army and in great physical condition. He took the civil service test while home on leave. He was in the patrol division five years before Chief McKenna promoted him to detective. Pat has a lot of prejudices. He considered anyone who was not a white Anglo-Saxon Protestant male police officer to be a "maggot." He disliked women except for emergency-room nurses. He was on his second marriage with a nurse.

Pat has a permanent scowl on his big moon-shaped face. He groused and growled about most assignments but followed orders and directions. He was the best pistol shot in the department and put in a lot of time on the shooting range. He does his job with little humor or emotion. The other detectives called him the Badge or just Badge.

On Wednesday morning, Pat came into the bureau strutting around the office, showing his certificate earned at shotgun school. He proudly boasted, "Best scores." The other detectives mocked him. Pat was proud of his certificates from the weapon-training classes. These certificates didn't mean very much, but he cherished them. He put the certificate on his desk and left the office to investigate a burglary.

Detective Dodge, who was present at the time, picked up the certificate and took it to the ID lab. He copied it and colored it so it looked exactly like the original. He then took the original and hid it under Pat's desk blotter. He took the counterfeit certificate, ripped it in half, stepped on it, and left it on the floor next to Pat's desk. This was going to be fun but dangerous. The detectives in the office could not wait to see Pat's reaction.

Most detectives would return back to the office around 4:00 p.m. to write their reports. The evening shift just reported for duty, so the office was full. When Pat arrived, the office was quiet. Everybody was waiting for Pat's reaction. When he saw the certificate on the floor, he exploded. "Who did this?" he bellowed. The guys were snickering, but they were afraid to laugh. Pat said, "I know Dodge did this." He stormed out, heading for the ID lab. Dodge heard him coming and snuck out the back door.

Pat returned to the bureau and hollered at all of us, "Tell me where he is!" He stomped around for a while, cursing Dodge, and then sat down at his desk. He called the police academy. We heard him requesting another certificate, explaining his was damaged. Apparently, Director Scott of the academy told him he would send another.

As a lieutenant in the bureau, I had an office just off the large room the detectives occupied. My phone rang. It was Dodge. He asked, "Is it safe to return to the office?" I told him I would sign him off duty. "Go home until tomorrow. Hide out."

Thursday, Al came in early. He took the certificate from under the blotter and left it on top of Pat's desk. He then went to the lab and hid. When Pat came into work, he found the certificate on his desk. He said nothing. He knew he was the brunt of a joke. Nobody looked at him and work went on in the office as usual. I gave out the assignments, and the detectives went out on the road.

Because the Badge was still angry, I took Dodge to lunch and then to a burglary crime scene. I wanted to keep him away from headquarters. At 3:45 p.m., a call came into the desk. A teacher from River Plaza Grammar School reported a domestic disturbance at the intersection of Nutswamp Road and Hubbard Avenue. Patrolman Pat Greaves received the call.

Dodge and I were nearby, so we headed in that direction as a backup. Patrolman Greaves was a smart officer. He arrived and parked his patrol car on Nutswamp Road and walked to the side of the house. The home was a ranch-style home facing Hubbard Avenue. He peeked in a window and observed a man holding a gun to a woman and female child. The woman was crying and looking frightened. The gunman was searching the bedroom.

Greaves backed to his car and called in the situation. It didn't appear to be a domestic case but possibly a robbery. Help soon arrived. We surrounded the house. Patrolman Pollinger parked behind Greaves's car and covered the back of the house. Patrolman Bert Grimm arrived and covered the front from behind a tree with a shotgun. The Badge arrived. He and I were at the front sidewalk without cover. Detective Deickmann arrived and drove into the driveway behind a Volkswagen, which was parked in front of the garage door. I was about to call for a bullhorn when the front door opened. The gunman held the woman around the neck with a gun pointed at her head. He hollered, "Get that car from behind the Volkswagen, or I will shoot her!" So I shouted to Detective Deickmann, "Slowly move your car to the road!" This situation was getting worse by the minute.

Dodge had forgotten his gun. He was hiding behind my car. Badge was standing next to me in a classic shooting position with his six-inch Colt Python revolver pointed at the gunman as he forced the woman down the front steps heading for the Volkswagen. She was hysterical. I had my snub-nosed revolver in my hand, but I could not shoot at that distance. We were about fifty feet away, and I was not that good a shot.

"Drop your guns!" yelled the gunman. No one did. The young girl was in the doorway, not in line with the gunman. While he was forcing the woman into the car, his gun fired. I thought he shot the woman. Before I could finish crying out "Shoot, Badge!" Pat Connell had fired and shot the gunman at the neck. Patrolman Greaves, who had worked his way around the house and near the garage, fired two shots. Three shots were fired in seconds.

We charged toward the gunman. He was lying on the ground in the driveway with the gun nearby on the ground. He was bleeding profusely from the neck. The woman wasn't shot. The burglar probable didn't know how to use the gun and it went off accidently as he was pushing the shaken and hysterical woman in the car.

Two ambulances arrived. The first one took the gunman to the hospital. Patrolman Furieto, an EMT, went with the gunman. He had administered first aid to him after the shooting. A second ambulance arrived to take Mrs. Mazza and her daughter to the hospital.

Before she left for the hospital, twelve-year-old Donna Mazza told me, "My mother had just picked me up from school. When we arrived home, we went into the house and surprised the burglar. When her mother attempted to run out of the front door of the house, the burglar dragged her back into the house at knifepoint. He took us into the master bedroom and searched the room. He found my father's gun. He held the gun to us and continued the search, looking for cash and jewelry He was gathering loot in a pillowcase when he saw or heard the police officers outside. He hesitated for a few minutes then dragged my mother to the front door." She added, "You know the rest. Can I go to the hospital with my mother?"

Patrolman Greaves went with the child and her mother to the hospital. I went back to headquarters with Dodge. He had to return to the crime scene with the ID van for forensics. The chief had already heard of the incident. I notified the prosecutor's office of the shooting and, as usual, started writing the official reports.

The victim's husband picked up his wife and daughter at the hospital. She was sedated and taken home. He thanked the officers many times.

The burglar survived. The doctors said he would be paralyzed from the neck down for life." The sheriff 's department posted a guard outside his room, but he wasn't going anywhere for a long while. His family arrived and caused a commotion with threats to the police. He was a career criminal with many convictions and was presently on parole. This case would never go to court. The criminal got his life sentence.

The Badge looked a little glassy-eyed when he returned to the office. I offered him time off and recommended a visit to Dr. Mohair, the department psychologist. Pat declined; I knew he would.

The mayor gave Detective Connell and Patrolman Greaves a commendation for their actions. Patrolman Greaves was given a trophy by the detectives at a luncheon. It was a toy replica of a Volkswagen with two bullet holes on it.

Case closed.

Post-Office Burglaries

||||||||||||||||||||||||||||||||||||||||||||||||||||||||||||||||||||||||||||||||||||||||||||||||||||||||||||||||||||||||||||||||||||||||

"Damn, damn, damn! Those bastards got my post office!"

When I went in to work on Monday morning, I saw the patrol report on the burglary of the Belford post office. The building was broken into on Sunday night or early Monday morning. The break-in was discovered Monday 5:00 a.m. by my old boss and nemesis, Assistant Postmaster Buttsy. I worked at the post office for nine months before I entered the police department. Buttsy said to me before, "Holiday, you are a lousy mailman and will never make it as a cop." What a jerk. I dreaded going to the post office for this investigation.

I went to the post office Monday morning at 10:00 a.m. with DetectiveVince and Dodge. Buttsy was there to harass me. He laughed and said, "You clam-diggers will never solve this burglary. I want the postal authority to investigate." Thank God the postmaster, Mr. Jackson, was cooperative.

The building was entered through the back door at the loading dock. There were tire marks, but too many trucks used the ramp, including the local Belford trucks. The metal doors were pried open with a heavy tool, probably some type of crow bar. There were sneaker prints on the floor possibly from the culprits. The box safe, which weighed about three hundred pounds, was rolled out the back doors onto a vehicle. A van or truck must have been used. Most post offices have their safes on rollers for movement within the offices. This US post office did not have a burglar alarm. I felt like punching Buttsy right in the face. What an a—hole!

Back at the bureau, I put out a Teletype to all New Jersey police agencies on the burglary. I had seen other previous messages on post-office burglaries and notified the patrols to check the offices prior to our burglary. District cars had too much territory to cover the five post offices in that district. The patrolman in that district checked the building at 4:00 a.m., and it was secure.

Two weeks later, at the monthly Monmouth and Ocean County Intelligence Bureau (MOCIB) meeting, the discussion centered on safe burglaries within Monmouth and Ocean counties. The MOCIB is an organization of detectives from the two counties. The meetings held once a month are no-nonsense meetings that conduct business only. Five post offices were hit. The first was in Old Bridge Township, and the last was ours. The other three were in shore towns. All had the same MO (modus operandi)—leaving very little physical evidence. The safes were not found. We discussed a task force but did not implement one at the meeting. Detectives from the federal postal service were at the meeting.

Two weeks after our post office's B&E (breaking and entering), we received a break. A Matawan patrol officer checked a van with three suspicious occupants near their post office at 4:30 a.m. Next to the van, on the ground, were burglary tools. The officer suspected the occupants threw the tools out the side door when they saw the patrol car. The patrolman arrested them for possession of these tools. Possession of burglar tools is a difficult crime for the prosecutor to prove.

Detective Sergeant Joe Booket interrogated the three suspects. The first one was Ray Folger, the renter of the van. He lived alone in Asbury Park in a new condo apartment. He had a criminal record in Texas for burglaries. At the age of twenty-five, he was well acquainted of police procedures and tactics. The second suspect was Jimmy Ellis from Red Bank. He was known to local police but not suspected as a person who would be involved in safe burglaries. He would not talk to Sergeant Booklet at all. He just asked for his lawyer. The third suspect was Jerry Casey from East Keansburg. I knew Casey from the Keansburg softball league. He was the league commissioner, a team coach, and a member of the Keansburg Recreation Committee. He was known as a rough guy but not a criminal. The three suspects were teammates on the O'Brien Tigers softball team.

Joe Booket called me personally and notified the other agencies interested in the arrests. Vince and I rushed to Matawan in hopes of speaking to the suspects before they were bailed out. Ellis's father had him out on a five-thousand-dollar bail before we got there.

Ray Folger was making arrangements with a bondsman when we arrived. He agreed to talk to us. He was bright, articulate, with a charming demeanor. He acted as if he enjoyed the interrogation. He said, "You will never be able to catch me. I am too smart for you." He was challenging us. "If I were the burglar and needed money, I could rob any post office." He was very cocky and laughed during the interrogation.

Jerry Casey was very nervous. He said, "I remember Vince and you from the softball league and the Country Tavern team." He had that right. He asked for his wife to be present during the interrogation. He had called her from the Matawan Police headquarters after he was arrested. She was a secretary in our police department a few years ago. She even worked in the detective bureau. We brought her into the interrogation room. Jerry, his wife, Sergeant Booket, Vince, and I were in the room. His story was that he went out drinking with Ray and Ellis in New York until 3:00 a.m. On the way home, they got tired and stopped to rest. He didn't see any tools in the van. He didn't even know where he was until he got arrested. I knew he was the "weak link" in the group. Mrs. Evelyn Casey appeared so scared I thought she would pass out. We couldn't make any charges at this time, but we knew they were our burglars.

Vince and I decided to do surveillance on Casey. Red Bank detectives were going to watch Ellis. County Detectives McCormick and Wilmore were going to conduct surveillance on Folger. They needed money after posting bail, and Folger's ego would not let us gain the upper hand. He practically told us he was going to commit another burglary. Casey lived in a converted bungalow on the bay.

He left for work at 5:30 a.m. He walked to the highway and got on a bus for New York City. When arrested, he gave his employment as a ticket salesman for Radio City Music Hall. His wife left for work at 7:30 a.m. She was a teacher's aide at a local grammar school.

Neither job was high paying, and their debts were piling. We found his problem was from his gambling on sports and horses.

The group had to have a place to peel open the stolen safes. Folger's condo was not a good place for this, and Ellis lived with his parents. The back of Casey's house or the beach was a possibility. That night after the arrest, Vince and I decided to snoop around Casey's bungalow. A van was parked in front of his bungalow. We parked a block away and walked the beach until we came behind his place. There was an alleyway between the bungalows. We sneaked through the alley, past garbage cans, to a window where we could peek into the Casey's kitchen. I asked Vince to boost me up since the window was about seven feet from the ground. I could see a light on in the kitchen. Vince put his hands together, bent over a little as I stepped into his hands as he lifted.

As I got my head to window level, Vince cursed loudly and dropped me. "You stepped in dog turds!" he screamed at me. I fell into the garbage cans, scattering them around. Their clanging together made a lot of noise. Lights came on in the bungalow next door and in Casey's house. Vince was already running. I ran out of the alley to the beach. I didn't see anybody chasing me. Vince was a hundred yards ahead of me. He was already in the car when I got there, still cursing. He was really angry with me. On the drive back to headquarters, he hollered, "I smell like dog shit!"

Back at headquarters, we washed in the locker room. Vince would not talk to me. He stormed out and went across the street to Muldoon's Bar. I finished the reports and went home after a bad night of investigatory work.

Although it was a weak document, I prepared a search warrant for Casey's bungalow the next day. I wanted to search for the Belford safe or parts of the safe. The judge was not happy with the weak affidavit but issued the warrant anyway. Vince was still mad at me and refused to go on the search. At 5:30 p.m., when Mrs. Casey had returned home, I executed the warrant with Patrolman Irv Beaver and the Badge.

We found a small amount of safe insulation on the kitchen floor. We found a torch and burn marks on the floor. Irv, looking around, found what we needed. In the washing machine were thirty coin wrappers containing pennies with "Belford Post Office" markings on the sides. That's when Jerry walked in the door. After entering, he expressed anger with the search. When I showed him the warrant, he calmed down. When I showed him the pennies, he broke down. He admonished his wife, "I told you not to take them." We arrested them both.

Back at headquarters, we booked the both of them, Jerry for burglary and Evelyn for possession of stolen property. Jerry wanted to talk to us in order to stop us from sending Evelyn to the county jail. I wanted a confession and information on the location of the safe and its contents. He gave us everything. He admitted to five other burglaries implicating Folger and Ellis. Folger had a fence in New York City, and the three of them got 10 percent of the face value of the stamps. He was singing all night to detectives from all over the county. I arranged for Evelyn to be released under her own recognizance. Warrants were issued for Ellis and Folger.

The next day, while detectives were hunting for Folger and Ellis, Casey took a group of us to the bridge on Route 36, which spanned the Shrewsbury River. He showed us where they dumped the peeled safes into the water. I arranged for a dive team to search the river under the bridge.

That afternoon, a police dive team recovered seven safes from the water. Five were from post offices. One was from the peanut-butter factory in Red Bank. Casey didn't know about the seventh safe. He wasn't in on that burglary.

Red Bank detectives arrested Ellis that evening. He confessed to his crimes. He gave the same story as Casey. They peeled the safes open in Casey's kitchen. He remembered Casey telling his wife not to take the pennies. Criminals always seem to make stupid mistakes.

Thursday morning, I went in early to prepare reports and confer with the other agencies. I almost fell over when Ray Folger walked into the bureau at 9:30 a.m. He had a box full of coffee cups and two dozen donuts. He said, "I heard that you were looking for me." He was cocky as usual. He was so charismatic you almost had to like him. He said, "My bail bondsman will be here before you finish your coffee." Ray admitted to the burglaries but would not give a statement. He said, "I will form a new gang and maybe switch to different crimes." He needed the money for lawyers and bail. Everybody liked this guy. I even asked the chief to come down to the detective bureau to meet him. He was bailed out by 11:00 a.m. He promised to go to any police station that wanted him. "Just call," he said.

I called Buttsy and requested him at headquarters to identify the safe. It wasn't necessary because postal investigators had already identified all the safes. I just wanted Buttsy to eat crow for saying we weren't competent enough to solve the burglary. I felt ten feet tall as I hovered over him.

Vince got over the dog-turd incident, and we went back to work as partners. He even helped with some of the reports.

Case closed.

The Chase

It was Tuesday night. A group of us rode to a softball game in Lumpy Slovinski's car. We won the game and went to Irish Red's bar after the game. The beer was flowing, courtesy of the Seaside Heights PBA team. It was party time; we were in first place in the league and expecting to win it all. At midnight, the owner of the establishment had a tradition. Big Red had the band play a funeral dirge while a plywood coffin was brought in and placed on the bar. When the song ended, the coffin was opened and a scantily clad barmaid jumped out and then the band played, "Happy days are here again." The bartenders gave all the patrons a free shot of Irish whiskey. It's great fun!

This evening, Big Red asked us to carry in the coffin. However, instead of bringing it to the bar area, we carried the coffin to the pool and threw it in. Sally, the barmaid, was screaming. She climbed out of the coffin and fell into the water. Vince and I dove in the pool and pulled her out. Her barmaid uniform was not waterproof and was quite revealing. She looked great. Most of the patrons came out of the bar to see what was happening. Some were laughing so hard they fell into the pool. Big Red didn't think it was funny. He kicked out the whole team from the bar. No problem. To us, it was just another fun night after a ballgame.

On the ride home, Lumpy was speeding along Ocean Avenue. We heard a siren behind us and saw flashing lights. Lumpy though it was an ambulance. He swerved off to the right and drove through a gas station. Meanwhile, the vehicle behind us, a police patrol car, passed us. Lumpy swerved back onto Ocean Avenue behind the police car. A block ahead of us, a roadblock was set up by Point Pleasant Police. When we stopped, we were surprised to find the roadblock was for us.

I pulled Doug Corrigan back down from the moon roof of the car. He was standing up though the moon roof opening, waving an Irish flag he had stolen from Big Red's bar. Sergeant Dennis Cahill of the Point Pleasant Police approached our car and looked in. He said, "Oh no, you guys got me in a pickle." There was a crowd of people on the sidewalks watching the action. Dennis walked back to his car and sat inside for a few minutes. He pretended to write a ticket. This would satisfy the crowd. He came back to the car and handed the cardboard cover of the ticket book to Lumpy. This appeared to be a summons issued but was a common police trick. He pretended to be angry and told us in loud-enough terms for the crowd to hear, "Get out of town!" Lumpy slowly drove away, and we headed home. I got home at 1:00 a.m., an early night for Tuesday softball. Nancy was surprised. I was ready to go to work in the morning without a hangover, get some sleep, and be fresh as a daisy.

But at three in the morning, the red phone rang. The red phone was a direct telephone line from police headquarters to my home. Chief McKenna had it installed to alert me early of problems. I didn't want the phone, but he insisted. The call was from desk sergeant Zemalkowski. He said, "Call Sergeant Cahill of the Point Pleasant Beach Police Department. They have Detective Bob Schnoor at their headquarters. He is in his underwear carrying a gun. His car had been in an accident. He arrested the driver of the car he smashed into."

It sounded like a real mess. I wished they called Captain Lutz instead of me. I called Sergeant Cahill. He said, "Holiday, I can't get rid of you guys. I got a cop in his underwear making an arrest on my street. Please get down here and straighten this out now!" Bob "Scooter" Schnoor was not hurt, only angry. I told Cahill I would be there in an hour. I picked up Vince, who had a hangover as usual, and raced to Point Pleasant.

At the Point Pleasant Police headquarters, I met Schnoor and Cahill and got the story. Schnoor said he got home from the game at 1:00 a.m. and went to bed. He heard a noise from his den. He grabbed a flashlight and his gun and confronted a burglar in his house. The burglar ran out the back door with Bob in pursuit. Bob lost him in the neighborhood, but when returning back to his house, he saw the culprit driving away in a Chevy pickup. Bob rushed to his house, grabbed the keys to his car, and gave chase."

Bob's wife called the police department, and they dispatched patrol cars. Other departments were notified. Tinton Fall Police reported that a Chevy pickup had been stolen earlier. "There has been a rash of car burglaries in our area." This time, the burglar picked the wrong house.

Schnoor said he chased the truck onto the Garden State Parkway. "The truck exited in Wall Township and headed east with me and a state police car in pursuit. The culprit went over the bridge onto Route 70 and was stopped at a roadblock on Ocean Avenue. I couldn't stop my car in time and ran into the back of the pickup truck, which slid into the side of Sergeant Cahill's patrol car." This was a big mess. The burglar was arrested. We knew him and suspected him of instigating other car burglaries in the county.

Cahill said, "Your detective was standing in the roadway in his underwear with his gun pointed at the burglar. He insisted on making the arrest and putting the cuffs on the criminal." It was a serious situation, but the cops couldn't help from laughing. They knew Bob was really mad.

Cahill lent Bob a police jumpsuit, and we went home. We would be back at 9:00 a.m. to process reports and records. I admire the tenaciousness of Detective Bob Schnoor. He was involved in two car chases that night. The first one was sitting in the back of Lumpy Slovinski's car as a passenger, the second one driving his own car. Both times Sergeant Cahill stopped him in the roadblocks.

I love being a cop. Life certainly is not dull.

Innocent but Found Guilty

The graveyard shift starts at midnight and continues until 8:00 a.m. Patrolman Doug Corrigan was on his last night of the shift. He was assigned to District I, covering Highway 36 from Keansburg to Sea Bright. During the week, the highway is quiet. On a clear night in the hills of Highlands, one could see the ocean shimmering in the distance. Doug was slowly patrolling the roadway when he saw two bodies on the ground next to the right lane.

He called for backup units. Doug got out of his patrol car and ran to the bodies. He discovered two females with major injuries. He ran back to his car and called for an ambulance. Neither victim appeared to be alive. He attempted to help them, but the only thing he could do was cover one with a blanket. They were not bleeding profusely but were awkwardly twisted in an unnatural position. They appeared to have been struck by a car.

The Highlands ambulance arrived and scooped up the victims. One was still alive and breathing. Patrolman Corrigan protected the crime scene with help from the Highlands Police.

I got the call on the red phone at 3:30 a.m. Sergeant Battle, who was on the desk, gave me the details. I sent Badge and Al Dodge to the crime scene. Badge spent two years in the traffic division and had the experience to investigate death by auto cases.

I picked up my partner, Vince, and went to the hospital. Both victims were in the emergency room on gurneys. Sally Rand, senior nurse told me the victim on the left gurney, was deceased. The victim on the other gurney was about to expire. I tried to talk to the victim who was still alive. I asked her what happened. She was murmuring, but even with my ear next to her mouth, I couldn't understand her. Nurse Sally couldn't hear her, either. After just five minutes, she closed her blue eyes and died. What a travesty. Life can be so unfair.

The victims were wearing white uniforms. They were probably waitresses. They didn't have any identification on them. Both were Caucasian females about twenty years old. They had blunt trauma to the body. One had a severe head injury. The back legs of one of the victims had impressions that looked like a front grill of a car. These needed to be photographed and enhanced. I was a little shaken as I had two daughters. Thank God, they're still babies. Vince was cool and calm.

Vince and I left the hospital and went to the accident scene. Sergeant Bray found a small piece of metal that appeared to be from a car grill. This and the dirt on the roadway were our only physical evidence. After Dodge took photos at the accident scene on the highway, I sent him to the hospital. Nurse Rand had said, "I will leave the bodies in the emergency room until you get your photographs. At 8:00 a.m., they would be sent to the morgue for autopsies by the county medical examiner." Al photographed the victims and collected their clothing for forensic evidence.

At headquarters, Vince worked on the identification of the victims. They didn't have any ID on them at the scene of the hit-and-run. I prepared a request for the examination of evidence. The clothing, a small piece of metal found at the scene and dirt, and dust debris from the scene were all we had. Al would package the evidence and transport it to the state police laboratory in Trenton. I sent a Teletype to all the Monmouth County police departments with the details of the crime.

The following morning, Detective Bob Farry from the Eatontown Police called. He reported he had a missing person reported. The missing report concerned a twenty-year-old female who had not returned home from work. She was last seen at the Americana Diner in Eatontown. With this information, Vince and I went to Eatontown to meet with Detective Farry. He obtained a photograph of the missing person from her mother. When I looked at the photo, I identified the victim.

The three of us went to the diner. The manager, a well-groomed black man with impeccable manners, ushered us into the diner office. He told us that the victim, Donna Hall, worked in the diner last night. She left at 10:00 p.m. after her shift with her girlfriend Patty Anderson. He heard them talking about a double date with two young soldiers from nearby Fort Monmouth. He could identify the soldiers if he saw them again because they were frequent patrons. We got the addresses of the victims. Detective Farry said he would notify the next of kin. Their relatives would have to go to the morgue and officially identify them.

Vince and I went to the Ocean Township Police Department. We met with Detective Sergeant Neil Taylor. Patricia Anderson lived alone in a condo in Wanamassa. The building superintendent let us into her apartment. There was a photograph of her on her bedroom dresser with Donna Hall. We identified both of them as our victims. Detective Taylor said, "I'll track down the next of kin." I took the photograph, and we went back to the office.

That evening, while I was at home the, red phone rang again. Mr. Pierre, the manager of the diner, called the police department. He had the two soldiers with him. The soldiers agreed to drive to police headquarters and meet me. I called Vince, and we went back to work. No sooner than we arrived, the two soldiers arrived. They were dressed in their fatigue uniforms. They seemed scared they would be arrested. I calmed them down and asked for their story. Private First Class Dominick Mullany was interviewed first. Private First Class Jackie Maywood sat outside the office, waiting for his interview.

Mullany said, "We met the girls at the Americana diner. I drove the four of us to a house party in Belford. Ebby Maxim invited us. There were about thirty people in the house drinking and listening to music. At about 1:00 a.m., Ebby's mother came home. She was angry with Ebby for having the party and chased everybody out of the house. Maywood and I ran out the back door. That was the last time I saw the girls. We went to my car and waited for about an hour. It was parked around the corner. When the girls didn't show up, we drove back to Fort Monmouth and to our barracks."

Maywood gave us the same story. Vince and I took statements from them and released them. I didn't notify their commanding officer, as it didn't appear they did anything wrong.

From the information I received, I knew the location of the house. It was a single-family home, the third house on the west side of East Road near Highway 36. Vince and I went to the house on East Road and found Mrs. Maxim at home. She was annoyed that her son had a party without her permission. She recalled two girls in white waitress uniforms running out the front door. She saw them scamper to Highway 36 and start hitchhiking. A few minutes later, a large white car stopped and picked them up. She didn't see the driver or anyone else in the car. We scheduled a time to interview her son, Ebby.

It was a long day. We went off duty.

I took Sunday off. After church, I spent the rest of the day watching football and resting. I couldn't stop thinking of the victims. I should had just gone to work.

Monday morning, I reported the weekend's investigation to Captain Lutz. We gave this investigation top priority, and the chief assigned two traffic officers to assist the detectives. With the victims identified, the next step was to interview the people at the party. Ebby Maxim gave us a list of those who were invited. I assigned the detectives and traffic officers to contact the witnesses and take their statements while I prepared the reports. At noon, Al Dodge and I went to the autopsy.

Tuesday morning, Jim Bruning called from the state police laboratory. One of the girl's uniforms had white paint chips on the back. The piece of chrome was identified as a piece of a front grill of a 1980 Cadillac. The bruising on the legs of Patricia Anderson matched the grill of the1980 Cadillac. From the evidence submitted, the lab technicians believe that the car struck both of them from behind. The grill hit Anderson, and then the hood hit her head and elbows as she flew over the top of the car. Donna Hall was hit and went under the car. We now had to search for a white 1980 Cadillac with a piece of the grill missing and small dents in the hood.

The Department of Motor Vehicles would not do the research into ownership of the car but invited us to Trenton to search their files. I sent Detective Schnoor and Detective Mulvey for this task. The county prosecutor's office sent Detective Molly Carroll to assist them. They had to search through thousands of registrations, and when they returned, we had a hundred and fifty cars in Monmouth County and sixty-seven cars in Ocean County to investigate. I notified the press. They wrote a follow-up story where they reported, "The police are looking for a white 1980 Cadillac with damage to the hood and grill."

We had our list and started the search. For two weeks, nothing turned up. Then I received a telephone call from a high school teacher in Leonardo. He had read the newspaper account of the deaths. He said, "My neighbor across the street has a car that matched the description, and I have not seen it at the house lately." I checked the list. Sergeant Thorne went to the home, but the car was not there and the house empty. I asked Jim Dowling, the teacher, to call if he ever he'd see the car.

The next week, Dowling called to report the car was in the driveway at 550 Dow Avenue in Leonardo. I sent Sergeant Thorne to investigate. He reported back to me that the owner, Ian McDermitt, was nasty and chased him off the property. He did look at the car and believed it had some recent work. I went the next day to the house with Al Dodge. Al took a surreptitious scraping of the paint from the car as Mr. McDermitt was castigating me. He scraped the paint from the wheel well where McDermitt wouldn't notice.

I asked McDermitt the same question Sergeant Thorne did the previous day. "Who drives the car?"

McDermitt said, "Get off my property. It's my car, and I am the only one who drives it."

Al Dodge took the paint scraping and submitted a forensic-test request directly to the lab in Trenton. We would have the results tomorrow. The state police considered the case a priority. We waited the rest of the day with our fingers crossed.

Friday, we received the call. The paint scrapings matched the paint on one of the victim's dress. We had enough information to apply for a court seizure of McDermitt's car. I prepared the documents, and Superior Court Judge Thomas Yacrelli signed the order. "Let's get the car," I told my men. The house and car had been staked out since we got the call this morning.

Armed with the court order and a flatbed truck we went to McDermitt's house. When McDermitt answered the door, he went wild. He screamed and hollered and came close to assaulting us. He made the same statement again, "It's my car, and I am the only one who drives it" It was a strange statement. It seemed he was protecting someone. We left an angry man and took his car. Sergeant Thorne followed the truck with the suspect's car directly to the lab in Trenton. He filled out the request forms, and now we wait again.

I took the weekend off. Vince and Sergeant Thorne did some background work on the suspect. McDermitt worked at a Dumont paint factory in Jersey City. He and his son, Dave, worked the 3 p.m. to 11:00 p.m. shifts. On the night before the killings, they both worked until 11:00 p.m. They had a parking permit at the plant for the 1980 Cadillac owned by Ian McDermitt.

Monday morning, I was anxiously waiting for Bruning to call. I had a lot of report writing to complete and planned to stay in the office. I assigned detectives their investigations and was relaxing in my office when I heard the commotion on the police radio. Detective Lumpy Slovinski, who had been tailing a suspect, a burglar named Miguel Ramos, was in a fight with him on the street. Backup patrol cars were dispatched along with an ambulance.

Lumpy returned to headquarters with a television and assorted jewelry that Ramos had just stolen. Ramos was taken to the hospital with a broken nose and bruises. Patrolman Beaver was at the hospital guarding Ramos. After preparing a preliminary report, I had to take Lumpy to the hospital; Ramos had broken Lumpy's pinky finger. Lumpy was still mad I had to make sure he didn't meet Ramos at the hospital emergency room. The fight would begin again, and Ramos would have more injuries.

While I was at the hospital, the state police lab called. McDermitt's car was the vehicle that killed the victims. The examination revealed hairs from one victim under the front end and dents

151

that had been repaired on the hood that matched the size of the victim being hit and bouncing on the hood. New chrome insignia had been installed on where the broken piece had been. The lab report was positive. I returned to the office for a Teletype of the report and signed a murder complaint against Ian McDermitt. The judge issued an arrest warrant. I was happy to make this arrest.

McDermitt had left Leonardo for his job in Jersey City. I didn't want to wait. I notified the chief and Captain Lutz of my plans to make the arrest in Jersey City. I called Jersey City Police Department and requested them meet us at the factory. Sergeant Thorne and I made the arrest at the factory. What a nasty guy! He cursed us all the way to Monmouth County jail. Bail had been set at one million, and he would probably stew in jail until the trial.

On Wednesday, McDermitt was brought back to the municipal court for a preliminary hearing. I was the only person to testify on the case. The judge, the Honorable Jerry Massell, held him over for grand jury. It didn't take long. Lumpy's case was next on the docket, so I stayed in court to listen.

Lumpy testified to the circumstance of the arrest and the fight. When the state rested its case, defense attorney Frank Morgan questioned Lumpy. He asked Lumpy, "What was my client, Mr. Ramos's demeanor before the fight?" Lumpy looked perplexed. He didn't answer. Morgan asked him again. When he didn't answer the second time, Judge Massell ordered him to answer the question. The judge said, "What was Ramos's demeanor?" Lumpy sat in the witness chair, thinking hard. Then Lumpy said, "Judge, the meaner he got, the meaner I got, and we fought. He broke my pinky." The courtroom broke out in riotous laughter, and even Judge Massell laughed. The judge pounded his gavel and restored order. Morgan, still laughing, had no further questions and the case was also held over for the grand jury.

Before the trial of McDermitt, the assistant prosecutor scheduled a meeting with all the state's witnesses. He had all the police reports and laboratory findings. I offered my theory on how the crime was committed. McDermitt and his son went to work together that Friday night before the crime. They left the plant in Jersey City together in the Cadillac. The father drove home, and then the son took the car from their Dow Avenue home. The son, Dave, was driving west on highway #36 when he saw the two victims hitchhiking He picked them up. They were in the car as verified by their fingerprints inside the car. Something happened between McDermitt and the girls that caused Dave McDermitt to throw them out, leaving them on the side of the roadway. He drove west to an opening in the median and turned around and drove east. He passed the girls on the opposite side of the roadway then turned into another opening in the medium. Now he was heading west again behind the victims. At a high rate of speed, he struck the girls from behind and left them on the roadway. We were ready for court.

Nine months later, the father, Ian McDermitt's, was tried before a jury. He was found guilty. It took the jury only one hour to reach a verdict. The prosecutor, Jack Mulvany, subpoenaed Dave for the trial and put him on the stand as a state witness. Mulvany asked him who drove the death car. Dave said, "It's my father's car, and he drives it. He was driving the car the night the victims were killed. I was not with him." What a liar! He would not admit to the crime. He let his father take the fall. He was the worst son and the biggest coward I had ever met. He committed the offense, but I could not prove it.

Dave's father was innocent. He did not kill the girls but took the rap for protecting his dastardly son. He received a sentence of three to five years on each count. The real killer got off scot-free.

My conscious is clear. Justice was not done, but it was served.

Drug Task Force

The Jersey Shore in Monmouth County had fifty-one separate police agencies. The departments were led by a chief of police and, in a few departments, by a police director. These leaders, knowing that the drug problem was not just a local matter, formulated a cooperative plan to combat the scourge. The chiefs agreed to a multijurisdictional task force that would place undercover police officers throughout county. Departments would lend the task force an officer for this dangerous assignment. The officer would volunteer for six months. The officer would be placed in an area where he was unknown to the local suspected drug pushers and users. The undercover would try to obtain a menial job in the area and hang out in the places where drugs were bought and sold. The officer would report only to a taskforce supervisor. He would be supplied with intelligence and money for the purchase of drugs. In the summer of 1982, ten men started working undercover.

This year, our department, although the largest in the county, did not assign an officer. I was assisting the task-force supervisor, Sergeant Joe Booket of the Matawan Police Department with intelligence and drug recovery. The prosecutor assigned Assistant Prosecutor Schuler as adviser and for the preparation of search and arrest warrants. The task force bought a lot of drugs. In October, the undercover officers were brought in from the field to the prosecutor's office for debriefing. The assignment had ended. In the next two weeks, seventy-one arrests warrants were issued and fifty-five search warrants authorized.

On October 15, Friday morning, the drug raid was scheduled. The prosecutor's office chief of detectives, Frank Licitra, called police departments requesting they supply two hundred and fifty police officers for the raid. Chief McKenna ordered me to assign two detectives. Captain Mudrock assigned a patrolman from the midnight shift. All officers were to report to the Monmouth County Police Academy at 3:00 a.m.

I did not have to go on the raid. However, I assigned two detectives so I thought I should be there. I was involved during the investigation. Detective Sage was a seasoned officer, and Detective Oakes was new to this type of raid. Patrolman Furieto was with them. They would be assigned to a team for an arrest and search. Chief McKenna would want to know what his men were doing. I got up at 2:00 a.m. and drove to the police academy in Freehold, the staging area for the raid.

When I arrived, the parking lot was filled with marked and unmarked police cars. The men were in the auditorium, awaiting instructions and assignments. They were enjoying coffee and piles of donuts. Chief Licitra told the men they would be in teams of three or four. They would be issued arrest warrants, search warrants and would kick in doors at exactly 6:00 a.m. Intelligence on the suspects and places to search would be in a packet supplied to the team leader.

Chief Licitra, Sergeant Booket, and Chief Bruce Phillips made the assignments. Detective Sage, Detective Oakes, and Highlands Detective Bray were assigned to make an arrest in Sea Bright. There was an inside joke about the assignment, but Booket would not tell me what it was.

At 5:00 a.m., Chief Licitra approached me with a request. Two officers from Sea Girt police department could not participate in the raid. There was a bad accident at the highway in Sea Girt, and they were needed at the accident. Their department had two officers assigned and could not participate. The chief seemed reluctant but asked me to fill in for them. I was to assist Detective Lynn Brown of the Asbury Park Police Department and Trooper Stanley Kowalski of Troop E, Wall Township. The arrest warrant and search warrant was for a bad dude in Neptune.

We left the academy at 5:15 a.m. I drove. En route, I found out that Trooper Kolowski recently graduated from the academy and had only four weeks experience on the road. DetectiveBrown was a juvenile officer with seven years' experience. Lynn was a five-foot-two, 130-pound black female with a lot of guts but little brawn. Thankfully, Stan was a six-footer and over two hundred pounds. I was supposed to be the backup, but it seemed now I became the team leader.

En route, Lynn read the file. The arrest warrant was for Hector Morales, a twenty-five-year-old Puerto Rican born in this country. He was released from the state prison eight months ago. He had done four years for weapons possession and drug offenses. The report said he was dangerous and would resist arrest—not very encouraging information for the team.

We found the house on Carter Avenue in Neptune, a dead-end street off Springwood Avenue. The house appeared to have been an old cinder-block garage converted into two apartments. There was a set of wooden stairs on the south side of the building to the upper apartment door. We had the warrant for the downstairs apartment. The place was narrow with an old wooden front door. I suspected there was a back door, so I sent Detective Brown to the back with instructions to enter at 6:00 a.m. or if she heard a commotion. There were no lights in the upstairs apartment, and there was a dim light in the front of the apartment we were going to enter. I parked right in front of the house at 5:59 a.m. There was a dirt front yard with a few broken toys next to a concrete walk. It was only about fifteen feet to the door. I instructed Stan to kick in the door and I would enter first. I had a bad feeling about the raid. It was dark, and our eyes would take seconds to adjust to the interior of the apartment.

At 6:00 a.m., Trooper Kowalski kicked in the door. I had taken my gun, a nickel-plated, snub-nosed .38-caliber Colt revolver out of my holster and had it in my leather coat. I had a flashlight in my left hand, and when I entered, I placed my gun in my right hand. Kowalski was in uniform and had a flashlight and his gun in his hand. The room we entered in was very dark.

"Police! Don't move!" I yelled.

It was a living room about ten feet wide with a couch on my left and a television on my right. The next area behind the living room was set up as a kitchen with a nightlight over a table. There was another ten feet to a dark area behind a counter that separated the kitchen from a bedroom. I heard a rustlings noise and saw movement over the counter. With my vision slightly impaired, I saw someone rising with a weapon. It was Hector with a shotgun. I cocked my Colt and had pressure on the trigger when I saw movement behind Hector. We had a standoff. He dropped the shotgun. This action took place in seconds, but it seemed like an hour. I holstered and quickly handcuffed the prisoner. His girlfriend, who was in bed with him, was handcuffed by Stan.

Lynn burst in the apartment from the back. The back door was not locked. We turned on the lights. Hector and Maria were placed on the couch, and I read him the warrant and the Miranda rights. He was screaming loud and abusive language. I had a difficult time understanding him, as most of his yelling and cursing was in Spanish. Maria was crying in a quiet manner.

Lynn guarded the prisoners while Stan and I searched. We found packets of heroin in the bedroom on the dresser with a set of works. On the kitchen table was a scale and hundreds of glassine bags. There was also a grocery-size bag containing marijuana. Next to the bag was a blender and Ziploc baggies. I went outside for evidence bags. When I returned, we packaged the evidence. It was time to leave. We finished the arrest and search within twenty minutes.

Stan hustled the prisoner outside and placed him in the back of my car. I removed the cuffs from the girlfriend and told her we were not going to arrest her. Brown and I were gathering the evidence together when a group burst through the broken front door. It was Hector's family that lived in the apartment above, his father, mother, brother and sister. They were now screaming in Spanish at Lynn and me. We pushed our way through them and out the door.

I placed the shotgun and shells in the trunk of my car, together with the narcotics. Then I remembered I forgot the bag of marijuana. While Stan and Lynn were in the car with the prisoner, I ran back into the apartment to get the bag of marijuana. I had to push past the family, who were still yelling. I grabbed the bag off the kitchen table when Hector's brother, Esteban, jumped on my back and got me in a stranglehold. The mother grabbed for the bag, and I struggled to hold on. We were swinging around with the bag when it ripped. Marijuana was flying around in the air. Hector's sister got into the fray and kicked me in my groin. I went down on my knees in pain with tears in my eyes. Hector's father was punching me. They were all pummeling me. I struggled up and started swinging and grappling. We crashed through the front door and out on the dirt front yard. Stan and Lynn jumped out of the car to help me.

I saw Esteban punch Lynn and knock her to the ground. She fell next to the house and was in a sitting position calling on her portable radio. I heard her screaming, "Officer down! Officer down! Send help!" Stan and I were busy fighting with the family. When Stan wrestled the family off me, he fell to the ground, and his trooper hat fell off. Everybody was flaying away at each other. Stan and I were getting them under control when he went down again and the fighting group rolled over his hat. I saw Stan scramble to his feet and pick up his squashed troop hat. His face got red, and he started throwing punches with a fury. I heard sirens in the distance. By the time help arrived, we had the family all on the ground and subdued. I retrieved plastic cuffs from the trunk of my car, and we cuffed them all.

During the melee, Hector tried to escape from the back of the car by climbing out the window. When Stan spotted him, he hit him so hard he knocked him out. We put Hector back in my car, and other police officers dragged the rest of the family into their cars. We headed back to the police academy in a caravan.

When we arrived back, there was a big group of cops outside to witness our arrival, including the judge and Chief Licitra. Detective Bunky Hearden, who was bringing in Hector's mother, removed her from his car. She was wearing only a torn muumuu, and her enormous breasts were hanging out. I heard the chief hollering for someone to get a blanket and cover her. At five feet tall and two hundred fifty pounds, she was the leader of the family and still very defiant. Hectors father's face was swollen and bloody, and his shirt had been ripped off. He could hardly walk. The sister was missing her front teeth and had a bloody mouth. The brother was also shirtless and bloodied. They were marched into the academy for booking. A doctor was requested to check their injuries.

Stan, Lynn, and I didn't look too bad. We were disheveled and our uniforms were dirty and torn, but we were not seriously injured. My right hand started to swell, but I didn't say anything. I knew it was broken. I would take it care of it later.

Chief Licitra was groaning that the raid was successful with seventy-one arrests and going smoothly until Holiday started a riot and arrested a whole family. The rest of the cops were congratulating us. Some knew the Morales family were bad people, and they were happy they got lumped.

That joke everybody was laughing about before we left the academy was that the three big officers, Bray, Detective Sage, and Detective Oakes were assigned to arrest a midget. At the academy, the prisoners was photographed with the arresting officers. Many copies were made of this group and were on police headquarters bulletin boards throughout the county. I was photographed with the Morales family. I treasure that picture.

That's the last raid I am going on. Ranking officers should be supervisors, not fighting in the trenches. I had to wear a cast on my right hand for six weeks.

Action Auction

Promotions were made in the police department. Six months ago, Captain McKenna was appointed chief after a long battle with the other three captains in the department. He recommended further promotions. After the civil service tests results were received, Lieutenant Lutz was promoted to captain and put in command of the detective bureau. Sergeant Vince Flynn, my partner, was transferred to the patrol division. I was promoted to a detective-lieutenant. At thirty-two years old, I had a responsible and reputable position. I was elevated as the executive officer in the detective division.

My ability was quickly tested. On Friday, Chief McKenna gave an assignment to Captain Lutz, who turned it over to me as soon as he could. When a group of citizens filed a complaint, the chief would always listen. This issue was a hot potato and was placed right on my lap. Captain Lutz told me to handle it personally. Mrs. Van Arsdale, chairperson of the zoning board requested me personally. The problem was in Action Auction. This was a new business recently opened in a former building that housed a grocery supermarket. The new owner divided the interior into separate shops with chain-link dividers. The building held thirty-five separate businesses. The main concern was with the second business on the left as you entered the building. It was a stall selling magazines and videos. Mrs. Van Arsdale said they were selling smut.

I took Detective Bob Swenson with me to inspect the operation. When we arrived, we saw the front counter filled with exotic magazines and comic books. The magazines had nude photographs on the covers, with titillating suggestions as to the content. A magazine with about twenty-five pages sold for five dollars. We witnessed two boys about twelve years old looking at the magazines. The second counter held newsworthy magazines such as *Time, Business Weekly,* and *Life,* and movie periodicals. It held some woman's magazines, such as *Glamour* and *Women's Daily.* There was a curtain at the back hiding adult videos.

The proprietor was a small man in his sixties. He had little hair, wire-rim glasses, a large nose and small mouth. He was dressed in a shirt with a heavy sweater. He sold the boys a pornographic magazine. I stepped in and cancelled the sale. I took the magazine for evidence. Detective Swenson got the names of the embarrassed boys. I got the name of the proprietor. His name was Sy Levy with an address in Philadelphia. I called for assistance to confiscate all the smut magazines. Patrolman Beaver and Patrolman Estoch arrived to help carry out his stock. Behind the curtain, we found one hundred and thirty porn videos. He was now out of business. I hoped Mrs. Van Arsdale and her ladies league would be happy.

Back at headquarters, I signed a complaint against Mr. Levy, and the court mailed him a summons. We stored the evidence in ten boxes and placed it in the vault. I informed the captain and the chief. The chief congratulated me for the quick action. I knew this wasn't going to be this easy.

On Monday, I was summoned to a superior court in Freehold. The confiscated property put Mr. Levy out of business, and he asked for immediate relief. The prosecutor argued the property was evidence of a crime, but the judge ruled against us. He said, "I needed an order for the court to seize the magazines"

Mr. Levy was back at headquarters about the same time as Swenson and I. We returned him his property. He wanted us to carry the stuff back into the store. Fat chance on that—if he wanted the smut, he had to cart it out of headquarters. He and his lawyer were pretty angry.

I went to work on obtaining a court order to seize the property back. With Prosecutor Dave Foley's help, the paperwork was completed, and we had a hearing set for the next morning.

Tuesday morning, things were moving fast on this case. We had our hearing at noon. Now the judge ruled that we could confiscate the materials and hold them until the criminal case was heard. I went back to Action Auction with Detective Swenson and Badge. Levy was really hot! He was jumping up and down and threatened to sue us all. I loved it; this was going to be exiting. The judge, the Honorable Patrick McClan, wanted the material brought to his chambers. Levy's lawyer called the judge, claiming first amendments rights were violated. When we turned the material over to the judge, he said, "I am going to read every magazine and view every video to determine if they violated the law by being lewd and lascivious." Good for us, Levy was out of business again. The material was raw and raunchy; we should prevail.

However, after three weeks, the judge ruled that the materials were disgusting but the complainant had a right to possess them. He also had the right to sell them to adults. Our charges stand against Levy for the sale to the juveniles, but all his garbage had to be returned to him again. The case would be heard in three months. In the meantime, he was open again for business.

The police department was served with a cease-and-desist order the next day. The order specified that "Lieutenant Holiday and his officers must stay out of the stall." I was really pissed.

There is more than one way to skin a cat, however. Two days later, I called Jimmy Keough, a new patrolman that still talked with an Irish brogue, into the detective bureau office He has been on the job for three months. I wrote a script for him and asked him to make a phone call. Jimmy called Fr. Ted Callahan, pastor of St Catharine's Parish. St Catharine's was where the two kids who were looking at the magazines attended grammar school. No doubt Fr. Ted knew of the incident. Jimmy, using the name of a parishioner with five children, berated Fr. Ted for allowing this pornography to be sold to our children. He said, "Fr. Ted, you are neglecting your duties as our spiritual leader!" Then Jimmy slammed down the phone. I knew what was going to happen next.

An hour later, a call came into the police desk from a Mr. Levy at Action Auction. He complained of a crazy man throwing his property out the door and into the gutter. A patrolman was dispatched. I sent two detectives to assist and had them call me back. They reported that a local priest in his ministerial frock was still throwing magazines out the door. The patrolman asked the priest to stop, but he didn't until all the magazines were in the gutter. He then was stomping on the videos, to the cheering of a group of elderly women. I had tipped off Mrs. Van Arsdale earlier; they had been waiting an hour for Fr. Ted to show up. Levy was out of business again. Ha. Ha.

The prosecutor, Dave Foley called the next day. Levy and his lawyer wanted a meeting. It was scheduled for that afternoon. I was scheduled for a grand jury appearance at 2:00 p.m., so the meeting was set for when I finished my grand jury appearance. When I arrived at the meeting, an accord had already been reached, if I agreed. The charge against Mr. Levy would be dropped. His property that were mostly destroyed by Fr. Ted would be returned. He would cancel his lease at Action Auction, leave Monmouth County and never come back. There would not be any complaints against the police department or Lieutenant Holiday.

No problem, good bye, Mr. Levy, I hope to never see you again. Case closed.

The Pagans Motorcycle Gang

There was a commotion at the police desk. Sergeant "Moose" Zemo was calling for assistance. I was in my office when Detectives Grimm and Mulvey called out to me. "They need help upstairs at the desk," Mulvey said. We rushed up the back stairs to see a group of bikers at the counter hollering for the release of two prisoners. Standing with them was bail bondsman Sy Seymour. Sy looked out of place among the big leather-jacketed bikers. Sy was about five-foot-two tall and one hundred twenty pounds, with a little tuft of white hair above his ears. He was wearing an expensive suit and shined shoes.

With the large police presence, that is, most of the patrol shift and three detectives, the bikers calmed down. The two prisoners were processed for release on bail. Both were arrested in the afternoon by the patrol officers responding to a call of a burglary in process. They were captured inside a home that they just broke into. The suspects had proceeds from two other homes that they burglarized in the neighborhood. It was a good arrest by the patrol shift.

One of the burglars was a skinny eighteen-year-old biker wannabe. He was the younger brother of Herman "Hammer" Hermanske. Hermanske was the president of the New Jersey chapter of the Pagan's Motorcycle Club. The other burglar was even skinner, with little chance to be a Pagan member. Both were being held on $2,500 bail.

The Badge, responding to the call for assistance from the police desk, raced into the parking area in front of headquarters. He noticed there were three cars in the police parking area, used for official vehicles only. There was a black Ford SUV, a big 1980 Olds, and a new white Caddy. In the SUV, Badge observed a club. It was a police-type club with a chain wrapped around the end—a serious weapon. Badge whispered this information to me while they were posting bail.

With knowledge of the weapon in the biker's car, we formulated a plan. We waited until all the bikers and the bails bondsman exited the front door of headquarters and got into their cars. They started the cars, but we surrounded them and stopped them from leaving the parking lot. I went to the side door of Hammer's car and told him, "You are under arrest for weapons possession." He was as angry as a trapped bear. He got out of the car ranting, and I put handcuffs on his wrists. I needed two sets of cuffs put together because of the size of his wrists. The other bikers were also arrested, including Seymour the bondsman. The group was marched back into headquarters for processing. We put them all in the bullpen after a pat down.

Badge and Mulvey went outside and searched the cars. They confiscated the chain club, a machete, a set of brass knuckles, and a small baggie with seven joints.

I signed complaints on the entire gang for weapons possession. Mulvey processed the paperwork on the arrests. Detective Dodge was called in for mug shots and fingerprinting. Detective Grimm was in charge of moving them around for the processing. The court clerk came into his office. Seymour bailed himself out and then arranged for bail on the Hammer and his crew. Judge Horan was called and set the bail at one thousand bucks each.

Their cars were towed from the police parking slots and left in the back lot of the municipal complex. The gang and Seymour had to pay for the towing. Seymour had cash and paid for all three cars. When they left, they were murmuring threats that they would return and get even for the harassment.

The patrol shift had been held over to handle the bikers and they were happy to receive four hours of overtime. Three detectives received four hours of comp time. I notified Chief McKenna, and he approved the OT and comp time. He agreed that these hoodlums would not intimidate us.

Three months later, the Badge and I went to the grand jury. Seymour was not indicted. However, all seven of the bikers were indicted and a date was set for a trial in the spring.

The state police had a task force concerning the activities of motorcycle clubs in the state. Senior Police Detective John Schrock called me with information concerning Hammer Hermanske and his gang. Schrock said, "I have an informant inside the gang, and they have discussed some type of retaliation against you and the officers that made the arrests." Schrock said he would notify us of any plans they made by the gang. I worked with John Schrock before on other cases and knew he would call. We weren't worried, just concerned.

Two months later, we received the call. The gang led by the Hammer and forty strong were traveling to a bar in Keansburg for partying and trouble-making. At 9:30 p.m., they were traveling along the shore roads and heading in our direction. An unmarked state police vehicle was following them with two state police detectives.

We quickly devised a plan. Patrolman Schnoor stopped the whole group on Highway 36 in an area that had a twenty-foot center median and two lanes on each side. He set up a one-car roadblock. As soon as they were stopped, we swooped in with two more patrol cars and three unmarked cars. The state police car was behind them. We closed the northbound lanes on the highway and diverted the other motorists.

I approached the group with the Badge and Richard "Dutchman" Deickmann at my flank. I told the gang leader, Hammer, and the others to shut off the bikes. We are going to inspect your bikes for registration, safety violations, and equipment."

Hammer was hollering his objections. I couldn't, however, hear him well because Rigo was revving up his motorcycle engine. (Rigo was one of the bikers arrested for weapons possession.) I yelled to Badge, "Stop that noise!"

Badge took aim with his shotgun and blasted the front of the bike. *Kaboom!* I almost peed my pants. There was smoke coming from the front of the bike and the hiss of the mangled wheel and tire. I now had the silence I asked for and the attention of all the bikers. Tank's bike was the first to be inspected. He was issued two summonses, one for a crack in his taillight and a tire with low tread. After the bikes and licenses were checked, we released them one at a time. A bike ridden by Trash Conklin had to be towed away for lack of registration. The bike Badge shot was also towed. In total, we issued fifty-five traffic summons. Now we wait for the courts.

We never heard anything concerning Badge shooting the bike. Those who weren't there couldn't believe it happened. Badge could scare me sometimes. I didn't tell the chief about the shooting, but he soon found out. He also wanted to keep this quiet.

Trial of the Pagan Motorcycle Gang

The trial was set in the spring of 1985. Seven defendants pleaded innocent to weapons possession. The prosecutor was the young and tough Steve Schular. The judge was the Honorable Tom Arnone. Burtum Slotnik represented the defendants.

The state subpoenaed Detective Pat, "the Badge", Connell, detectives Barry Grimm, Ron O'Mack, and myself. Sy Seymour, the bondsman, was also subpoenaed as a witness. Sy had been charged with the defendants but not indicted by the grand jury. He could testify as to the weapons being seized in the defendants' vehicles.

The proceedings were set for Monday morning, April 8, in courtroom #320. This was the last room on the third floor and at the end of the corridor. We arrived at 8:30 a.m. Hammer and the gang were hanging out by the door in front of the courtroom. The prosecutor and Slotnik were inside the room in a heated discussion. Slotnik had filed a motion to exclude the evidence because it was seized during an illegal search.

At 9:05 a.m., Judge Arnone entered and took his seat on the bench. Steve called the Badge as our first witness. We were not allowed to hear his testimony. Witnesses were sequestered and forced to stay outside in the hallway. Hammer and his crew sat inside the courtroom, around the defendant's table. They could see us near the door, which was left open. They were glaring back at us. The judge could not see us from his position. Rigo, a gang member, gave us the finger and a menacing stare.

No other witness was called. The defense argued for exclusion of the evidence. The prosecutor argued for the state to be allowed to introduce the evidence. The judge called a recess to deliberate on the motion. At noon, the court officer told everyone to return after lunch at 1:00 p.m.

We had lunch at Frederica's restaurant. The bikers left town; they rode out west to a local biker bar. The state police followed them.

At 1:00 p.m., we returned. Hammer and the gang were still out to lunch. Court resumed, and the judge ruled the weapons were admissible evidence. Slotnik requested time to discuss this decision with his clients. Court was recessed until tomorrow morning. Jury selection would be done at this time.

Tuesday morning we were back in the hallway waiting for the prosecutor. The hallway was crowded with the bikers, sheriff officers, court officers, and the usual group of senior citizens that attend trials. Somebody must have spread the word that there might be trouble in the courthouse. The judge had requested extra security. I said "Good morning" to Hammer and his boys. They snarled at me like a pack of dogs. I just smiled and stared back at them.

Hammer told Tank to go downstairs and get him a cup of coffee and a roll. When Dirt, Rigo, and Ink chimed in wanting coffee, Hammer said, "Just get mine, Tank. They can get theirs later. Go." Everybody else was waiting in the corridor for the court door to open. The judge was late. Ten minutes later, Tank returned with Hammer's coffee and roll. Before Hammer could drink his coffee, the court door opened, and the defendants were summoned into the courtroom. Hammer placed his coffee cup and roll on the windowsill and went inside. He took his usual seat at the end of the defense table. He was sitting so that he could see me standing near the open door. The judge could not see me.

A jury panel was brought into the court. The voir dire was beginning. I peeked in the doorway, and Hammer gave me the finger. I just nodded and smiled at him. I then noticed his coffee to my right on the sill. The window was open. I picked it up and showed it to Hammer, opened the top, and took a sip. Wow, that infuriated him! I then pointed the cup at Hammer and threw it over my shoulder out the window. Hammer jumped. The judge was rapping his gavel, and defense attorney Slotnik was trying to calm him down.

Slotnik and the judge couldn't see what I did and didn't know why got Hammer so riled up. They might have thought a juror caused it. When Hammer calmed down, they all sat down again. Hammer looked back and saw me peeking in the door again. I smiled at him again and reached behind me to pick up his roll off the windowsill. Hammer had an incredulous look on his face. I unwrapped the roll, pointed it at him, and took a bite. I then threw it out the window just like the coffee.

In the hallway, the sheriff's officers, the detectives, and a few others knew what I did. They were holding their hands over their mouths so that they wouldn't laugh out loud. There was commotion in the courtroom again. I left the hallway with Detectives, O'Mack, Grimm, and the Badge. We went downstairs to a room that was for police officers waiting to testify. We stayed there until noon until we received word from a court officer that we could leave and go to lunch.

We stayed in the building and had lunch in the court cafeteria. At one o'clock, we tentatively went back to the hallway outside the courtroom. The bikers were at the end of the corridor, leaning against the wall. I was expecting trouble as I walked up to Hammer, smiled, and said, "Good afternoon, Mr. Hammer." He gave me a strange look and quietly said, "'Lo lieutenant." The rest of the bikers nodded to me. I took this as a sign of respect or capitulation or they thought I was nuts.

Court was called to order. The jury was recessed right after they entered the courtroom. A plea bargain was taking place. The prosecutor, Steve Schular, came out of the courtroom and told us one of the defendants was taking the weight. He admitted the weapons belonged to him and then lied to the judge. He told the judge, "The other defendants did not know I had the weapons." The state accepted the plea, the judge accepted the plea, and we were satisfied with the conclusion.

After the judge rapped the gavel, signaling that court was over, everyone filed out. In the hallway, Hammer came up to me. He said, "I hear you have a bike." I told him I ride a Triumph 650 and my buddy has a 48 Indian. He said, "Your bike is a piece of junk, but the

Indian is as good as a Harley." We were in a conversation, just like old friends. He said, "You should ride with me if I go through the Bay Shore again. I will call you at police headquarters if it's okay." I said, "See you then."

We returned to headquarters. I reported to Chief McKenna. I said, "Picture this, Chief. I threw Hammer's coffee and roll out the window of the courthouse."

The chief said, "You're nuts, and Hammer must have believed you're crazy too...and he's probably right." He added, "I love it. Great job! Tell the boys I commend them."

True to his word, Hammer called in June. I was home on a Saturday evening when my red phone rang. This is a direct landline from headquarters.

The desk sergeant said, "Hammer wants you to call him, and he left a number." I called him. Hammer and the Pagans were taking a ride, and they were going to O'Brien's Bar in Keansburg. He invited me to meet them at the Sea Bright Bridge at eleven thirty and ride with them. I told him I couldn't make this ride, but I would arrange for a police escort if he wanted one. He said, "Hey, Lieutenant, that would be f—n' great."

I called the police desk. Sergeant Hannafey was on duty, and I made the request. He said it would be fun to take the assignment. I talked to Hannafey a few days later. He led them west on Highway 36 for twenty miles and dropped them at Main Street, Keansburg. He said the Pagans liked the escort; they all waved to him when he left them. They were all grinning. A half-mile behind was an unmarked state police car following the precession.

I never had a problem with the Pagans again. A few years later, Hammer and five others were arrested for the rape of a pole dancer in an Asbury Park bar. They were sentenced to prison. I would meet him years later at Rahway State Penitentiary; he was still big and nasty-looking. We had a cordial conversation about motorcycles.

FBI National Academy

In the spring of 1977, I was selected to attend the FBI Academy. I applied two years ago. It takes that long to process an application. The academy is known throughout the world as the best and finest in law-enforcement training. Twice a year, the academy selects two law-enforcement officers from each state and a few from other countries. A Scotland Yard police, an Egyptian detective, and an Australian police officer were on my floor in the dorm. I specialized my training in forensics and psychological profiling. I graduated in Sept of 1977. I was now ready to go back to work.

Prior to attending the academy, I took the civil service test for the rank of captain. Fourteen lieutenants were eligible. While I was in Quantico, the results came out. I was no. 1 on the test. The second place went to Lieutenant Scott, who was seven points behind me, a considerable margin. I know there will be no promotions until Captain Lutz is made department chief. Now that I was back as commander of the detective division, he would be moved upstairs into the deputy chief's office. Captain Lutz had the ear of Chief McKenna and didn't want me get promoted until he got his stars. He would not want to compete with me on a civil service test for the deputy chief's job. I would just have to wait. Such is office politics.

While I was away training, the department had an interesting investigation. "Sewer Rat" Barness was found in his car parked at the beach, shot dead. A patrolman on the midnight shift first observed him in his car. He didn't take any action; he didn't realize he was dead. While on his day shift at 10:00 am, Officer Blunt (son of Detective Sergeant Blunt), checked on Sewer Rat sitting in his car. When Officer Blunt opened the car door, Sewer Rat fell out of the car. He had been shot in the right side four times with small-caliber bullets.

Captain Lutz led the investigated with the assistance of Lieutenant Collins. They suspected Sewer Rat (a known drug dealer) was involved in a drug sale that went bad. The victim's last contact was with local junkies he supplied. Statements were taken, and a local user was suspected. He was subsequently arrested even though he had an alibi. The weapon was not found. The case was sent to the prosecutor's office for presentation to a grand jury.

I read all the reports. The department jumped the gun with the arrest. The alibi witness had to be broken. The evidence was weak and the other witnesses unreliable. The assistant prosecutor called me and requested the investigation continue. The first assistant prosecutor was angry with the department. The prosecutor's office and Chief McKenna were in a feud over home rule and our department's tactics. Captain Lutz did not request the assistance of county detectives on the case. This made things worse. I assigned two detectives to reinvestigate at the request of Assistant Prosecutor Elliot Katz.

I spent the first week back in the office catching up on the personnel changes and investigations. The chief promoted two new detectives and reassigned two others to patrol. The chief was difficult to work with. I just got the men trained, and he changed their assignments.

On Monday morning, I assigned the weekend cases. I needed to get out of the office. I took the Badge with me and hit the road. I wanted to check on the concert to be held this weekend at Brookdale College. It's a heavy metal concert and expected to draw a large crowd.

Badge and I met with Captain Folks of Brookdale security at his office at 11:30 a.m. He too was concerned about the size of the crowd and the drugs that might be used. He would request assistance officially from the chief. I would send Detective Stover, our narcotics detective, to meet with Brookdale Police.

My next job was to find Foxie, my female informant. I had gotten two tickets for the concert from Folks and would send her as my spy. She would enjoy the show and let me know what is happening. Foxie would call me at home if anything happens. She worked at a restaurant called Sissy's in Belford. When Badge and I stopped for lunch, she was working. We ate lunch, and I gave her the tickets. She had my red phone number. It's a separate landline telephone to my home for emergencies and some informants.

Now I wanted to find Fast Freddie, another of my acquaintances. He knew what's going on in the streets and gave me information if it benefitted him. We found him in his beat-up truck behind the Keansburg Diner. He was casing the back of the diner. One of his nefarious enterprises was to steal the grease barrels and sell the grease. He was the only thief in our area in the stolen-grease business. We had a conversation concerning Sewer Rat. He said he didn't know who killed him but thought we got the wrong guy. Someone shot him because they bought bad drugs. He said, "I will ask some junkies." I doubted if he would find any answers.

We next rode around in the area of Hillside. I was looking for an informant that we called Ipana. County Detective Corrigan gave him this nickname because he had excessive large buckteeth. We rode the area for over an hour but could not find him. I did leave him his payment; I dropped a bottle of Ripple wine in the creek under the bridge on First Avenue. We have been using this drop for over three years. Ipana was a hopeless alcoholic but a valuable informant who knew what was happening in the area. I hadn't seen him in four months, but when he'd find the wine, he'd sit on the bridge wall looking for me.

Leaving the liquor store in the shopping center where I bought the wine, I spotted Stuart Woods at the parking lot. Eight years ago, I investigated a murder of a nightclub singer killed at a gas station on Highway 35. Woods was charged with the murder and pleaded guilty. He was eighteen years old at when he committed the crime. He was sentenced to twenty years in the state penitentiary for the murder. The lenient sentence outraged many involved in the case. I wondered what was he doing out on the street now.

We stopped Woods before he got into a truck. He said, "I got out on parole last month." He is working for a local contractor doing cleanup work at construction sites. He drove away with a smile.

We went back to the office to check this out. I called the parole office. Parole Officer Lester Snyder confirmed his release. The state prisons were so overcrowded even murderers were being released early.

This was the major discouragement of doing my job. Woods should not be out of prison. He was a psychopath. I'm sure our paths would cross again. In the meantime, "I was back to work after a great summer in Quantico."

Professional League Gambling

Professional football was in season. Gambling is big in New Jersey with two pro football teams in the state. A small amount of gambling takes place in virtually every bar in the state.

Fast Freddie owed me a favor. He was caught stealing chicken fat from behind Howard Johnson's restaurant by police patrol on a routine check of restaurant at 4:00 a.m. He was upstairs in our local cell asking for me when I arrived in the morning. He didn't want to be sent to the county jail in lieu of bail. He offered me information for ROR, or "release on your own recognizance" with a promise to return court.

The information better be good. Fast Freddie was brought down to the detective-bureau interrogation room. He said, "The owner of the Midnight Club on Route 35 is betting heavy on football and taking bets at the club for bookies to ease past debts." Acting as our informant, Fast Freddie agreed to place bets at the bar. I made the deal and called the judge and arranged for his release.

I called my good buddy, county Detective Bruce Corrigan, and filled him in on the information. He wanted to be part of the investigation. We set up Fast Freddie with money and recording devices, and he went into the bar and made bets. We did this on two separate Saturday nights, betting on Sunday's professional games. We now were preparing search warrants for a raid.

The following Monday morning, I got a surprise phone call from Omar Suliman, the owner of the Midnight Bar. He and his co-owner, Betty Newman, wanted a private meeting with me. They wouldn't tell me why until we met in person. I agreed to meet them at their apartment over the bar that night.

I immediately called Detective Corrigan. I told him to stop the process on the search warrants and don't meet with the judge. I said, "Put everything on hold until I meet with Omar Suliman and Betty Newman. I think our cover was blown." I hoped Fast Freddie didn't tell them we were investigating the owners. If he did, he was going back to jail.

Monday night, I went to the meeting with Suliman and Newman. They said they would not talk if Corrigan was present. I had to go alone without any recording devices. The three of us met in the living room with Omar's dog present. He looked like a big wolf. Here is Omar's story:

"I started betting small on pro football. I got in over my head and was behind on payments. Betty did not know about my gambling. They forced me to take bets from customers. I took the bets for them and turned them over on Saturday nights. The payoffs were on Tuesday afternoon. I just kept betting, trying to get even. I even made bets using false names. I owe over twenty grand, and they are coming for the money on Tuesday. If I didn't have the money, they threatened to kill me. The only thing I can think of is to 'rat them out' and hope you can arrest them when they show up to collect the money. They also want to collect any bets I take on Monday-night games. I am scared."

He gave me a description of the two collectors. Big Paulie was five foot eight tall, three hundred pounds, had a ponytail, and was a flashy dresser. His cohort was Vinnie ("the Eel"), six feet tall with long sideburns and jet-black hair. They drove a new cream-colored four-door Lincoln sedan. The car had New Jersey plates. They told Omar that they worked for Sam the Plumber.

With all the information we had available, Corrigan and I applied for arrest warrants for the two bookie collectors. County Judge McHoney signed the warrants. We could not get a search warrant for the car because we didn't have enough information. The judge did say, "Call me when we make the arrest and if enough information to warrant it, but I will allow a search of the car if it is used by the suspects," said the judge. We now had arrest warrants for a

John Doe (aka Big Paulie) and an arrest warrant for John Doe #2 (aka Vinnie the Eel).

We started planning for the arrests on Tuesday. I employ six officers (one would go undercover at the bar) and three cars (one at the Pancake House parking lot on the south side of the club, one at a gas station in the north side of Route 35). Corrigan and I would be at the back of the club on the road behind it. When the perpetrators arrived, we would arrest them before they entered. We didn't want anybody getting shot.

We set up on Tuesday morning at 11:00 a.m. I called Omar in the morning and told him we were staking out the bar. He said, "I am taking a big chance. If this doesn't work out, I am in big trouble with the mob." Detective Irv Beaver and Sergeant Blunt were in a car on the highway. Badge and Swenson were in the Sears store parking lot; Corrigan and I were parked behind the bar on Gillville Lane. The Greek was going to the bar at noon. Waiting is the dullest part of the job.

Just before 2:00 p.m., Beaver spotted the car pulling into the parking lot in front of the bar. He saw two big men in a new cream-colored Lincoln. Badge and Bob Swensen were the first to arrive. I knew Badge would make sure he was there first after his fiasco with the bank arrest of Big Louie Rickey. Badge had missed his assignment and was the butt of jokes for months. We were all there before the culprits had a chance to exit the car. Paulie was so fat it took a lot of hollering before Badge dragged him out of the car. They were cuffed, searched, and given their Miranda rights. We had to double-cuff Paulie; his wrists were so big. They didn't resist; they just wanted to know what was happening. Beaver and Sergeant Blunt took Vinnie to headquarters. Badge and Swenson transported Paulie. It was a smooth takedown of a couple of badasses.

When they left, Omar came out the front door with the Greek. He thanked us and asked "what's going to happen next." I told him they would be booked and then bail would be set. When they were released, we would cover the bar as much as possible. I knew we, or the county detectives, could not protect him for long, but we would try. We didn't have manpower for a lengthy coverage. Besides, he was not a popular person with our police department or the county police. I wished him good luck.

With Omar and Betty back inside the bar, Corrigan and I looked inside Paulie's car. We found a lot of junk food wrappers on the floor and a blackjack under the front seat. I called for a tow, and Murphy's towing brought the car back to headquarters, unhooked it, and left it in the back lot. I had Paulie's keys, and Corrigan took a surreptitious peek into the trunk. *Wow!* We closed the trunk lid and went into the bureau.

I called the judge. I asked the judge if he would be available later in the afternoon to review an affidavit. I wanted a written warrant to search the car. I suspected I would find gambling records and money. It was easy to write the affidavit and prepare the search warrant and return.

At 4:30 p.m., Corrigan and I were at the judges' chambers in Freehold. Judge McHoney reviewed the paperwork and congratulated us on the arrests. He gave us the authority to search and seize the contents of the car and send him the results.

Back at headquarters, we were excited to execute the warrant. I ordered Badge to take Paulie out of his cell. I wanted him to witness the search. Paulie's lawyer, Raymond Brown, was in the court clerk's office attempting to arrange bail. I asked him if he wanted to come outside in the parking lot to witness the search. He refused and said, "If you search my client's car, I will sue you." I must have had heard that a thousand times. I said, "I'm giving you the opportunity, counselor. It's your choice." He did not leave the clerk's office.

In the back lot with Paul Scotto in handcuffs, Corrigan, Badge, Veronica McKier (a recording secretary), Detective Beaver and I opened the trunk of the car. We found records of bets on football and basketball in the hundreds. We found forty-five thousand dollars in cash with slips and notes concerning where the money came from. With this evidence, I can call the judge and get the bail higher. Big Paulie was in a lot of trouble; he should not have had all these records with him. He was in more trouble with his bosses than the government. The mob needed these records. A lot of betters were going to claim wins and want their payoffs. This arrest and seizure was going to hurt organized crime where they don't like it—in their pocketbooks.

Bail was set at twenty-five thousand dollars. A bondsman posted bail for Paulie Scotto and Vinnie Acentino that evening.

I prepared the case for the grand jury. I love this job. The mob will try to obtain copies of the seized records and the prosecutor will oppose. Those records are worth a million dollars. The mob must pay off the betters even though they couldn't prove what bets were made. Even organized crime has rules.

Omar was going to need protection. I hoped we can give it to him.

Murder of Ninety-Five-Year-Old Mrs. Ludlum

It's September and harvest time in the farms of Monmouth County. Migrant workers from Latin American countries are in state looking for work. They live in communal buildings on the farms, staying to themselves and moving on after the crops are harvested.

The Ludlum family has owned a farm in Lincroft since the turn of the eighteenth century. Her family had moved from the farm, but Mrs. Ludlum chose to live alone and stay in the house that was built by her ancestors in the late 1790s. She leased her acres to farmers who owned adjacent lands. They had been growing corn, soybean, and hay for many years. Neighbors would visit Mrs. Ludlum daily, but she was fully capable of taking care of herself. After an early supper, she usually took a walk to a neighbor's house or somewhere on the farm.

Neighbor Irv Henderson became concerned when he did not see Ida Ludlum on Monday or in the early evening. He decided to walk to her home and check on her well-being. It was a warm evening for the last day of September, and there was a full harvest moon in the sky. As he approached the house, he noticed all the lights were on. He hurried his steps until he came to the back porch. There he found Ida Ludlum on the floor. She had bled profusely from the back of her head. He checked for a pulse and found none. Her body was cold. Irv ran inside and called 911.

I received a call at 7:45 p.m. at home on the red phone. Sergeant Zemo on the police desk told me we had possible murder at the Ludlum farm. I had promised my girls I would help with homework and take them to gymnastic practice. Things can be difficult for a cop's wife. Now Nancy had to handle these chores for me.

I arrived at the Ludlum house at 8:08 p.m. Patrolman Furieto had secured the scene. The ambulance arrived ten minutes after Henderson's call. They found her unresponsive. Furieto told them not to touch or move the body.

Sergeant Zemo dispatched another police unit to the call and the roadway from West Front Street to the house was sealed off. The good work by the patrol division made my job easier. En route, I called for additional detectives. The Greek was on duty and arrived just before me, followed by Detectives Swenson, Moon, Omak, and, a few minutes later, Detective Dodge. My posse was assembled, and we went right to work.

Patrolman Furieto recorded the presence and arrival of every one at the scene. I ordered Moon and the Greek to enter the house to help Irv Henderson with a search. They did not touch or disturb anything. We wanted to make sure there was no other person injured or perpetrators hiding in the house. After they cleared the house, Detective Dodge entered to shoot photographs and get fingerprints of the inside rooms. The Greek reported to me that the victim's bedroom had been ransacked and other rooms had been disturbed.

Aloysius Jones, the medical examiner's assistant, arrived. He told me, "The medical examiner will not be coming to the scene, and I have his authority to handle the body." Furieto had dutifully logged in Jones on arrival. I think Furieto wants to be promoted to detective; he seemed to be enjoying working with us. He didn't have much of a chance, however—the chief didn't like Italians.

I called Detective Dodge outside of the house to photograph the body while Jones did his examination. When Jones rolled over Mrs. Ludlum, it was clear she was struck on the back of the head with a blunt object. Near the body was a piece of firewood. The wood had gray hairs embedded in the fibers. We believed it was the murderer's instrument. Furieto was right there with his notepad, recording the time and place the firewood was found. He was being so diligent and serious I almost had to laugh. It was his first murder scene, and he was really following the book. He was well trained. I was proud of him.

The Greek came out of the house with Detective Moon. They found a boot print on a piece of paper on the floor from the victim's bedroom. Mrs. Ludlum didn't wear or own size-10 work boots. In all probability, the perpetrator left this print. Hendricks, who was present when they found the boot print, told us the migrant workers wore similar boots. He said, "Their quarters are in the back of the farms about one half a mile from the Ludlum house.

I sent Dodge back into the house for evidence collection and fingerprinting. Detective Bert Grimm was assisting him. Jones finished his victim examination; he photographed the body and crime scene and prepared the body for transportation to the morgue.

Time is of the essence when investigating a murder. With Irv showing the way, Detectives O'Mack, Moon, Greek and I went to the migrant's quarters. The building was a square wooden structure with one large room containing about twenty bunk beds. The place was dark. We entered and woke everyone up by turning on the overhead lights. They sat up on their bunks looking surprised and dazed at our entry.

"Everyone stay where you are! Don't move!" I yelled. "Round them all up. We are taking them all to headquarters." I could see that the workers took off their boots when entering the building and left them near the front door. I whispered to the Greek, "Make sure they put their boots on."

Outside the building, we transported the migrants in our personal and patrol cars. We had thirteen suspects to bring in. They were jabbering in Spanish until O'Mack loudly yelled at them to shut up. They understood his big mouth.

Back at headquarters, we separated them as best as we could. They denied being able to speak English. Hendricks, who came along to assist us, said, "They can understand some English and even speak a little English when they want too." We found Inocencio Barreto, the foreman and leader of the group, to be cooperative, and he helped with translations. While detectives were attempting interrogations, I was on the phone with the prosecutor's office for legal advice. The prosecutor sent county Detectives Dick Manson and Sal Mouseillo to assist.

While this was going on, the Greek was doing a surreptitious examination of the boots the suspects were wearing. It didn't take him long to find a match. Barreto told us that four of the men went out of the encampment at 4:30 p.m., supposedly going to Red Bank for groceries. We concentrated on this group. Ismael Mendoso was the suspect. He owned the matching boot and was one of the foursome that left camp.

I called a translator from a list of volunteers to help us. At 10:30 p.m., I talked to Molly Goldon, a Spanish teacher in a local middle school. She said she would come to headquarters to help. I sent a patrol car to pick her up. She arrived at 11:00 p.m. I told her what we needed. I didn't think this would work too well because she was a charming, soft-spoken, and only twenty-two years old. She said, "I am excited to be of assistance." After the detective's attempts to interrogate them, they seemed relieved to have a pretty young blonde in the room.

I was right; the interrogations were all smiles and denials. I needed a police officer that spoke Spanish—someone to holler and scream, maybe even terrify the suspects.

We kept the four suspects and sent the others back to facilities on Cat Bird Alley in Holmdel Township, a local migrant camp. Detective Ramone Diaz from the prosecutor's office arrived at 1:00 a.m.

After the group was separated and with Diaz leading the questioning, they started making admissions. Now they were trying to save themselves. Three of blamed the assault and battery on Mendoso. He was the lookout, and when he saw Mrs. Ludlum approach, he hid on the porch and struck her when she got close to him. The group then fled back to their quarters. On the run back, Jose Rios hid the loot in the hollow of a willow tree. They stole some worthless costume jewelry and thirty-four dollars in cash.

Rios, Mateos, and Triado gave us written confessions regarding their involvement in the burglary. Mendoso, after receiving his Miranda warnings, refused to answer questions or give any written statements.

Detectives Crapapolis and Moon returned to the farm and found and recovered the loot. We now had statements, a boot print and Mendosa's matching boot, the recovered loot, and the murder weapon.

I signed criminal complaints and requested the judge to convene court for the arraignments. I sent all the detectives off duty and asked the secretaries to clean up the paperwork. The case was solved within twenty-four hours. All I had to do now was to notify Chief McKenna and I could go home and get some sleep.

Paroled Too Early,
Convicted Killer Rapes Woman

Badge was back to work. He was in Montana on vacation. Along with his other prejudices, he now hated Native American Indians. He was assigned to the evening shift this week. He called me at midnight. "Lieutenant, we got a rape case, and I am at the hospital with the victim." Badge liked going to the hospital. He was on his third marriage, and all his previous wives were emergency room nurses.

I arrived in fifteen minutes. Badge was in the waiting lounge drinking coffee. He was waiting for me to start the interview. The victim was almost finished with her examination. We asked the receiving nurse if the victim was able to talk to us. She ushered Badge and me into the examining room. The victim was ready and anxious to tell us what happened.

Sara Ann Compton was a thirty-year-old single mom living with her five-year-old daughter in a small cottage. The home was located on the hill behind the town of Atlantic Highlands. It was a beautiful location with a view to the Atlantic Ocean to the east and a view of Sandy Hook Bay to the north. She worked in Atlantic Highlands as a secretary for a law firm and rented the cottage because it was close to her job and near her daughter's grammar school. She appeared distraught and disheveled. Her hair was a mess. She wore no makeup. She was still wearing her pajamas and a terrycloth robe and was very eager to talk.

She told us that she was in her living room about 11:00 p.m. when she heard the noise of a loud truck in the neighborhood. Ten minutes later, someone entered her back door and was walking through her kitchen. She had not locked her doors yet. She usually locked the front and back doors just before going to bed. A man dressed in black with a ski mask covering his face and head star-

186

tled her. He said, "Be quiet! We don't want to wake your little girl." She suppressed a scream and asked him what he wanted. He didn't answer but approached her as she was standing up, blocking the way to the hallway and her daughter's room.

"He pushed me down on the floor and pulled off my robe and pajamas bottoms. He then raped me on the floor in the living room. I was afraid to resist because he knew my daughter was in the house. After the assault, he got up and left through the front door without a word. I was on the floor lying on the rug when I heard the door slam. I got up and went to a front window and saw dark-colored pickup truck leaving. It had a loud muffler. I called my mother who lives nearby and then called the police.

"I know who raped me. It's my babysitter's son. His name is Stuart. He drives a big pickup truck. I also recognized his voice. He recently got out of jail and is living with his mother." I asked for the babysitter's name and address. She replied, "Mrs. Woods and he lives on Seventh Avenue in Atlantic Highlands."

Badge and I transported Mrs. Sara Compton back to headquarters for a formal statement. Her mother arrived to babysit while we were at police headquarters. I called in Joyce Krieger, our secretary, to take the shorthand statement. Badge called Atlantic Highlands Police Department for assistance. At 3:30 a.m., they reported the suspect's truck was in front of the Woods's home. All the lights were off.

Detective Bob Ochs was called to work. Bob was our case investigator for sex crimes. The detectives took Sara home at 4:00 a.m. after she signed her statement. En route to her home, they drove her past Stuart Woods' home. She spotted the truck and exclaimed, "Oh my god, that's his truck."

I prepared an arrest warrant, a search warrant for the truck, and a seizure warrant for clothing he was wearing last night. We waited until 7:00 a.m. to wake the judge. Badge and Ochs went to Judge Massell's home. He reviewed the paperwork and signed the warrants. I called Detective Sam Guzzy of the Atlantic Highlands Police Department and requested he meet us at the Woods's home on Seventh.

We arrived at 9:30 a.m., and Sam knocked on the door. No answer. Sam pounded on the door until we heard shuffling in the house. Stuart Woods opened the door. He was wearing only boxer shorts. He saw us and started running for the back door. Sam had prepared for this and had Patrolman Venti watching the back of the house. Venti arrested Woods as he came out of the back door. We all went into the house.

Mrs. Woods woke up and started screaming that we were there to persecute her son again. Guzzy, Ochs, and I went into Stuart's bedroom. On the floor lay his black chino pants and a black sweatshirt. We didn't find a mask. After being advised of his rights by Detective Ochs, he refused to make a statement. Ochs and Badge transported him back to headquarters for booking. Detective Dodge came to the house and picked up the clothing evidence. Dodge noticed strands of carpet on the trousers. Sam had an idea. The last time we arrested Woods for murder ten years ago, he threw the victim's clothing in a dumpster behind the first-aid building. The first-aid building still used a dumpster and had one behind the building. This building was near the Woods's home.

Patrolman Venti, Detective Guzzy, and I checked the dumpster. Sam boosted Venti over the edge, and he fell into the dumpster. Right on top of the refuse, Venti spotted a black ski mask. Sometimes, detective work can be a matter of insight and memory. Before returning to headquarters, Detective Dodge stopped at Sara Compton's home. He informed her of the arrest and took a sample of the new rug in the living room. We wanted to match fibers from the rug with the fibers on Woods's trousers.

We had plenty of evidence and a solid case. Stewart Woods was going back to the state penitentiary where he belonged. He was arraigned that afternoon. Bail was set at one hundred thousand, and he was sent to the county jail. I notified his parole officer, and a parole sticker was placed on him. I would be hearing from the public defender shortly, but there would be no deal made. We would go to trial.

We know Stewart Woods from ten years ago when he murdered a nightclub singer. We went to trial for that crime, and Woods was convicted. He received a twenty-year sentence at the state penitentiary. I testified for the state, and he swore revenge on Detective Dodge and me. Well now, he was going back to prison without getting his revenge.

As usual, I prepared all the paperwork. I finished at midnight. It was a long twenty-four hours. Too bad I didn't get over time.

Case closed.

The Mob Comes for Revenge

I knew it was going to happen. Last fall, we broke up a gambling ring that was operating in the shore area. Two mobsters were arrested and charged with collecting gambling bets and paying off winners. Their gambling slips were seized, and other records were confiscated. The mob lawyer attempted to get copies of the records seized, but this was denied in superior court after a heated legal battle. This meant the bookies not only lost the forty-five thousand cash that was seized but they had to pay off all their customers (their betters) who claimed they won their bets. That could amount to a million dollars. Only they knew how much they had to pay out. But it was a big loss.

The defense lawyers did apply for a copy of the search warrant obtained to search the vehicle of the arrested hoods. The defendants were entitled to these documents. In the warrant affidavit, I referred to a confidential informant as part of the basis to search the suspect's vehicle. From this warrant, it would be easy to figure who was the confidential informant. Omar, the bar owner, would be their target. How and when they would exact their revenge would be up to them. I would have patrols spend more time near the Blue Moon Bar and have a detective on stakeout when possible.

On June 6, Tuesday, collection day for bookmaking bets and payoffs, the mob decided to pay Omar a visit. The bar was open since 10:00 a.m. and had seven customers. Betty was sitting near the cash register when a tall, lanky man in jeans and work shirt entered. Potsy, the bartender, knew the mob might show up to seek revenge. He was nervous when a customer he did not know approached. The customer asked for a beer and then asked, "Where is Omar?" Potsy was scared and told the stranger that Omar was not around. The stranger said, "His car is in the back. I'll look around."

Betty was suspicious and quietly dialed 911. The police desk was on alert for the call. The district patrol car was dispatched; Patrolman Dick Heller was assigned to respond.

I was in the bureau office when I heard the call to dispatch a car to the Blue Moon. I ran out with the Badge. We were only three miles south of the bar on Highway 35. En route we heard Heller call in; he had arrived and was going to the front door.

A minute later, we arrived. There was a group of men running out the front door. We could hear Betty screaming for help. When Badge and I entered, Potsy was crouched behind the bar. "I heard two shots," Betty said. "They were in the beer cooler out back."

"Who?" I yelled to her.

"Omar, a killer, and the cop," she answered.

Badge followed me as we ran to the back and into the cooler room, guns in our hands. When I entered, Omar was standing with a gun in his hand.

Patrolman Heller was bent over a beer barrel, vomiting. The assailant was on the floor, bleeding from a facial wound. I took the gun from Omar. Badge went to attend to Patrolman Heller. Heller was not injured but shocked because a bullet whizzed by his ear and he dove into the beer barrels for cover. The scene was secured. I called for an ambulance.

Betty came back to the beer cooler with Potsy and a few patrons who returned to the bar. More patrolmen arrived; then first responders rushed in with a gurney. The assailant was transported to Riverview Hospital with two officers guarding him. The cooler was sealed off, and everybody was escorted into the bar area.

While statements were being taken, I interviewed Omar. He said, "I was in the back taking an inventory when this guy walks into the cooler. He demanded money for the losses his boss was taking for the arrests made last fall. I knew he was referring to the bookie goons. He pulled a gun on me. I had a gun hidden in my desk. I thought he was going to kill me. Just then the door opens and a cop walks in. I pulled out the gun and shot at the killer and hit him in the face. The killer shot back, but the bullet missed and almost hit the cop. It all happened so fast. That's when you came in. I shot in self-defense."

I transported Omar and Betty back to headquarters for formal statements. Badge went to the hospital to talk to and try to identify the gunman. Detectives Graves and Schnoor took the statements from the patrons at the Blue Moon. Detective Dodge handled the forensics in the beer cooler.

After consulting with Prosecutor Steve Hornacek, I released Omar and Betty. The prosecutor will present all the witnesses to a grand jury for indictment. Judge Yaccarino got the details and set bail at one million dollars for our unknown prisoner.

Back at the hospital, Badge took the prisoner's wallet and clothing. He was identified as Louis Ferreira, aka "Louie the Killer". He was a known associate of the Newark mob. His long rap sheet aided in obtaining the high bail.

Badge was staying at the hospital guarding the prisoner. Badge loved being at the hospital. He was married three times all to emergency room nurses. When I arrived, Ferrare was just coming out of surgery. He had a bullet enter his chin at an angle that exited under his right ear. The wound was not fatal. The surgical nurse gave me the bullet that the doctor removed from the skin next to Ferreira's ear. The bullet was evidence; it came from Omar's gun.

The sheriff's office had been notified and sent two officers to guard the prisoner. Badge and I went to a diner for dinner. After a dangerous, exciting event, it takes time to unwind. I got home at 4:30 a.m. I would catch a couple hours sleep and be back in the office at eight for all the reports.

At 3:00 p.m., when the reports were completed, Badge and I returned to Riverview Hospital to interview Louie Ferreira. He was alone in a single room with one wrist handcuffed to the bed. Outside the room were two sheriff's officers. They knew me and allowed us to enter the room.

Louie was awake. He had bandages around his face, and his jaw was wired shut. I advised him of his rights, but he could only mumble. He gave me the one-finger salute with his free hand. I understood what his gesture meant. He did not want to be interviewed. Badge thought it was funny. He seldom laughed.

I had hoped this attempt at revenge was over!

The Sid Gross Murder Case

We were overdue. We hadn't had a major crime in the past four months. The holiday season was over. With the exception of two fatal hit-and-run cases, the detectives were not too busy. The detectives had a chance to clean up some cases. Burglaries were down, and there was an overall lull in crime.

On Saturday, January 9, at 6:27 p.m., a resident called to report an injured and badly beaten man on the side of his driveway. A resident named Joe Truex was returning home from work when he discovered the injured man. The driveway was three hundred yards long, with his home set back from the road near the woods. On the left side of the drive was a fallow field he leased to a local farmer. On the right were weeds and brambles with a light coating of snow. The victim was lying on the weeds and snow.

When Mr. Truex stopped his car to check on the victim. It was very dark, and the victim did not respond to his calling. Mr. Truex threw a blanket on the victim and then hurried to his house to call for help.

When the 911 call was received, the shift commander, Sergeant Hannafey, dispatched district patrolman Fred Deickmann and an ambulance. Deickmann was met by Joe Truex at the entrance to his driveway, and they walked back and checked the victim. The body was cold. This person was surely dead. Deickmann called in a 10-40, requesting assistance. He returned to the entrance of the driveway and sealed it off. He sent Mr. Truex home and advised him to stay there and not return to the immediate crime-scene area until called.

Sergeant Hannafey called me at home while I was having supper—another dinner spoiled. "A possible homicide," he said. En route, I radioed Sergeant Hannafey and requested he notify

Detectives O'Mack, Blunt, McConnell, and Dodge to report to the crime scene. I also requested he notify the prosecutor's office.

When I arrived, Deickmann was guarding the entrance to the driveway. I noticed tire imprints in the snow near the entrance. Vehicles ran through edge of the snow before entering the driveway macadam. One set of the tire imprints appeared to be made by a vehicle with dual wheels on the rear and large tires, indicating they were from a truck. I had a patrolman Bob Johnson guard and preserve these imprints until they could be photographed and casted.

Detective O'Mack and Detective Richard "the Dutch" Deickmann arrived. Detective Richard Deickmann was the father of Patrolman Fred Deickmann. The three us walked up the driveway toward the victim. There were no footprints in the snow near the body, only tire imprints. From about ten yards, I observed the area where Truex stopped his car and walked toward the body. There were also tire imprints from Fred's patrol car and his footprints in the light snow. There were tire imprints from a truck with dual wheels. From the prints it appeared that the victim was dumped from the truck and then the truck backed out of the driveway and headed north toward Highway 35.

I requested Detective Dodge to come directly to the area of the body. Before we got any closer to the body, I needed photographs. When Detective Dodge arrived, we put on latex gloves and conducted cursory examination of the body. Dodge took photographs. We didn't disturb the body, but with the aid of flashlights, we could see the victim was a middle-aged white male with possible gunshot wounds to the head. I assigned Fred to guard the scene around the body. I had Sergeant Hannafey call the medical examiner's office and request his presence.

Detective Jones from the ME's office and Dr. Becker arrived within the hour. With the scene preserved and Dodge doing the ID work, the body could be moved and searched. When Detective Jones rolled over the body, it became apparent that the victim was shot on the left side of the face and in the left ear. Dr. Becker ordered the body moved to the morgue in Freehold for the autopsy. The doctor said he would perform the autopsy in the morning at 11:00 a.m. I was going to assign the Dutch to witness the autopsy. He was going to be the lead on the investigation. He still got sick looking at scrambled eggs, but he would have to endure the procedure. I would probably accompany him.

While the body was being placed on a gurney for removal, Jones found a .38-caliber revolver tucked in the victim's waistband. The weapon was loaded. Jones turned the gun over to Detective O'Mack. The victim had a set of keys in his right front pocket and a wallet in his right rear pocket. The victim did not have any cash in his pockets. Detective O'Mack took the wallet and keys for identification purposes. A complete search would be conducted at the morgue.

With the crime scene in the capable hands of Detective Dodge, I returned to headquarters with detectives Deickmann and O'Mack. I called in Veronica, our secretary, for notes and reports. Detectives Charlie Conner and Andy McCormick arrived from the prosecutor's office. Detectives Oakes and Graves arrived. I assigned the detectives the tasks that needed to be accomplished, for example, statements from witnesses, police reports, and evidence collection and preservation.

I notified Chief McKenna and Dep. Chief Lutz. They did not want to come to headquarters but wanted me to call them with updates on the investigation. This was my case. I started a murder book.

Patrolman Johnson was assigned at the crime scene to stop all vehicles traveling on Timber Avenue near the entrance to the Truex's driveway. He reported a local resident, James Conroy, stopped to ask what was going on. He told Johnson that he was on Timber Lane at 5:30 p.m. and observed a box truck on the road in the vicinity of the Truex driveway. I sent a detective to pick up Conroy for further information and a written statement.

O'Mack and McCormack, examining the victim's wallet, found a New Jersey driver's license. The name on the license was Seymour Samuel Gross, address in Maplewood. The height and weight matched the victim. The photograph didn't help; the victim's face was bloody and a mess. The Maplewood Police were contacted.

Detective Jerry Barbatos investigated and called back. "I believe we have the identified the victim," he reported.

Detective Mulvey took a statement from Conroy. He lived on Cherry Tree Farm Road near Timber Avenue. Conroy reported that at approximately 5:30 p.m., he observed a large gray box truck in the vicinity of the Truex's driveway. There was a large symbol on the side of truck in the shape of a Z. "I should be able to identify the truck if I see it again," he said.

At 9:30 p.m. Detective Barbatos called again. He said he had spoken to Mrs. Gross at her home. She explained, "My husband did not come home from work. I expected him at six, his usual time. I called the store where he worked, Rahway Auto Parts. I was told that he was not in the store or shop. This was unusual for him." Since this was a homicide investigation, Detective Barbatos offered to drive Mrs. Gross and her son to headquarters.

Dutch sent a Teletype issued to all New Jersey police departments, a BOLO on a gray truck, dual rear wheels, with a large Z on the right side.

I requested Rahway Police Department to check the store and shop. A few minutes later, Detective Bender called back to report the store was closed and locked. There was no sign of the owner, Carl Gross. I made arrangements to meet with Bender on Monday morning at the store.

At 10:30 p.m., Mrs. Gross arrived escorted by her son and Detective Barbatos. Based on her physical description of her husband and the description of his clothing, we were pretty sure the victim was Sid Gross. When we told her we believe her husband was murdered, she became hysterical. She said she was too distraught to talk to detectives at this time. I did ask her if she knew who would shoot and kill her husband. She said, "Yes, but I don't want to talk now. I am too upset. I will tell you all about it tomorrow." Her son wanted to take her home and contact her doctor. They promised to be back tomorrow morning to identify the body and give a statement.

At midnight, I sent everybody home. We would be back in the office at 7:00 a.m.

Sunday morning, I called for a meeting with all the detectives. We discussed the case and tasks were assigned. Detective Graves was in charge of tire-imprint casts and to return back to the crime scene for daylight photos. The casts of the tire prints in the snow came out well, and the impressions should be identifiable.

Mrs. Gross, her son Robert, and her lawyer arrived at 9:00 a.m. I set up the interview room. After coffee, we started the interview. Detective O'Mack operated a tape recorder. I asked Mrs. Gross to identify herself and tell us who she thought killed her husband. She stated, "Max set him up." I didn't have to prep Mrs. Gross; she was anxious to talk. I let her continue.

"Max is a mobster. He insisted Sid owed him money, and they had an argument about it. I heard them talking on the phone Friday night. Sid told him not to send Kelly around. Sid was extremely upset. An hour later, Kelly called. He spoke to Sid, and I heard Sid hollering. He told Kelly to stay away. He did not owe Max any money. That's all I know."

I asked her if she knew any more about Kelly. She said, "Kelly had just been released from prison. He works for Max as a collector and enforcer. He worked for Sid, driving his delivery truck, before he went to prison. He always carried a gun, and he probably shot Sid."

O'Mack called in Veronica, our secretary, and took a formal statement in the presence of Mr. Justin, her lawyer. Detectives Conner and Oakes went to the Rahway store with Robert Gross. He had a key to the store and shop. We needed a list of employees present on Saturday.

Detectives McCormick, Deickmann, Dodge, and I went to Freehold Hospital, which was the location of the morgue. We arrived at 11:00 a.m. Before Dr. Becker started the autopsy, Detective Dodge took the fingerprints of the deceased. He would take photographs during the autopsy. As soon as the sheet was removed from the body, Detective Deickmann got sick. He ran outside and vomited on the entrance ramp. I won't force him to go to an autopsy again, my mistake. Detective Dodge, however, could eat an egg salad sandwich during an autopsy.

Dr. Becker noted two entrance wounds, one on the left check and the other near the left ear. Both exit wounds were in the right side of the head. Preliminary measurements were comparable to a .38-caliber bullet. Bullet fragments were in the skull. A full report would be sent us in a few days. The doctor ruled the death a homicide.

While we were in Freehold, Detectives Mulvey and Oakes contacted the parole office regarding Kelly Rogers. His parole officer, Nick Scudito, was off duty but was tracked down at home. He said he was assigned to supervise Kelly, a convict released last month. Scudito returned to his office in Newark to pull the records he had on Kelly Rogers.

An hour later parole, Officer Scudito called Detective Mulvey. He gave us very useful information.

Kelly Rogers was in prison for a murder he committed ten years ago. Rogers was a forty-two-year-old black male, six foot tall and two hundred eighty pounds. He had been a trustee for the past three years. He was released to a halfway house in Newark in November. Kelly had to report in weekly and continue to work daily. The state parole system got him a job driving a delivery truck for a company in Newark. Economy Trucking Company on Ulyas Avenue, Newark, employed him. Rogers had not reported to his PO for last two weeks. Scudito was going to issue a warrant to pick him up Monday morning.

Back at headquarters, we had another meeting. We had our suspect. Tomorrow we would start at 7:30 a.m. to put our case together. But right now it's time for a break, some pizza and beer. We headed to Muldoon's Bar to use some of the petty cash fund.

Monday morning, 7:30 a.m., Detective Mulvey was assigned to obtain suspect Rogers's rap sheet and photo. Detectives O'Mack and McCormick sent to Rahway Auto Parts store for information and statements. Sergeant Blunt and Detective Oakes were assigned to Economic Trucking in Newark. I am staying at headquarters preparing reports and coordinating investigators. Detective Dodge was in the ID room processing film and tire casts.

Detectives O'Mack and McCormick reported from Gross's store. Two employees observed Gross leave the store though the front door and enter a gray box truck that was parked in the front. One employee, a clerk at the front counter, described the driver of the truck as a large black male, short hair, wearing a red flannel shirt. The truck had a large Z painted on the side.

Detectives Sergeant Blunt and the Badge reported an interview with Angelo Speziale, manager of Economic Trucking. Speziale reported that Kelly Rogers was assigned to deliver a load of furniture on Saturday morning. His destination was in Atlantic City. He returned late, approximately 10:00 p.m. He also added that the truck cab was washed clean, an unusual occurrence. Truck drivers usually bring back the truck dirty, filled with wrappers, mud, and garbage. Kelly was typically a slob with his truck.Sergeant Brunt learned that the truck was presently at the Farmers Market in Brooklyn, picking up a load of fruit and vegetables for grocery stores in Long Island.

I sent the detectives to Brooklyn to find the truck. I needed a photograph of the truck and tire-imprint samples.

Mrs. Gross and her son arrived at 11:30 a.m. She identified a photograph of Rogers as the person who worked for her husband before he went to jail. She said, "I believed that was the person Sid was arguing with during the previous week." She also wanted Sid's wallet, which I did not release. I did have her read the statement taken yesterday and sign the copies.

At noon, Detectives O'Mack and McCormick arrived at headquarters with the witnesses from front of the store. They took statements from both.

Badge called from the Farmers Market in Brooklyn. They located the truck. The market manager, Mr. Pokus, refused to give them the truck. The truck is almost loaded and ready to leave for deliveries. I asked Badge if he had his "baby" with him. The baby was the Badge's six-inch nickel-plated Colt .45-caliber revolver. Badge said, "Yeah, Captain." I told Badge to show baby to Mr. Pokus and tell him we were taking the truck.

I called NYPD. I was directed to the 1-7 precinct. I spoke to Detective Sergeant Flanigan. I explained the problem, and he said he would go to the market immediately. Badge called back. Sergeant Blunt was on the back of the truck, throwing the boxes off the truck.

Mr. Pokus was irate and, along with his other employees, was making threats. Badge said a riot might start. I told Badge, "Get the truck! That's an order!" Badge always followed orders.

Half an hour later, Badge called back. New York detectives arrived and were great. They told Mr. Pokus the Jersey detectives were taking the truck and if he interfered, they would lock him up. Mr. Pokus asked Sergeant Blunt to please get off the back of the truck; he would have his men unload the boxes. Many of the boxes Blunt threw off the truck were broken open. I felt bad, but if they had cooperated in the beginning, this would have been a lot easier.

Sergeant Blunt would drive the truck, and Badge would follow. They would be back in Monmouth County in two hours. It was a great job by determined detectives. I just hoped I followed proper legal procedures. I need the truck as evidence. At 3:00 p.m., the truck was back at the parking lot at headquarters. I sent detectives to find Jim Conroy. I hope he could identify the truck.

Detective Graves would photograph the truck tires for a comparison with the photos taken of the tire imprints at the crime scene. Graves sometimes assisted Dodge with photography. Detective Dodge took photos of the exterior of the truck showing the large Z on each side. The inside was clean and smelled of Lysol. Detective Dodge noticed some gray matter on the ceiling of the cab. He scraped a small amount off. We both knew what it was right away. It was brain matter. Detective Dodge was one of the best identification officers in the state. I was lucky to have him.

I notified Prosecutor Hornacek. I started my affidavit for the seizure of the material inside the truck. The prosecutor and I would take my reports to a superior judge for approval.

I notified the state police laboratory in Trenton to expect the truck. State police Sergeant Williams said, "They would work that night to identify the matter inside the truck. It would take a couple of days comparing the tires, but they would give the work a priory status.

I decided I had enough evidence to sign a complaint against Kelly Rogers. Prosecutor Hornacek wanted to wait for the official laboratory reports. I was afraid Kelly Rogers might run. I am going back to the Judge for the arrest warrant.

Tuesday, four days since discovery of Sid Gross's body, I had a warrant to arrest the killer. The chief was pleased with our progress. The prosecutor thought we had moved to fast and should have developed more evidence.

Give That Man a Cigar

I had a warrant to arrest Kelly Rogers for the murder of Seymour Gross. Four days of intense investigation led to the charge. A third of the work was accomplished. We would find Rogers, seize him, and hold him for arraignment. Then we would finish our mission by convicting him in a court of law.

Parole officer Nick Scudito gave us his last known address as a halfway house on Clinton Avenue in Jersey City. I requested the assistance of the Jersey City Police Department. I was directed to the office of SWAT team leader, Lieutenant Joe Pellico. After giving him a rundown on the murder and investigation, we set up a meeting for the following morning to execute the arrest. In the meantime, Lieutenant Pellico was going to stake out halfway house.

I notified the prosecutor's office and Assistant Prosecutor Hornicek. County chief of detectives Licitra assigned Detective McCormack and Detective Manning to assist with the capture. I notified Chief McKenna and received his approval to take officers to Jersey City for the arrest.

At 1:00 a.m. on January 13, we assembled our group in the detective bureau. Along with the county detectives McCormick and Manning, I had Sergeant Blunt, Detectives O'Mack, McConnell, and Mulvey on the team. We arrived at the police headquarters in Jersey City at 3:00 a.m. We met with Lieutenant Pellico and his SWAT team members. We followed the SWAT team truck to 677 Clinton Avenue in two unmarked cars. Lieutenant Pellico knew the house layout; his officers had been at the location on previous arrests.

When we arrived at the house, it was dark and quiet. The house was an old Victorian-style home with a wraparound front porch and a rear entrance. Joe and I took the front door. The door was unlocked. We entered the house, turned on lights, and made some noise. The rest of the team entered the rear door when they heard Joe and I at the front.

The house had two bedrooms downstairs and five bedrooms upstairs. The team rounded up all the occupants, sixteen men and five women. Rogers was not among them. One resident told us that Kelly sleeps on a mattress in the front bedroom. Joe and I searched the area and found some clothing, toilet articles, and a telephone address book.

The SWAT team arrested a man named Rufus Johnson on an old warrant. We questioned him about Rogers. He said, "Kelly was sleeping at his girlfriend's apartment." We got the address. It was in Kelly's telephone book.

We left the house and went to 1149 Bergen Street, the apartment of Ms. Pam Williams. We arrived at 6:30 a.m. The apartment was on the third floor in the center of a group of row houses. There was only one entrance in the front of the building. There was a fire escape for emergency exit in the rear.

There was a set of twelve steps in the front that led to a small porch that had a sturdy door, which opened to a foyer. To the right of the steps was a door to the front apartment. Joe sent men to cover the back fire escape. The rest of us would enter the front. Joe and I quietly climbed the steps and entered the foyer. A door to the right had the name Rodriguez on a nameplate. To the left were the steps to the Williams's apartment. I did not want to go up the steps to the apartment door. There was no cover. If he opened the door and he shot at me, I didn't think he could miss. I was scared. Why was I the cop to go first? What did I have to prove? I did this before when I arrested a murderer in Keansburg. I hoped and prayed I was lucky again. I had my bulletproof vest and a borrowed SWAT helmet, but it might not be enough. Rogers had killed before; I didn't think he would hesitate to shoot.

Against my better judgment, I went first. Lieutenant Pellico, Detective O'Mack, and one of Joe's men were behind me. Every cop had a gun in his hand. When I reached the top step, I pounded on the door. Nothing happened. I waited a minute and pounded again. After a short while, a voice from inside said, "Whose dat?" I yelled, "Police! Open up!" Quiet again. I pounded on the door again. Inside a voice asked, "Who are you?" I hollered, "Look out the front window!" There was a SWAT truck parked in front. We backed down the steps. After a few minutes, I yelled for Kelly to come down the stairs to the foyer. If you don't come down, we will shoot tear gas through the windows." He answered, "I'll be right down." We retreated to the foyer.

Rogers came down the stairs. I placed him under arrest. Joe handcuffed him, and we brought him back upstairs into the apartment. Pam Williams was in the living room when we entered the apartment. I asked her if we could look around. Miss Williams said, "I know what you want." She took Joe and I into the bedroom. She lifted a pillow off the bed and a gun was there. Joe picked up the gun and I got a plastic baggie from the kitchen and Joe put the gun in it. The gun was a nickel-plated, colt. 38-caliber revolver. I thought we had our murder weapon. We searched the rest of the apartment. I told Ms. Williams I would need a statement from her. She said, "No problem." After talking to Pam Williams, I could not understand her relationship with Rogers. She was a pleasant, educated woman who worked as a registered nurse.

Rogers was placed into the SWAT van and driven to the Jersey City, first precinct. Our two cars followed. At the precinct, Rogers was booked, photographed, and fingerprinted. A Jersey City detective in the bureau told me to be careful with Rogers. He was a mean dude. He said Rogers was only happy when he was drinking whiskey and smoking cigars. While we were waiting for Lieutenant Pellico to release Rogers to us, Roger's lawyer arrived. He introduced himself as Raymond Green. He shouted out, "My client will not answer any questions. You cannot question him."

Green demanded to see his client. Rogers, who had been in the identification room, was now in the detective bureau office, handcuffed to a railing. Lieutenant Pellico told Mr. Green he could talk to Rogers for a few minutes before he was released to us. Mr. Green advised Rogers not to say a word. "I know that cop Holiday, and he will lie to you." I arrested a burglar three years ago, and Green defended him. Green did not like my testimony or the fact that his client was convicted. Rogers was giving me a mean stare since his arrest. He narrowed his eyes and mumbled some threatening words. I just looked back at him and grinned. I remembered what I learned about him earlier. This gave me an idea. While Rogers was talking to Green, I went out of the precinct and to a nearby *bogoto* and purchased three Macanudo Cigars.

Rogers was released to us. I thanked Lieutenant Pellico, and we took Rogers and placed him in the back seat of my car. He was handcuffed, and we had him in leg irons. Badge drove and Sergeant Blunt rode shotgun. The other officers followed close behind.

For the first half hour nothing was said in the car. We were on the turnpike heading south when I reached into my inner jacket and took out a cigar. I took off the wrapper, licked the cigar, and bit off the end. I didn't smoke, but I thought this was how it was done. I waited for a few minutes. I could see Rogers watching me. I finally lit the cigar and took a puff. Rogers turned his head, smiled, looked at me, and said, "You got any more of them cigars?" I said, "Yep." A few more minutes passed with me puffing away, and Kelly said, "You wouldn't give me one, would you?" I said, "Sure." I waited another couple of minutes before I took out another cigar. I unwrapped the cigar and gave it to a happy Kelly. He licked it, bit off the end, and I lit it for him.

After a few minutes of puffing away, Kelly said to me, "I know where you be from. I drove the laundry truck from Rahway prison and picked up stuff from the hospitals down your way." I asked him how that happened. He said, "I was a trustee in the prison and got the job. It got me out three days a week, although a guard was always with me."

We had a nice conversation all the way back to the Monmouth County jail. He did most of the talking. I didn't ask him any further questions. When we arrived at the jail, Detective McCormick took over the processing of Rogers. I left for my office. I had reports to write, people to notify, and more tasks to assign. The first of which was for Detective O'Mack to process the gun we recovered in Jersey City. I wanted the gun taken to the state police laboratory in Trenton as soon as possible.

Finding the Murder Weapon

Bad news! Monday afternoon, the laboratory technician from the state police called concerning the authenticity of the weapon submitted. The ballistics did not match the bullet found in the skull of victim Gross. The weapon found in Williams's apartment was not the murder weapon.

Where is the gun? Rogers's had probably gotten rid of the gun after he shot Gross. But where? We discussed the problem in the bureau. McCormick suggested Rogers threw the gun away after he shot Gross and the gun was lying along the roadway. The gun might also be where he washed out the truck. We didn't have any other ideas.

We organized a search party to go from the crime scene to the turnpike. We would walk the roadway that Rogers would have used to return the truck. He washed the truck somewhere on this route; there was a chance that is where he ditched the gun.

Volunteer off-duty officers, police reserves, fireman, and the Boy Scouts joined us Wednesday morning. There were over fifty men and woman to search. We met at 10:00 a.m. at police headquarters and assigned the streets to be searched. Search groups left at 11:00 a.m.

I didn't have a chance to leave the office before a call came in from a group of searchers. A Boy Scout found a gun twelve foot off the roadway in the weeds. He was only three hundred yards from the driveway where the victim was found. The search lasted less than thirty minutes.

I went to the location on Timber Avenue with Detective Dodge. He took a photograph of the gun and picked it up. He placed the gun in a paper bag. The gun was a nickel-plated .38-caliber revolver and easily observed in the sunlight. The reflection of the sun off the gun barrel helped the Boy Scout spot the weapon. We returned to headquarters to call off the search and thank the volunteers. I hope the chief wouldn't get too angry when the bill comes in for the coffee and donuts. He shouldn't because we found a gun.

Detective Dodge prepared the request for examination. As soon as the request form was completed, he left for the lab in Trenton. I hoped this gun was a match.

Thursday afternoon, bad news turned into good news. The gun we recovered was the weapon used to kill Sid Gross. A partial thumbprint was found on the gun. The print matched the right index fingerprint of Kelly Rogers. That report was submitted to the prosecutor's office, along with the murder book. The murder book consisted of all the police reports, witness reports, photographs, and laboratory reports.

The next step was the grand jury.

The *State vs. Kelly Rogers* Trial

The defendant was being held in county jail awaiting disposition of his case. His bail was set at one million dollars by the municipal judge. The court system demanded a speedy trial before one hundred days. A grand jury presentment was set for March 2. I testified, and so did the medical examiner. The hearing lasted less than one hour. The jury did not ask me any questions.

Two weeks later, the prosecutor's office notified me that Kelly Rogers was indicted as a convicted felon for murder and possession of a deadly weapon. Trial date was set on April 15. The state was ready.

In early April, the defense requested a postponement of the April trial date. It was granted by the superior court judge and reset for April 28. The defense requested more time to prepare. This was a usual occurrence.

The defense now requested a pretrial hearing on the admissibility of the evidence the prosecutor would present. The defense had applied for and received the list of state's witnesses and evidence. The defense claimed that the guns seized were in violation of the Fourth Amendment, an illegal search and seizure. The contention was also that the actual murder weapon was seized in violation of the Fifth Amendment, a defendant's right not to incriminate himself. The truck seizure was in violation of the fourth amendment; the contention was the truck was seized without a warrant.

At the pretrial hearing, the prosecutor called Lieutenant Pellico first. He testified that he gave Rogers the Miranda warning in the apartment. He said, "Mrs. Williams gave him a gun, which she pointed out under a pillow in her bedroom. The weapon was under her control, and she volunteered to turn it over to the investigators".

I testified next. I stated that I advised Rogers of his rights under the Fifth Amendment in the apartment after the arrest. Lieutenant Pellico and Mrs. Williams were present during the reading.

Green did not challenge Lieutenant Pellico. He had plenty of questions for me. He asked me why I searched the roadway looking for the gun. He wanted to know if it was the result of Rogers telling me about the driving of the laundry truck for the prison. I told him, "I would have found that information from a background investigation of Rogers's activities as a prisoner." He asked me, "Did you give my client a cigar as an inducement to confess?" I told him, "I did not expect a career criminal to confess." This got Green angry, and he complained to the judge that I was not responsive to his questions. He was overruled. He then asked me why I gave a cigar to Kelly. I said, "I was smoking one, and I was being polite." The jury laughed. I said, "When your client asked me for one, I gave it to him."

Green appeared very frustrated. He also challenged the seizure of the truck. He said that we needed a warrant. The prosecutor countered with a statement by the truck company manager. The manager gave permission to us take the truck. We had told the manager we suspected it was used in the commission of a crime.

It didn't take long for the judge to rule. Both guns could be admitted at the trial. The truck and the brain matter inside were admissible. This decision would be the crux of the case. Those in attendance predicted a guilty verdict.

One week later, the trial was started. A jury was selected on the first day. The second day was for opening statements. Prosecutor Steve Hornicek was brief and direct to the point. Green was long-winded. I thought he was boring the jury. After they finished their openings, the state's first witness was called, Mr. Joseph Truex. He spoke of finding the body and calling the police. Hornicek followed with the medical examiner. Detective Dodge testified next; then the first police responders. That ended the first day of the state's case.

I was the first witness called the next morning. The prosecutor finished with my testimony in an hour. The cross examination started at 10:30 a.m. and lasted the rest of the day. Green tried to discredit my testimony, but I was too experienced to allow that to happen. He dwelled on the car ride from Jersey City to the county jail. He insinuated I was manipulating Rogers to talk when I answered his request for a cigar. He repeatedly asked me about the conversation. Did I ask questions? I said to him, "Kelly did most of the talking. I just listened."

Halfway through the cross-examination, Green requested a side bar hearing with the judge. Green was complaining that I was looking at the jury during my testimony. The judge told him that a witness should look at the jury when testifying. Then Green complained that I was nodding at the jury when I testified. The judge asked me not to nod and asked if that satisfied Green. He angrily walked away from the sidebar conference.

I have used these nonverbal signals to jurors in the past. They were suggestions given to me to me by a former prosecutor, Tom Smith. When a question is asked, I single out a juror, look straight into that person's eyes, answer the question, and slightly nod. If the juror nods back, it works. That juror and I were together on the issue. When the next question was asked, I look at a different juror and do the same thing. This method was very subtle and not illegal. Green noticed this and complained. His irate complaint did not work with the judge. The jury was mine. When my testimony was finished, the state rested its case.

The following day, the defense called witnesses. Mrs. Williams was called back to the stand. She told the jury that Kelly was a gentle man and would not shoot anyone. The jury was looking at me when she testified. I don't think they believed her. On cross-examination, Prosecutor Hornicek asked her if she knew he had been in prison for a previous murder. Green jumped out of his chair and objected. Before she could answer, the judge stopped her. He then admonished the prosecutor. This information was inadmissible and prejudicial to the defense. This was a mistake by the prosecutor and could help the defense on appeal. The defense called Detective Jones from the medical examiner's office. Nothing was accomplished by the defense.

The defense did not call any other witnesses. Court recessed. When court resumed, Green had some motions for judge to decide. The first was for dismissal on all charges, as the state did not provide any evidence against the defendant. This is a standard defense motion. It was quickly denied. All the other frivolous motions were to be decided by the judge over the next two days. Court recessed for the weekend.

On Monday, the court did not resume until noon. The judge had others matters to consider. Both attorneys were prepared for summations. Green went first. He was long-winded; he was in his opening statement. Again after an hour, I thought he was boring the jury by repeating his contentions. He finally finished at 2:30 p.m.

Prosecutor Hornicek was brief and summed up the state's case in less than an hour. The judge delivered his charge and sent the jury home. They would report to court in the morning for deliberations.

On Tuesday morning, the jury was assembled and sent into the deliberation room. The prosecutor and I waited for the verdict. All the other witnesses had left. The jury delayed until noon. I think they just wanted to appear to be working until they ordered lunch.

At 1:00 p.m., the jury sent word through the bailiff that they had a verdict. Court was resumed. The verdict was guilty on all charges, sentencing set in two weeks.

On May 5, Roger Kelly was sentenced to life in prison plus thirty years.

Case closed pending appeal.

The Cowboys

On the way returning from superior court in Freehold, I heard a lot of chatter on the radio. I just finished a two-week trial and needed some time off. It's not going to happen. Something was amiss in the Bay Shore. I knew I would eventually be involved. I might as well find out what was happening now. I requested information from the desk at headquarters. Chief McKenna came on the radio. "Report to me at the Spy House. Now!"

The Spy House was located on the beachfront. It was a mile of beachfront that was hit by a heavy storm last year. The county of Monmouth owned the beachfront with the Spy House and some other structures. A fishing pier off the property was destroyed in the storm and was being rebuilt.

When I arrived at 2:30 p.m., there were at least seven official vehicles at the entrance to the beach construction area. There was only one entrance in the area. The roadway was blocked by a large tandem dump truck. Beyond the truck off the roadway were two construction trailers and other construction vehicles, including a crane. Two groups of men were in the area. There were about ten men in helmets and work clothing. Other groups were dressed in suits. Nobody appeared to be happy.

When I found the chief, I asked what was happening. "Two problems," said the chief. The first one was a report to the Monmouth County Improvement Authority that the contractor was in violation of state laws by removing beach sand from the site and selling the sand out of the county. The jobsite foreman denied those accusations. The construction company owner claimed that he had a right to removing the sand and sell all the cubic yards. Officials from the authority, the environmental commission, FEMA, and a group of local citizens were there to protest. A lot of arguing was going on between these groups.

I said, "It's not our problem, is it, Chief?"

Our problem started when the county administrator called the chief and requested him to put a temporary stop on the sand removal. The chief agreed. He then had a phone conversation with the owner, Sal Costello. Costello had the contract to rebuild the sand dunes on that stretch of beach. Costello also had the contract to rebuild the fishing pier. Costello told the chief that he had a right to remove the sand. The chief and Costello got into a heated argument. Threats and ethnic slurs were exchanged. The chief called the patrol office and ordered Lieutenant Freibott to send a patrol car to stop the trucks. He called the detective bureau and spoke with Lieutenant Flynn. Lieutenant Flynn sent Detectives Sergeant Blunt and Swenson to the beach to stop the trucks. As usual, the chief "stewed" about this problem for a while and then went to the beach himself.

When Chief McKenna arrived, he saw a truck blocking the roadway. It had two flat tires on the front. A pickaxe was imbedded on the tire on the driver's side. Sergeant Blunt had flattened the tires after the truck driver threatened to drive over the patrol and detective cars. Sergeant Blunt and the truck driver were face to face and arguing. The owner of the truck company arrived and joined the shouting match.

The truck owner shouted, "These tires are worth three thousand dollars each!"

I was trying to calm down the tire-flattening problem when two more official cars arrived at the scene. Three men from the Army Corps of Engineers jumped out of a car and went to the construction trailer. The first assistant prosecutor Schuler and County Detective Cavanaugh approached the chief from the second car. A heated discussion followed. It seemed that the prosecutor was blaming the chief for all the problems. The prosecutor was responding to a call from a Sal Crispino that a detective threatened to shoot his truck driver. Crispino owned the trucking company that Sal Costello had contracted with to remove the sand. What a mess that we had! Crispino was at the site to protect his truck drivers.

The prosecutor told the chief, "You don't have any control over your *cowboys*! My office might have to exert its authority and take over."

The chief countered to the prosecutor, "Your office is a Mickey Mouse operation. Stay out! You have your home rule, and I have mine. This is my jurisdiction and my problems."

It was finally discovered that the Army Corps of Engineers had a cease-and-desist order from a federal district court judge in Newark that ordered the stoppage of all operations. When the order was shown to all concerned, the situation cooled down. Everybody eventually left the beach.

I noted in the following weeks that the work had completely halted. Our department received a notice that we were being sued for the cost of the truck tires and work stoppage. It would all work out in the courts with the lawyers making a lot of money. The incident continued the animosity between the chief and county prosecutor.

Allegations of Police Brutality

The Greek approached me with a plan for a drug raid. The narcotics team had been developing the plan all week. They received their information months ago but did not make this a priority because of the small amount of drugs being sold; the majority of sales were marijuana. Detective Graves and rookie detective, McNulty, had prepared a search warrant. I wanted to review all search warrants before detectives presented them to a judge.

The warrant was for a home in the Leonardo section of the township. The target was the home of Anna Paget. I know Mrs. Paget; she was one of the animal-control officers for the township. I had worked with her on occasion and found her very compassionate and competent. However, her seventeen-year-old son and his two buddies had been selling drugs. She was a single mom, and the team believes she didn't not know about the drug-dealing. The facts in the affidavit were substantial and a judge should approve the search and seizure. I suggested another approach to the problem, but the detectives did not believe Mrs. Paget would give them consent to search. She was law-abiding and antidrug but very protective of her son. They wanted to go the house on Friday night when the activity was at its peak. Mrs. Paget was not usually at home. I gave them permission to go petition a judge.

On Friday night, the detectives set up surveillance of the home. The district patrol car and shift sergeant were in the area if the raid was to take place.

At 10:30 p.m., a car pulled up in front of the home. Kyle Paget and his buddy, Billy Woodward, game out of the house and had a conversation with two occupants in the car. Kyle returned to the house. He was only in the house for a couple of minutes when he returned to the car. He had something in his hand. The detectives hidden nearby burst out and attempted to corral the group.

Kyle Paget pulled out of the grasp of Patrolman John Estoch and started running down the street. Two detectives chased him to the corner of Center Avenue and Hamilton Avenue, where they tackled him, and they all fell to the ground. Kyle was screaming that the policemen were going to kill him. His screaming and yelling was so loud it attracted the people in the nearby homes. A scuffle ensued, and Kyle was finally subdued and handcuffed.

They walked back to the house, and Kyle was bought inside to witness the search. Cocaine and marijuana were found in Kyle's bedroom. The amount was small, less than an ounce of cocaine and about thirty ounces of grass. Some oxycontin pills were in Woodward's jeans pocket. They were arrested and brought to headquarters for processing.

Someone called Mrs. Paget about the arrests. She came storming into headquarters. She was angry with everyone. She demanded to know who assaulted her son. The shift commander called me at home. He asked me to try to diffuse the situation. Mrs. Paget had left before I arrived at headquarters. I met with the detectives and patrolman that were at the scene. It did not appear to be a major issue. The suspects were arrested, the house searched, and the contraband seized. Because Mrs. Paget alleged her son was assaulted, I interviewed him in the cellblock.

Kyle told me he was beaten up on the street by Detective Crapapolis and another detective after he was caught running away. He knew the Greek was watching him and afraid the police were going to assault him, so he ran. I asked him if he was injured, and he said yes. I did not observe any injuries, nothing to substantiate an injury. Kyle did not have on a shirt. I had a flannel shirt in my locker and gave it to him. I did note a bruise on his right rib cage. Because he complained he was injured, I told him we would take him to the hospital to be examined by a doctor. I requested the patrol commander handle the transportation.

The shift commander was Lieutenant Zemko. The lieutenant assigned two patrolman to take the prisoner to Riverview Hospital.

One man rode in the ambulance; the other followed in a patrol car. I told Patrolman John Estoch, who was in the ambulance with Kyle, to make sure the hospital took a blood sample. I suspected Kyle was under the influence of drugs during the incident.

I called Mrs. Paget and arranged for Kyle's release. She could pick him up at the hospital. She was calm and cordial and thanked me for getting him released. She did ask me why Kyle was beaten. I said, "I was not there, but I am looking into the situation." She seemed satisfied. Billy Woodward's uncle posted one-thousand-dollars bail for his release.

I notified the chief on Monday morning. He already knew of the arrests. He received a call from one of the witnesses. It was probably Dave Heiser, but he didn't tell me who actually called. He did not seem concerned.

It didn't take long for the prosecutor to call me. He wanted all the reports on the raid and arrests. He said, "I have a complaint from Mrs. Paget that her son was punched and kicked by the police." The defendant was a juvenile, and I prepared the reports as if the case would be heard in juvenile court. I sent the reports to the prosecutor's office.

I received a telephone call from Dave Heiser. I had known Dave for many years as a teacher in our local high school and a citizen serving on various boards. He had an excellent reputation in the community. He was as well respected in the county. Dave had witnessed the arrest. He said the punching and kicking of Kyle Paget was unnecessary. He also told me his neighbor Johnny Brown saw the assault and arrest.

I telephoned Johnny Brown. Johnny told me, "I heard screaming on the street and looked out his window. There is a streetlight on the corner. I was able to observe two men punching and kicking Kyle Paget while he was on the ground in the street. I did not know the assailants. Kyle was screaming that they were going to kill him. The men put handcuffs on Kyle and walked him toward his house. I assumed then the men were plain-clothed police officers."

The telephones were buzzing all weekend. It seemed everyone knew about the incident. I called the three detectives into my office.

We had a bad situation, an angry mother, a juvenile claiming injury, and two citizens witnessing part of the event. The amount of drug seized was small, and we would have difficulty proving a drug sale took place. I intended to request a meeting with the prosecutor the next morning.

First Assistant Prosecutor Paul Shanley agreed to meet with me in his office. When I arrived at ten o'clock Wednesday morning, he was waiting for me. We had a lengthy discussion and reached a deal that we felt could appease everyone. There would be one drug charge for Paget and Woodward—that is, possession of a controlled dangerous substance, all other drug charges dropped, no jail time for Woodward and no juvenile incarceration time for Paget, no charges against Mrs. Paget. Most importantly for us, there would be no charges against any police officers.

Thursday, my next task was to get all involved to agree. I telephoned Anna Paget first thing in the morning. We met for lunch and had tuna sandwiches. She wasn't really happy with the plea bargain but agreed. I used all my powers of persuasion. Anna and I had been friendly for years. She would convince her son to accept and Billy Woodward to agree to the deal. I called Shanley. He said that the prosecutor reluctantly agreed. I informed the detectives of my progress.

Late Thursday afternoon, I was called to a meeting in chief's office. Chief McKenna was behind his desk. Deputy Chief Lutz and Detectives Crapapolis, Graves, and McNulty were present. As soon as I entered, the chief started a negative tirade about my actions in the case. The chief admonished me for interfering. "We are not making any deals with the prosecutor," he insisted. "The prosecutor is out to get us and make us look bad. As soon as the criminal charges are settled, we all will be sued civilly." Then he ordered me to "get the hell out of my office and don't do anything more on this case!"

Wow! I was shocked and embarrassed. I was also angry. I was protecting the detectives and the department. I left headquarters and went home to cool off.

On Friday morning, I placed a call to Shanley. When he got on the phone, I addressed him formally. "Prosecutor Shanley, this is

Captain Holiday. I am requesting that all negotiations we conducted on the Paget case be dropped and that the charges continue through the court system." Shanley addressed me back formally and said, "The case will take the normal course. Thank you, Captain." Just yesterday we were talking to each other as Paul and Bill. I knew Shanley concluded that Chief McKenna had quashed the plea bargain.

A month later in April, I received a subpoena to appear at the grand jury. The prosecutor was presenting evidence to indict police officers Steve Crapapolis, Kevin Graves, and Patrick McNulty for assault and police misconduct. Court was set for April 15.

On April 15, I testified before the grand jury. I gave evidence before the jury that Kyle told me he was assaulted but I did not see any injuries on his body, except for a bruise on the right side of his ribs. I testified that I had Paget taken to the hospital emergency room for an examination and blood tests. I suspected he was under the influence of drugs. That's all the questions I was asked by the prosecutor, and I was excused. I saw Dave and Johnny in the waiting room. I knew the detectives would be indicted. A jury is heavily influenced by the testimony of uninvolved citizens who witnessed an event.

The indictment was slapped on the detectives. An arraignment was set for the defendants. A trial date was set and preliminary arrangements made for attorneys placed on record. The defendants (the three detectives) pleaded not guilty. I had hoped the case could be resolved by an offer from the prosecutor.

I waited for a plea bargain and feared a trial.

The Detectives' Trial

The trial of the three detectives was set to start this Monday morning. I was a subpoenaed witness. I did not have to be in court until called. It should take a couple of days to hear the pretrial motions and select a jury. The Greek seemed confident on an acquittal. Pat and Kevin were not so sure. I feared the worse.

On Tuesday morning, the Greek called from the courthouse in Freehold. He wanted to know where the chief was. He and the defense lawyers wanted Chief McKenna in the courtroom in full dress uniform. The defense said it was important that the chief appear in solidarity with his detectives. The defense lawyers believed his presence would make a positive impression on the jury.

I walked upstairs to the chief's office. His secretary was at her desk. When I asked for the chief, she told me, "He called Monday morning from his condo in Florida. He is taking two-week vacation. He will not be back to New Jersey for the trial."

I couldn't believe the chief would take a vacation at this critical time. This was the first time in the history of our department that our police officers had ever been charged with a crime. The judge would not postpone the trial. I was not going to call the chief in Florida, but I knew the Greek or his lawyer would. I asked myself, *Why is Chief McKenna not here?* Deputy Chief Lutz said, "He has no knowledge of the case and could not add anything to the defense. He didn't want to attend the trial." But just his presence could help. The chief's absence at the trial would not look good for the detectives.

The prosecutor started to present the state's case on Wednesday morning. The witnesses were called, starting with Mrs. Paget. She was emotional but believable, a mother telling the jury what a good boy her son was. The next witness was a county detective. He presented the hospital report. This report was not very damaging. The victim had minor bruising and a contusion on his right rib cage. This ended the first day of testimony.

The second day of testimony started with Billy Woodward. He was not present when the arrest of Kyle was taking place, but he set the stage for the event. He ran when the police arrived but was caught at the back door. He said the police roughed him up during his arrest. On cross-examination, he admitted the possession of drugs. He also admitted smoking marijuana with Kyle before the police arrived. He was the prosecutor's witness and got a deal for his testimony. He was not going to be charged for drug possession if he testified. The defense brought out this deal during cross-examination.

Sherry Johnson was called next. She was Kyle Paget's girlfriend. She was in the house smoking pot when the raid took place. She didn't witness the arrests. She stayed on the couch in the living when the police entered and stayed there the whole time.

The next witnesses were neighbors, Dave Heiser and Johnny Brown. Their testimony was devastating. They testified that they saw the detectives kicking and punching Kyle Paget. They said they witnessed Kyle on the ground and heard his screams, "They are going to kill me!" They saw a detective pull Kyle to his feet, handcuff him, and walked him toward his house. Neither witness could identify the detectives nor which one of them did the kicking.

The third day of testimony started with Kyle Paget. He admitted smoking pot with Billy and Sherry before the police arrived. He denied the charge of selling drugs. He said, "I knew Detective Crapapolis was out to get me. I had a problem in school with the detective's daughter. I dated Mary Crapapolis and broke up with her. Since then, Detective Crapapolis has had it in for me. I was scared, and that is why I ran." His testimony of his arrest coincided with the witnesses. On cross-examination, he held up well for the prosecutor. He was a teenager who was easy to dislike but sounded believable. The state rested after he testified.

I was called for the defense. Unusual for me, I usually testify for the prosecution. I told of my interview with Kyle when he was in the juvenile detention room. I said, "I believed Kyle was still under the influence of something even three hours after his arrest." I testified concerning the blood sample taken at the hospital. Kyle Paget had THC [tetrahydrocannabinol] in his system when he was examined at the hospital. The prosecutor did not ask me any questions. I left the courthouse and returned to headquarters. The defendants did not testify on the advice of their lawyers.

The defense rested its case, and court was over until Monday. The chief was a no-show during the trial.

Court resumed Monday morning with the prosecutor's summation. When he finished, the defense asked for a motion of acquittal. It was quickly denied. Each defense lawyer had his own summation. I thought Atty. Jim Butler was incisive and eloquent for Detective McNulty and gave him the best chance for acquittal. The judge charged the jury with the fate of the defendants.

We did not have a decision until Tuesday. I came to court to hear the verdict. When the jury entered the courtroom from the deliberation room, they did not look at the detectives—not a good sign.

The sentence was guilty! I felt a lump in my chest. *No, no, no!* I wanted to holler. Sentencing was set for three weeks. I left by myself. I could not face Steve, Kevin, or Pat.

Three weeks later, I was in the courtroom again. Friday was sentencing day. The court was crowded with reporters and friends. The defendants were allowed to present character witnesses. I was going to vouch for the detectives. These men worked for me, with me, and at times protected me. I would be sincere and hope for the best.

After hearing the character witnesses, the judge said, "It is a sad day for law enforcement." He pronounced his sentence. He did not give them jail terms. Each received probation for three years. They lost their jobs, their pensions and were forever banned from employment with the government. This was the worst day of my career. I wanted to protect the men who worked for me. My efforts failed.

Chief McKenna did not appear for sentencing. He took another vacation to Florida. When I started my career in law enforcement,

Chief McKenna was my mentor. I admired him. I respected him. Now my attitude changed. He wanted no part of standing behind his accused officers. He seemed more concerned about his own reputation as chief of police.

My New Career as an Educator

I believe I was born to be a cop. I like people. I enjoy watching people and how they live their daily lives. It gives me pleasure to help people. Maybe I should have become a priest. My personal life was fulfilled when I married Nancy Marshall. We have two daughters that light up my life like a Christmas tree. I am grateful for my marriage and subsequent police career.

My father was influenced by the Depression's work ethic. He believed a man is only a good man if he worked every day. My father went to work at 5:30 a.m. each weekday morning and returned home at 6:30 p.m. On weekends, he worked in the family tavern on Friday night, Saturday, and Sunday. He did not have much time for my sisters or me. However, I always had a roof over my head and food on the table so I can't complain.

When I was fourteen, we lived in a house in Belford. A new family moved into the house next to us—Ralph Simon with his wife, Florence, and four children. Ralph was a Newark Police officer. He was in the horse-mounted patrol assigned to downtown district. Ralph took me with him on occasion to work. I would help clean the stable and walk the street following him on his rounds. He would get me into any movie house I wanted. After a movie, we would have lunch, and he would resume his patrol.

When Minski's Burlesque opened, he would ride his horse Sunny into the back of the theater. Ralph walked around the backstage as if he owned the place. The actors and showgirls all knew him. He introduced them to me, and I felt older and worldly. I fell in love with Cupcakes La Tour, the featured stripper. When the show started, I stood in the front row of the stage and collected her costume. I was supposed to be in school at this time. I would return home with Ralph at 4:30 p.m. My mother thought I was attending classes at Red Bank Catholic High School. Little did she know I was getting a "street" education.

Ralph Simon taught me how to ride a horse. He showed me how to fish and ice skate. More importantly, he sparked my interest in law enforcement. He was my go-to guy when I had questions about policing. He was both my friend and mentor.

My career lasted twenty-seven years. I retired with a pension and a college education. During my career, I was an instructor at the police academy. McKenna also assigned me as a public speaker for the department.

After retirement from my police career, I wanted to share my knowledge and experience in police work with the next generation of law-enforcement officers. For several years after retirement, I taught courses to students on the subject of criminal justice at a local college. I unabashedly admit I was one of the most sought-after professors in my field. Many of my students have gone on to successful careers in the field. It is gratifying to know my contributions helped others continue this important work—protecting the public.

CPSIA information can be obtained
at www.ICGtesting.com
Printed in the USA
BVHW030827060121
597114BV00008B/56

9 781648 011252